THE CAYENNE MATRIX

H. Weslee

Part I
Bliss
Chapters 1 – 22

Part II
Chaos
Chapters 23 – 31

Part III
Matrix
Chapters 32 – 76

Part IV
Reckoning
Chapters 77 – 104

Part I – Bliss

Chapter 1

September 6, 2005

Jonathan Delacroix zig-zagged his ATV through the rain-soaked pasture, dodging one rotting carcass after another from his prized herd of Black Angus. Suddenly, a stream of white hot volts exploded several feet ahead. Jonathan veered sharply right, lifting the vehicle's oversized left tire off the ground and nearly tipping it over. The crackling sparks provided a cruel reminder. Downed power lines snaking their way across the landscape remained lethal, poised to sizzle any bumbling trespasser.

Frantic, Jonathan navigated the rover up a small bluff hoping for better news. He found none. The ranch's sugar cane crop, eight feet tall a week earlier and nearly ripe for harvest, was leveled as far as the eye could see. Hands trembling, Jonathan retrieved the phone from his pocket, fumbled it, then snagged it an instant before the device disappeared into the muck below. His 200 acre farm bordering the Louisiana marshlands lay in ruins.

"We've lost everything," he shrieked into the receiver's microphone, gasping for air. "Gone. Every last bit of it. All we worked for . . . it no longer exists."

Concluding his tour of despair, Jonathan reached the outer limits of his property abutting the lake. "Damned Katrina," he muttered to himself, wiping away the tears from his eyes.

Ready to turn back, Jonathan noticed a curious cream-colored object a few yards away. Pulling closer for a better look, Jonathan suddenly stopped dead in his tracks. The hair on the back of his neck stood up.

Protruding through the mud and staring right back at him were the hollowed-out eyes of a human skull.

Chapter 2

(1981)

The aqua green, rust spotted 1955 Ford f100 pickup barreled down Louisiana Highway 23 and chugged along the west bank of the Mississippi towards the river's swampy delta. The driver was a man about 5'8", with slicked back gray and black hair, crusty, weathered skin, light brown eyes and a dimpled triangular chin that came to a rounded vertex just below his jawline.

The passenger, an adolescent girl about ten years old, watched the churning driveshaft through a hole in the truck's floor, her hand tightly gripped to the arm rest on the door as a broken seat belt hung limp under her thigh. Her hair was reddish-brown and neatly parted in the middle with two ponytails extending down the back of her neck.

"I haven't talked to you about this yet Kathryn," the driver lied as he surveyed the road ahead, "and I don't know when your mama's going to let me see you again, so listen up. Make sure you stay away from all the riff-raff out there. You don't want somebody who promises the moon so he can take advantage of you. You need to find yourself a nice young man with the proper schooling, someone who will treat you right and treasure you."

Katy knew what was coming next. Her father was not inclined to stop until he had worked himself into a lather and said his piece. When agitated, Dudley Duvall's voice constantly rose and fell as he vacillated between English and French.

As expected Dudley continued, his voice building to a climatic crescendo. "Don't fall for sweet talkers. Il est tous le temps apres chasser du trouble (he's only looking for trouble). Fait comme si tu les voit pas (pretend you don't see them) and keep going."

Katy nodded in agreement. She knew that assent, real or feigned, was the only way to cut the lecture short and even that didn't always work. Katy already loved her fifth grade class, had no interest in boys or platitudes and figured the rest of the message could wait until later. What mattered at that moment was that she was going fishing with her father and the sooner they arrived at Lake Hermitage, the better. Redfish and speckled trout awaited and Katy was anxious to bait her hook and cast her line.

A few miles past the town of Alliance, the truck exited the Belle Chase highway, proceeded half a mile further and then turned right onto a hidden gravel road that headed down towards Dudley's favorite fishing spot at the lake. As the pickup bounced along the bumpy path and kicked up pebbles that struck the windshield, Dudley Duvall repeated his missive.

His statements were matter of fact and any irony dripping from his lips was completely lost on him. Dudley saw no contradiction in trying to steer his daughter away from young ne'er do wells even though he himself had seduced well over a dozen father's daughters during his youth.

In fact, one got the distinct impression that if Dudley had to do it all over again, he wouldn't change a thing. True, he wished he hadn't lost half of his left pinkie in a slicing accident years earlier at the shrimp processing plant where he worked. Although Dudley blamed the mishap on faulty machinery, in truth he had become momentarily distracted when peering down the blouse of a co-worker who leaned over in front of him.

Other than that though, he had few regrets. Dudley pursued his own lusts, drank hard corn liquor brewed by local bootleggers and held down a decent paying job for most of his life. He had attended Mass from his teenage years a couple of times a month, sitting in the rear of the local parish church with the other Creoles and any Hispanics and blacks who were there, while white parishioners occupied the forward pews.

Through all this, Dudley had managed to save $8,875 for retirement, a tidy sum in that time and place. He never married but his periodic forays with the ladies had produced five children by three women, including Kathryn who was born in 1971 after Dudley's brief fling with her mother whom Dudley met while working as a waiter on a New Orleans riverboat.

As he aged, Dudley realized that his time as the "Bayou Casanova" was coming to an end. He still whistled at high skirts, but now instead of winks, the whistles only returned contemptuous stares, exasperated sighs and disgusted murmurs of "creepy old man."

Dudley's most recent social outing had not gone well. Anxious to make a good impression on a first-time dinner companion, Dudley so over-perfumed himself with cheap drug store cologne that the aroma nearly incapacitated his date, causing an allergic reaction. The last Dudley saw of her she was stumbling out of the restaurant, coughing and sneezing, never bothering to retrieve the high-heeled shoe that had fallen off her foot. Dudley started to follow to see if he could assist, but figured it was a lost cause so he sat back down and finished the appetizers instead.

Despite his recent series of bungled encounters with the opposite sex, there was still fishing and Dudley knew that no one could take that away from him. He loved being out on the water. No worries, no cares, just himself, the boat, his rod and reel and the serenity of the lake. Although Katy's mother and grandmother despised him, Katy loved to fish with her father, so the times that Dudley was able to take her with him were extra special. Once or twice a year, the two took a weekend trip south to Lake Hermitage in Plaquemines Parish where Dudley had fished as a boy.

As the afternoon wound down, father and daughter anchored the boat to a dock at the local marina. Satisfied with their catch, they began the trek back to the truck. On the way they passed a small wooden lean-to that served as a bait shop. Inside was a middle-aged Cuban man, dressed in overalls, high mud boots and wearing a faded Grambling University cap. He had just pulled down the storefront's roll-up door and secured it to the front counter.

"How'd ya do?" the man yelled as he locked up the back of his shop. "Just fine Earl," Dudley replied. "I got a couple of bites, but Kathryn here landed some specks and reds. We caught enough for supper, so it was a pretty good day."

"A pretty good day indeed," Katy thought as she beamed with pride to herself. A pretty good day indeed.

Chapter 3

Lafitte Public Housing, 6th Ward, New Orleans, Louisiana (1982)

The sudden jolt in the back came without warning. It propelled Katy forward and downward, thrusting her face first into the dirt, the weight of her backpack providing added force to the violent impact. Stunned, Katy cleared the debris from her eyes, then extended her left arm and swept it from side to side in an arcing half circle, groping blindly in a futile attempt to locate her eyeglasses on the ground.

At that moment, Katy heard an infuriated voice.

"I bet you'll help me now, you kiss-assed teacher's pet. I should beat the shit out of you," the voice chided.

Katy could not see who was doing the yelling, but she recognized the voice as one from school. It was the class bully, Cassandra Ransom. Although Katy and Cassandra were in the same grade, there was a two-year age gap (and twenty-five pound weight difference) between the two. Katy skipped the sixth grade because of her advanced test scores, while Cassandra had been held back and was repeating the seventh grade.

Katy was usually careful about avoiding Cassandra, but a week earlier Cassandra's ire had been raised when Katy, a noted bookworm, refused to do Cassandra's homework for her. Cassandra had not forgotten and was intent on payback.

Disoriented, her nose and mouth pressed against the hard dirt and unable to retrieve her glasses or gather herself, Katy knew she was in trouble. There was no telling when, or if, Cassandra might strike again.

Katy brushed the dirt off of her clothes. She did not want to fight. It wasn't in her nature and even if it was, there was no way Katy could stand up to an enraged Cassandra. As Katy started to lift herself up, Cassandra shoved her down once more.

"If you ever pull that shit again, I will kick your ass," Cassandra repeated.

Then, for good measure Cassandra added, "you yellow-assed bitch," drawing oohs and aahs from the gathering multitude.

It wasn't the "N" word but it was close. The slur served as a reminder to light-skinned Creole girls like Katy that just because she wasn't white didn't mean she could expect to always be accepted as black. The slight pierced deep; and that was before even getting to the "bitch" part.

Katy tilted her head up slightly to expand her field of vision. Everything was a blur. She reached out again for her glasses, using her hands to scan the surface of the ground within her reach.

"Those glasses have to be here somewhere," Katy thought to herself in desperation.

Finally, Katy felt the metal frame. She gripped the glasses with her left hand and tried to place them on her face. The right temple was broken so the glasses no longer fit snug over Katy's ear. Katy considered trying to sit up but feared that would only prompt Cassandra to push her back down again, or perhaps worse, kick her. She knew Cassandra was not simply going to walk away.

With her glasses tumbling off her face, all Katy could see from ground level was dirt, blades of grass and several pairs of feet against a hazy backdrop, as shadowed figures moved in the distance amidst the sound of curious, muffled voices. As Katy scanned the surface, she thought she picked out the feet that belonged to Cassandra by the pink tennis shoes Cassandra often wore.

The pink shoes started to move towards her. Katy heard a gasp from someone in the crowd. As the pink shoes got larger and closer, Katy realized that she was in immediate peril. There was no time for indecision.

Spurred on by instinct and gripped with fear, Katy suddenly sprang cobra-like at one of the advancing shoes. She quickly wrapped her arms tightly around it, twisted Cassandra's ankle like she was wringing out a wet shirt and chomped down on Cassandra's foot as hard as she could.

Cassandra let out a high-pitched shriek, then tried to kick Katy with her free foot. Flailing wildly, Cassandra lost her balance, tumbled backward and crashed to the ground with a resounding thud. The force of Cassandra's impact sent ripples across the earth. With her head still just inches from the ground, Katy sensed the vibrations as if she were at the epicenter of a massive earthquake.

A pall of silence fell over the assembled crowd, many of whom stared open-mouthed at what they had just witnessed.

"Damn," exclaimed one stunned onlooker breaking the eerie silence. Then a couple of the neighborhood kids started to giggle. The giggling quickly morphed into uproarious laughter. Goliath was defeated.

The sudden tumble terrified Cassandra. She figured Katy would be easy pickings and had expected little if any resistance. The embarrassment of being tossed to the ground by a frail do-gooder was too much for her to take.

She slowly picked herself up and started to sob. "She broke my foot," Cassandra screamed. "That yellow-assed teacher's pet broke my foot."

As Cassandra limped off, Katy wasn't quite sure how to feel. She was relieved but remained terrified, and was as befuddled as anyone by the skirmish's outcome. Katy was certain she hadn't fractured Cassandra's foot. She probably hadn't even broken the skin with her teeth. But Katy knew she had surprised and humiliated Cassandra in front of a sizeable audience.

And that meant there would be repercussions. Street credo demanded it. The incident was not over.

Chapter 4

In short order, Katy's life become infinitely more complicated. There were periodic threats, dirty looks and "inadvertent" forearm bumps in the school hallways from some of Cassandra's friends. Unnerved by the incident, Katy was constantly looking over her shoulder. Her study habits deteriorated; her grades plummeted.

Katy's mother, Francine Bernard, who made her living by cleaning the homes and scrubbing the floors of New Orleans's wealthiest families, initially thought the taunts were nothing more than harmless schoolyard banter and would soon pass. She was wrong. Francine was slow to realize that long gone were the days when grade school scuffles would be quickly forgotten. The unwritten code of the public housing projects was quite the opposite. Scores had to be settled, revenge exacted.

Realizing that Katy's safety could be shattered by unseen threats at any moment, Francine reluctantly concluded that it would be in Katy's best interest to move her out of New Orleans for a while. There was plenty of room in the house on the family farm across Lake Pontchartrain, where Francine grew up. Nana Bernard, Katy's grandmother, would be more than happy to have Katy stay with her. Francine hated the thought of being separated from her daughter, but ultimately concluded that she could not risk Katy's safety.

And so, eleven year old Katy Duvall found a new home with her grandmother in rural St. Tammany Parish thirty-five miles across the Lake, leaving her mother and younger brother Jerome behind in the 6th Ward. Except for occasional weekend trips to New Orleans to help Francine with her domestic work, it was a place Katy rarely left until she finished high school.

Chapter 5

(1993)

"The Mississippi River flows where it damn well pleases." —Unknown Union solider at Vicksburg, 1863.

Natchez, Mississippi, located on that portion of the Mississippi River characterized by a series of tight loops and sharp curves that extends for over a hundred miles, is the seat of Adams County. That distinction, although perhaps notable, is not particularly significant given that Natchez is the only city in Adams County.

For several hundred years the River's aimless wandering, caused by tons of sediment that shift from bank to bank, has cut off large swaths of land and made a mockery of the Louisiana-Mississippi border. There are parts of Mississippi that now extend west, surrounded on all sides by Louisiana. Conversely, a chunk of Louisiana territory sits wholly within Jefferson County, Mississippi.

Confusion over state boundaries is one thing. The equivocating River's impact on private property lines is another. Prime fishing rights and oil deposits buried deep beneath the river bed often hung in the balance. The resulting land disputes were occasionally resolved by a handshake and friendly pat on the back. In this part of the country, however, the settling up was more likely to be accomplished through fisticuffs, pearl-handled daggers and errant .12 gauge shotgun blasts.

On a steamy summer day off of US Highway 61 just outside the Natchez city limits, Bryan Stirling paced back and forth on the front porch of the Lawson residence, his every move increasing the saturation level in his short sleeve polo shirt. An inviting glass of sweet tea offered by Wanda Lawson rested gently on the porch railing nearby, begging to alleviate Bryan's misery. The glass sat untouched, spurned by Bryan's tunnel vision.

A timorous breeze offered hope of a respite, but invariably the breeze waned and frittered away, smothered by the dense air. As he wiped the moisture from his brow, Bryan paused when he thought he saw the dust of an approaching vehicle, but realized it was just a twirling wind gust providing one final tease from the departed current.

Bryan, a student at Westchester School of Law in Los Angeles and President of the school's Black Law Students Association, had volunteered for a summer program designed to provide free legal services to impoverished residents of rural Adams County. His primary summer assignment was to assist Burl Lawson, a forklift operator for a local warehouse, and his wife Wanda. Burl believed in accepting an honest day's pay only if he provided an honest day's work. When he shook your hand, his grip was firm and he looked you right in the eye.

The Lawsons had been married for forty-one years. Despite being diligent workers all of their lives, the pair had watched themselves gradually become part of Mississippi's white working class poor. They could no longer afford vacations, kept their vehicles for at least fifteen years and anxiously awaited the weekly discount coupons in the Sunday paper.

Several months earlier, Burl had taken out a "payday" loan from a local grocer who also ran a bail bondsman business. The grocer advanced Burl $375, a portion of which Burl used to purchase an anniversary gift for Wanda. To obtain the loan, Burl signed a loan agreement and also wrote the grocer a $525 check. The grocer told Burl the check would be cashed in two months, but the fine print which Burl did not read, indicated that the check could be cashed as early as the following week.

When the grocer attempted to cash the check two weeks later, it bounced. Burl was then sued for breach of contract. The grocer had been pursuing collection action ever since.

When the Lawsons started receiving phone calls threatening Burl with jail time, the couple reluctantly sought the assistance of the local Legal Poverty Association who promptly designated Bryan to handle the case as his summer assignment. The Lawsons had not enjoyed a good night's sleep since the entire ordeal began.

Bryan eventually represented the Lawsons in an arbitration hearing before the Mississippi Department of Banking. He was now nervously awaiting word of the Department's decision which was to be delivered by courier that afternoon.

As Bryan continued his vigil on the porch, he snuck a quick peek into the house to check on the Lawsons. They sat on the couch, gazes fixed on their nineteen inch black and white television set. The Lawsons washed all dishes by hand and used twenty-year old appliances. They had no microwave and Bryan noticed a curious pattern of tin soup can tops that had been nailed flush to several floor boards throughout the den and living room.

When Bryan asked about the can tops earlier in the summer, Burl laughed and said Wanda had insisted on them after she was startled one morning by a young water moccasin slithering its way through the house. The juvenile had entered the dwelling through a hole in one of the floor boards that was created when a knot in the board fell through to the ground, a common occurrence during periods of high humidity when the wood grain in the boards expanded.

Burl chuckled as he finished the story, remarking that "the only time during all our years together that Wanda threatened to leave me was if I didn't get those damn holes plugged. I'll tell you one thing. I ate a lot of Campbell's Soup that week!"

Most of Bryan's friends had accepted summer positions at prestigious law firms, but Bryan opted for the unpaid Mississippi assignment. He convinced himself that he had done the right thing no matter what the final outcome of Burl's case but as the moment of truth approached, Bryan fretted about the decision. He had done all he could, but could not bear the thought of letting the Lawsons down.

Just then, a courier's delivery van rounded the corner. The driver exited the van and asked for Burl Lawson. Bryan summoned Burl from the house. Burl emerged wearing his customary work boots, dungarees with carpenter pockets and John Deere cap. Usually upbeat and positive, this time Burl's demeanor was downcast. The legal proceedings had worn him down and eroded some of his dignity. All of a sudden the moment seemed too big for him. After signing for the package, Burl hastily shuffled it to Bryan to open as he and Wanda held hands and prayed. Bryan knew the entire summer was riding on the words that he was about to read.

Bryan scanned the contents until reaching the critical text, which he read aloud. "Now, therefore, this Department being duly authorized by the State of Mississippi hereby finds that the loan agreement signed by Burl A. Lawson was usurious and illegal and is therefore null and void. This Department now orders that . . ." and the rest was drowned out by joyous shrieks from the celebrating Lawsons.

Now sopping wet, Bryan caught his breath and quickly guzzled the tea that was still waiting patiently on the porch. Then he grabbed the pitcher, poured another glass and inhaled it just about as fast as the first one. After some reflection, relief and many hugs, the trio returned inside, continued to celebrate and finally collapsed on the sofa and chairs in the living room.

Later, Wanda would prepare a dinner of fresh picked turnip greens, black-eyed peas, corn bread and fried blue catfish, followed by pecan pie smothered in bourbon-laced whipped cream for dessert. In between mouthfuls, Burl still tightly clutching the letter, handed it back to Bryan and asked him to read it all over again.

Chapter 6

A couple of days later, his summer work complete, Bryan prepared for the journey back to the West Coast. He would be joined by two other law students, Tony Ramirez and Rusty Newman, who had also participated in the Mississippi program. As they loaded up their belongings, Bryan asked the other two if they were up for a slight detour to New Orleans on the way back. Bryan's elderly cousin, Josephine Taylor had fallen ill and Bryan's mother asked him to check in on her during their return trip.

Tony and Rusty readily agreed, as visions of a couple of nights on Bourbon Street danced in their heads. None of the three had been to New Orleans before, so the anticipation of a short visit to NOLA sounded like a fitting way to cap off the summer.

Two hours into the drive, the car merged onto Interstate 10 as it paralleled Lake Pontchartrain toward New Orleans. As they continued east, the distinctive marble colored roof of the New Orleans Superdome and the City's downtown skyline, slowly came into view.

Bryan could not possibly have imagined the twists and turns Louisiana had in store for him.

Chapter 7

As their car entered New Orleans, the law students felt a rush of anticipation despite their accumulated fatigue from the preceding weeks. They made their way to the Lafitte Housing Project where Josephine lived, the setting sun now painting a masterpiece of brilliant orange and turquoise in the western sky.

The housing project was comprised of a series of parallel brick structures with each dwelling unit containing eight, three-story apartments. The buildings were separated by common lawn areas approximately twenty yards wide, with a meandering sidewalk running through the middle of each patch of grass.

Josephine resided at 611 N. Miro. As the trio drew closer to her apartment, Bryan observed several people conversing on the porch next to Josephine's, including a striking young lady with shoulder length auburn hair. She wore jeans and a short sleeve shirt and as Bryan passed by he heard playful laughter and noticed a shy smile out of the corner of his eye.

The young woman turned in Bryan's direction but he quickly looked away and pretended not to see her as the weary travelers arrived on Josephine's front porch.

Chapter 8

Josephine was elated to have company and immediately welcomed the guests into her home.

"Y'all come on in and relax and let Cousin Pheen take care of you," she said to all three of them, although in truth "Cousin Pheen" could barely take care of herself.

Josephine's apartment unit featured a living room on the entry level ground floor, and a den, dining room and kitchen on the second floor. The third floor contained the bedrooms and a bathroom. The entire living area was less than 650 square feet.

After Josephine made the beds and gathered some towels so the young men could shower, she explained to Bryan that her diabetes had been acting up and that she felt tired most of the time and was having some trouble with her vision.

Just then, the doorbell rang. Josephine went downstairs to answer it. It was Katy Duvall, her next door neighbor's daughter and the young woman Bryan noticed as he and his friends were arriving at Josephine's. Katy always referred to Josephine as her aunt even though they were not related.

"Just checkin' in on you Aunt Jo," Katy said, "is there anything I can do for ya?"

"I'm alright Katy," came the response, "or at least I'm doing as well as I can," Josephine laughed. "Come on in for a spell and meet my cousin Bryan and his friends. They're here all the way from California."

Katy said hello to Bryan and also met Tony and Rusty. After a few minutes of small talk, Katy told the three young men that she and two girlfriends were going into the City that evening to take in some live jazz.

Katy then added, "if I didn't invite you along, I wouldn't be showing the proper Louisiana hospitality, so y'all are more than welcome to join us if you like."

That was all Bryan needed to hear. He eagerly accepted without even asking the others. In a couple of hours after a second shower, the group of young twenty-somethings was off for an evening of food, jazz and people watching in the French Quarter.

The experience did not disappoint. New Orleans was at its vibrant best and there seemed to be action on every corner. There was no shortage of both tourists and natives in extravagant dress, celebrating everything and nothing at the same time and decorated in all manner of beads, boas and sequin masks.

At one intersection, the group stumbled upon a local street ensemble led by a talented trumpeter wailing the blues on his muted horn. A little further down the street, the young adults encountered an over-exuberant band of New Orleans Saints football fans, well on their way to full inebriation and screaming "Who dat?" a popular team slogan, at the top of their lungs.

Moving on, the youthful contingent finally settled in for some hor d'oeuvres and live music at a bar and grill on Frenchman's Street. When one of the bands struck up a series of Zydeco tunes accentuated by lively accordion solos, the young women began dancing and yanked the law students out of their seats to join them.

Bryan tried to keep up with Katy, but he was overmatched. He could only watch in amazement as Katy swiftly launched herself across the floor in a series of twirling, athletic half circles. When she finally ran out of space, Katy stopped and giggled. She made eye contact with Bryan, whom she had left in the dust clear across the room, winked at him and then giggled some more.

"Where did all that come from?" Bryan asked, when he finally caught up with her.

"I love dancing," Katy said. "My Nana enrolled me in a dance academy when I was twelve, but two years later I had to withdraw because it was too expensive for us."

"Complete freedom," continued Katy. "That's how it feels. Especially with Zydeco where you can really express yourself anyway you want to. Anything goes."

At that moment, Bryan desperately wanted to find out exactly where this was leading and in particular, what "anything goes" meant. He would not get the chance, at least not yet, but he was beginning to learn that Katy was unpredictable, marched to her own drummer and could not be put in a box. That intrigued him. Bryan was eager to learn more.

After leaving the restaurant, the group continued to explore the eccentric nooks and crannies of the French Quarter. Rusty's interest was piqued when they approached "Lady Cecile's House of Mediums and

Madams." He insisted on going in. The others agreed to tag along and humor him. All except Katy that is. As Bryan purchased his ticket, he noticed her looking on from a sidewalk bench.

"You comin' Katy?" he asked.

"I think I'll sit this one out," Katy replied. "But you go ahead. I need to cool off a bit. I'll wait here for you guys."

"Ok," said Bryan as he shrugged his shoulders and joined the group entering Cecile's. "See you in a few."

Katy bought herself a shaved ice and waited for her friends to return. They were back in fifteen minutes, all seemingly no worse off for their troubles.

A little over an hour and a couple of Pat O'Brien hurricanes later, the exhausted Louisiana girls and California boys decided to call it a night and return to Lafitte. The French Quarter festivities having reached their apex, were in a gradual decline. A few of the late night revelers had partied themselves into submission and lay passed out on the sidewalk, the end of their jubilant but short-lived reign symbolized by a hollow whiskey bottle clanking down the street.

Chapter 9

After arriving back at Lafitte late that evening, Bryan's friends staggered their way up the stairs to one of the bedrooms in Josephine's apartment, while Katy and Bryan loitered for a bit on Katy's mother's porch. They talked for nearly an hour and discovered that they had much in common, including professional aspirations, apprehension about the future and a humorous streak.

Katy told Bryan that she lived in an apartment downtown but regularly returned to Lafitte on weekends to check in on her mother and younger brother. She worked as a medical assistant and attended night classes in pursuit of her goal to become a registered nurse.

As Katy explained to Bryan, "I was born in New Orleans but at heart I'm just a country girl raised on a good ol' Louisiana farm. City life is a bit fast for me although I enjoy all the different things New Orleans has to offer. After I finished college a few months ago, this is the only place I could find a job that pays anything. So here I am. I've learned a lot working with my boss Dr. Curry. But I want to help the people who live out in the swamps and bayous. There are tons of folks out there who can't afford basic medical services."

Bryan was impressed.

"A beautiful girl with a social conscience. That's quite a combination. I'm surprised somebody hasn't already taken you off the market," he said.

Katy thought she knew what Bryan meant, but she wasn't sure. But even if she was right, she wouldn't mind luring Bryan into a more robust explanation.

"What do you mean by 'off the market?'" said Katy, feigning naiveness with a twinkle in her eye, all the while becoming more delighted with the course of the conversation.

"I mean you must have to fight off all of the guys who are knocking on your door," said Bryan. "Is there anyone special?"

"Well, I sort of have a boyfriend," said Katy, "but it's an on-again, off-again kind of thing."

"Well," said Bryan, "right now is it on or is it off?"

"Depends on who you ask," replied Katy. "If you ask me, it's off and will probably stay off. If you ask Francois, he always thinks it's on."

Katy then went on to describe how she started dating Francois LeBlanc while the pair were in high school. After graduating, Katy moved back to New Orleans for college while Francois stayed in St. Tammany Parish and began attending trade school to land a position in the ship repair industry. As Katy put it, the two had been drifting apart ever since but Francois was having difficulty letting go.

"You know how you reach a point where you become exposed to different things and what you want for your future might not be the same thing the other person sees for themselves down the road. That's where Francois and I are. I want to see and experience different things, but still continue to be a part of my community."

"Francois is from Lacombe and doesn't care if he ever sees anything other than southeastern Louisiana. He will probably be happy getting up and going to work in the same place, living in the same house for the next forty years. That's not me. I told Francois that breaking up is what's best for both of us. So far he hasn't accepted that. But sooner or later he's going to have to."

"I can certainly see why he wouldn't want to lose you," said Bryan in a further attempt to catch Katy off guard and flatter her. "Any guy would have to count themselves very lucky to have someone like you."

It worked. Katy blushed with embarrassment at the words of this handsome, worldly newcomer. She was not used to these types of compliments but was certainly amenable to accepting a few more. Bryan seemed almost like a foreigner to her, so different was he from any of the young men she had met in Louisiana.

Then Bryan added, "I'm going to take you at your word."

"What do you mean by that?" said Katy.

"That any other relationship you had in the past is now 'off,'" continued Bryan with a slight laugh.

Katy's cheeks turned pink, the exhilaration apparent all over her face. "I'm not sure that's exactly what I said," Katy replied coyly. "But I think I can live with your interpretation!"

As late evening turned to early morning, the pair discovered something else they had in common; a mutual affinity for slow, passionate kisses by moonlight.

Their eventful evening ended at 1:13 a.m. when each headed back to their apartment to get some well-earned sleep. The tingling excitement of the evening would keep both of them wide awake until dawn.

Chapter 10

There were no early risers the next morning, but Bryan awoke before his friends. When Katy offered to show him the rest of the French Quarter, he happily agreed. The pair later returned to the 6th Ward for lunch at Dooky Chase's where Katy introduced Bryan to the restaurant's owner Leah Chase, one of New Orleans' most revered chefs.

After being seated, Bryan quickly doused the glass of water in front of him. The New Orleans heat and humidity had been getting the best of him.

"I'll have the tallest glass of lemonade you can pour," he said to the server. "Katy, what about you?"

"A lot of us down here prefer sweet tea," she said, "so I think I'll go with that."

"I had some of that famous sweet tea in Mississippi. Have you ever mixed them?" asked Bryan.

"Haven't done that yet," came the response. "But sure, I'll try it."

"Check that," said Bryan to the server. "We'll have two Arnold Palmers instead. One heavy on the lemonade, the other heavy on the sweet tea."

Katy giggled. She enjoyed Bryan's company and marveled at how his quick wit allowed him to instantly adjust to evolving circumstances.

Then Bryan began twiddling his thumbs and fell silent for a few seconds. He had something on his mind.

"I really enjoyed last night," he said to Katy.

"Which part?" Katy replied with a smile.

"Some parts more than others," Bryan answered, "but all of it was fun. Be sure to thank your friends for showing us the town."

"I will," said Katy. "It was a nice diversion and something new for us too."

"I don't want to belabor this," Bryan said slowly, "but I was just curious why you were avoiding Lady Cecile's. Or did I imagine that?"

"You didn't imagine it," Katy replied. "I didn't want to go in there. I have my reasons."

"Which are?" Bryan probed, "if you don't mind my asking."

Katy took a deep breath.

"A number of years ago right after I moved to live with my grandmother, my cousin Eloise who was a few years older than me had a crush on one of her school classmates. Now you have to understand that Eloise is one of those people that is easily influenced. She made up her mind to try and find out how things were going to end up between her and her love interest. Well, Eloise had heard about a local tarot card reader who could tell fortunes. She was determined to go see him, but afraid to go by herself so she snuck me out of the house and dragged me along."

"Well, the next thing I knew Eloise and I were deep in the swampy backwoods entering the card reader's rundown shack. He called himself Clovis and said he was a divine oracle, but we couldn't see his face because of the bright red witch doctor mask he wore. The place was repulsive. All I could think about was getting out of there as fast as I could. I was so terrified of being bitten by the spiders and roaches crawling all over the place that I wasn't paying very close attention to what was going on, but finally Clovis pulled some cards out of his deck. He stared at them for a few seconds, looked at Eloise and then told her what she didn't want to hear."

"Which was what?" asked Bryan.

"He warned her that the fellow she was interested in was bad news and that she should stay as far away from him as possible. Eloise was devastated, but it turned out to be good advice."

"Ok," said Bryan. "So what does that have to do with you not wanting to go into Cecile's?"

"Well, as we were about to leave," continued Katy, "Clovis picked all of the cards up off the table and said he could give me a reading as well even though we only paid for one of us. I told him 'no thanks.' But Eloise insisted that he draw a card for me."

"And?" said Bryan, becoming more interested in Katy's story.

"It creeps me out even thinking about this," Katy said, "but after shuffling the deck, he pulled the first card off the top and turned it face up."

Katy paused. "It was The Three of Swords."

"So what?" replied a perplexed Bryan. "What does that mean?"

Bryan couldn't believe he was immersing himself in this conversation but he was drawn to Katy like a magnet and anything involving her was of interest to him.

"Clovis hastily picked up the cards and at first refused to continue," replied Katy. "He just said that I should leave and that it really didn't matter what The Three of Swords meant. But Eloise insisted. Apparently she didn't want to be the only one going home with bad tidings."

"With cousins like that, who needs enemies," replied Bryan in disbelief.

"Right," Katy replied. "Anyway, Clovis' reading of the card was that I would find myself in some very difficult situations, three of them to be exact. 'Trials by fire' he called them. He also said that the third time . . .," then Katy paused.

After a few seconds she gathered herself. Katy continued.

"Clovis said that the third trial would overwhelm me. I was frightened of course, although I really didn't believe in any of that stuff."

"Then I got to thinking about how I ended up at my Nana's house in the first place," continued Katy as she recounted to Bryan the story about her seventh grade encounter with Cassandra.

"Looking back on it, perhaps I had already been through Round One. So maybe this psychic actually knew something. I don't know. I didn't want to believe it, but I was very confused. And scared. Aren't there words to a famous song that warn you about that? Something like 'your life will be filled with misery if you can't figure out what you're following'?"

"That sounds sort of familiar," Bryan said slowly, "but I can't quite place the lyrics. Never mind that though. Katy, this guy Clovis was obviously a fraud. Three bad things will happen to you? What kind of prediction is that? Everybody has at least three bad things happen to them during their life. Most of us have a lot more than that. So then when something bad happens, does that make him right? Come on. Like I said, he sounds like a phony. It's the type of prediction that anyone could make and if you wait long enough, something will eventually happen that will make the warning turn out to be correct."

"I . . . I guess you're right," said Katy. "I never quite thought about it that way. But I was very young and impressionable. I was frightened. So now I just try to stay as far away as I can from any soothsayers, palm readers, mystics, just the whole group of them."

"Amen to that," said Bryan. "Now I understand why you didn't want to be bothered with Lady Cecile's. No additional explanation needed. But I hope you don't carry that prediction around with you anymore. It's just not worth it. I was just curious, that's all."

Then Bryan continued. "Katy, did this Cleophas mention any good things that might happen to you?" he chuckled.

"Clovis," corrected an exasperated Katy. "No he didn't. I assume that positive predictions might be bad for business. In that line of work, there always has to be some negative, mysterious angle to everything I guess. Why do you ask? Do you foresee some favorable events in my future?"

"I think so," said Bryan smiling.

"Good, let's talk about some of those," replied Katy hoping to change the subject.

"Agreed," Bryan replied. "I think I've heard enough about talismans and tarots."

"So what happens when you finish law school?" Katy asked Bryan, eager to move on to something else as they waited for the server to return with their drinks. "Do you get to go into court the next day?"

"No," Bryan laughed. "You can't go straight to court. I won't even be an official lawyer until I pass the California bar exam. And that's not guaranteed."

"Aw, I'm sure you'll have no trouble," said Katy. "You seem to have a knack for getting what you want!"

"I haven't quite gotten everything I want," replied Bryan slowly as he raised his eyebrows in Katy's direction, "but I'm working on it." They shared a quick giggle as both realized the chemistry that was now developing between them.

Katy was interested in Bryan's law school and career plans, but shifted gears slightly to what she really wanted to know.

"Soooooo," said Katy pausing slightly. "Are you coming back to Mississippi next year?" hoping to hear that Bryan would be returning to the South soon.

"Not likely," said Bryan. "That was just a one-time summer assignment."

"Well I guess you will just have to make a special trip to New Orleans to see me, won't you," Katy said, leaning slightly into Bryan.

"Either that or become a Louisiana lawyer," Katy laughed, only half-jokingly. "I've heard that we need some new lawyers down here," she added, having heard no such thing but nevertheless hoping Bryan would catch the hint.

"Or maybe you can become a California nurse," Bryan shot back.

"Be careful what you ask for," Katy responded.

Sensing that Bryan was good-natured enough to handle some playful needling, Katy decided to double down. She seized on his formal manner of speaking and precise sentence structure, a rarity in the neighborhood where Katy grew up, to have a little fun. Katy wasn't used to hearing words and phrases like "indicative" or "stream of consciousness" in the rural Louisiana countryside. Also not going unnoticed was Bryan's correction a few minutes ago of her use of the phrase "words of a song," to "lyrics." Katy decided to cast Bryan as the outsider and jerk his chain a bit.

"Why do you talk so proper?" Katy asked Bryan.

"You mean 'speak' proper," said Bryan in all seriousness. "Why do I speak proper?"

"You're making my case for me," Katy replied with a smirk. "You just can't help yourself, can you? Too much California sophistication I guess. Straight talk plays just fine down here in Louisiana you know."

Bryan laughed. He knew he had taken the bait but considered it of little consequence. Bryan liked Katy's unpredictability and spontaneity and he didn't mind that it rendered him slightly off balance. He could never be quite certain if Katy's insinuations and flirtations were intentional or inadvertent and it kept Bryan guessing what new direction their next interaction might take. Although Bryan dated occasionally in Los Angeles, he did not have a steady girlfriend. It did not take him long to realize that he had never come across anyone quite like Katy before.

Katy also was certain that the attraction between the two of them was mutual. Deep down though, she wondered if someone like her could fit in Bryan's future or whether the path Bryan was on could ever intersect with her own. The two of them were certainly a long way from that point, but still it was something to think about. Katy decided that she wouldn't mind finding out just how far this relationship might go.

Bryan and Katy continued to see a lot of each other over the next couple of days. As the week progressed, they both dreaded that their brief encounter was coming to an end. When Wednesday morning arrived, Katy woke up listless. She was surprised at how downcast she was knowing that Bryan was about to leave.

"Katy, get it together," she said to herself. "You've only known him for a few days."

Josephine was also feeling a bit despondent. She was not accustomed to having company and the presence of the young men created a lot of activity and social interaction around her place that she had not experienced in years. The hustle and bustle invigorated her and Josephine considered it only a minor nuisance that none of her guests put the toilet seat down when they finished using the bathroom. She secretly wished they would stay longer.

Having loaded their car for the long trip back to the West Coast, the law students prepared to depart New Orleans. They had originally planned to start the return trip on Tuesday, but stayed an extra day at Bryan's urging. Bryan said he needed to make sure Josephine was properly situated before he left, but Tony and Rusty knew better.

As the would-be lawyers prepared to journey back across the country, Bryan hugged Katy and gave her a quick kiss on the lips. A tear rolled down her cheek as she turned away. They had previously exchanged phone numbers and promised to keep in touch.

"Let me know when you plan to be back in New Orleans," Katy said, barely able to get the words out of her mouth without choking up. She was secretly convinced that she would never see Bryan again.

"You're welcome here anytime. And call me when you get to California."

Bryan felt the same way but he was better at concealing his emotions. "I will," he said. "Promise. And you might just see me sooner than you think."

Bryan thought about Katy all the way across the 1,900 miles of Interstate 10 back to Los Angeles. He called her on Saturday right after he made it home. It did not take long for the two of them to plan their next get together.

Chapter 11

Although Katy told anyone who would listen that she was not "from" New Orleans, as time passed the City grew on her, especially the multi-cultural and heritage rich Treme' neighborhood that bordered Lafitte. In addition to taking in occasional concerts at Congo Square, Katy also frequented a number of local shops and restaurants in Treme'.

When she took a break from her native Louisiana cuisine, Katy's favorite spot to eat was El Barrio, a hole in the wall, Mexican food joint where Katy loaded up on street tacos and pico de gallo. She developed a fast friendship with Jose, the eatery's owner, and the two talked extensively each time Katy stopped by. Katy frequently asked Jose to recite different phrases in Spanish. Through these mini-lessons and eavesdropping on Jose's conversations with his staff and some customers, Katy picked up some basic Spanish over time.

One afternoon Katy showed up at El Barrio for a late lunch. She noticed that Jose was not his usual chipper self. His skin was pale, his eyes bloodshot and a worried look was strewn across his face.

"Jose, como esta? Que pasa?" Katy said, asking Jose how he was doing and what was going on, all while cracking a slight smile out of pride in her halting but discernable Spanish snippets.

"Hola, senorita Katy," Jose replied with no enthusiasm.

"What's wrong Jose?" quizzed Katy. "You can tell me."

"I have a visitor coming by today at two o'clock," Jose said. "A visitor I do not want to see. I am supposed to give him $300 to protect me."

"Jose, what on earth are you talking about?" asked Katy almost sneering.

"It's true," replied Jose. "I don't understand this. They first come by a few days ago and tell me to be careful because there are some dangerous criminals in the neighborhood. I don't see these criminals they are talking about. Then they tell me if I pay them three hundred dollars every month, they will protect me from these outlaws. I tell them no, I feel safe already. I don't have three hundred dollars. The next day I came into work and the back window of my restaurant, si' it is broken into little tiny pieces.

So the men came back and tell me 'see what happens when you don't have protection?' What is this thing Senorita Katy? What is this?"

Katy smelled a rat. She could feel her blood boiling. Katy had heard rumors that a long time street hustler had recently formed a new crime syndicate and was operating in the area but until now she paid little attention to it. As far as Katy knew, the local shops and businesses in Treme' had not previously been targeted for strong arm tactics by low level organized crime outfits.

"Jose, don't worry. I am going to stay until these men get here," she said, "and we'll get to the bottom of this."

At precisely 2 p.m. sharp, a tall, thin man in his mid-twenties, showed up. He wore dark shades and had a couple of days-worth of scraggly facial hair growth with a long, blonde, unkempt ponytail sticking out of the back of his baseball cap.

"Jose mi amigo, what's up?" the man said in a heavy southern accent. Jose refused to look at him.

"Who are you?" Katy interrupted, "and what do you want here?"

"I don't believe I've had the pleasure of making your acquaintance ma'am," said the man as he extended his hand to Katy. "Name's Quentin, but everyone calls me Q. And who might you be?"

Katy ignored the offered handshake, which she would have done even if she hadn't noticed the grease stains smeared on Q's palms.

"I'm a friend of Jose's" she said.

"Well I'm here to complete a business transaction with Jose," Q said. "And it doesn't involve you. I'm going to take excellent care of our friend Jose here. Nothing for you to be concerned about. Right Jose?"

"From what I hear," said Katy, "you're demanding money for 'protection.' That sounds an awful lot like extortion. Is that what you're doing?" Katy asked pointedly. "'Cause a shake down's not going to go over very well with me."

The smile disappeared from Q's face. His entire demeanor changed. Q leaned over, grabbed Katy's wrist, twisted it tightly and then whispered menacingly in her ear.

"Here's some friendly advice for you cutie pie," Q said as he dropped his voice to a point where it was barely audible. "Make sure your life preserver is inflated before you wade into the deep end of the fuckin' pool."

Then Q released Katy's arm and slowly pulled away. "Or else you just might find yourself submerged without a way back up. Understand what the hell I'm sayin'?"

Then turning to Jose, Q continued. "I can see you're busy Jose but I'll be back. We're offering you a good deal. This is a nice place. Great customers, hip music. I hear the food is first rate. You never know. You could wake up one day and it could all be gone. Poof. Just like that," said Q, snapping his fingers for emphasis.

"Now that would be a shame. There's some bad apples out there. We know who they are and we can keep them away from you. A lot of your neighbors wised the hell up and appreciate the value of our services. It might be in your best interest to do the same. Think about it Jose. Comprende'?"

"Punk," yelled Katy. "Asshole," she screamed, kicking her leg at Q as he walked by.

Q just tipped his cap.

"I'll see you around Jose," he said. "And next time, tell Wonder Woman to stay her pretty ass at home if she knows what's good for her."

Chapter 12

Bryan began his third and final year of law school a couple of weeks after arriving back in Los Angeles from New Orleans. He also started interviewing for a permanent job that would begin after he graduated and took the bar exam the next summer. Bryan narrowed his employment choices to two. The options could not have been more different.

First, there was Winter & Black, a national law firm anxious to add Bryan to its environmental defense practice. The position came with a considerable starting salary along with a significant amount of prestige. It was the type of job that many law students coveted but few were offered. For most students, accepting the associate position at Winter & Black that Bryan was offered would have been a no brainer.

Bryan's other choice was serving as a staff attorney on criminal cases with the Los Angeles County District Attorney's office. The idea of continuing in public service after his rewarding summer in Mississippi appealed to Bryan, even though the starting salary was far below his other offer. But Bryan thought that beginning his legal career with the County DA would make him a "real" courtroom lawyer since he would be responsible for writing briefs, reviewing crime scene evidence and appearing before judges, almost from his first day on the job.

In the meantime and in order to earn a little extra money, Bryan accepted a part time job as a teaching assistant in Professor Foster's first year Criminal Procedure class. Foster was one of the most popular instructors at the law school. Thirty-five years old and comfortable fraternizing with students outside of class, Foster drove a Corvette and hung out with A-list Hollywood celebrities in his spare time, representing a few of them when they got into legal trouble.

Much to his surprise, Bryan found the reality of working with Foster to be much different than the professor's jet-setting reputation. Foster was unfocused, erratic and forgetful. These signs didn't mean much to Bryan, but they raised the antennae of Matt Collins, one of the students in the class.

Collins hailed from an affluent family in the Dallas suburbs and only attended law school at the insistence of his father. "There's a long line of prominent attorneys in the Collins family," the father said, "and you're going to be the next one." Matt, however, preferred to spend his time partying and taking day trips to Venice Beach instead of attending class or studying.

Now, on the verge of failing Professor Foster's class and flunking out of law school, Matt desperately sought to escape his predicament. He too had noticed a change in Foster's classroom behavior. The professor's blistered lips and irritability confirmed Matt's suspicions. Foster was probably doing crack cocaine.

Anxious to capitalize on the professor's demons and break free of the dire straits he had created for himself, Matt invited Foster to a late night social get together.

"We'll have lots of leftover Halloween candy," Matt promised with a wink.

Foster couldn't resist the invitation. The need to feed his habit overwhelmed him and practically led him by the nose to the gathering. After luring the professor into a compromising position and snapping some damaging photographs, Matt had all he needed to pull off a bribe.

When Bryan graded Foster's final exams, he noted an unusual number of scores in the high 90s from several students in the bottom third of the class. After another student complained about the exam results, the law school investigated. The probe concluded that Foster had slipped a copy of the exam to Matt Collins before the test was given. Collins, not satisfied with improving his own grade, had then distributed additional copies of the exam to some of his friends.

Collins and several other students were expelled from the law school, while Professor Foster was suspended. Bryan was reprimanded for not notifying the administration of the questionable exam results. The reprimand proved costly. Winter & Black withdrew Bryan's offer of employment.

Chapter 13

The reprimand and withdrawn offer devastated Bryan. He couldn't believe what was happening. The constant sacrifices, the midnight study sessions, all of it was being flushed down the drain for something he had nothing to do with.

Meanwhile, back in New Orleans Katy continued to work full time for Dr. Curry while taking nursing classes two nights a week at Loyola University. She spoke to Bryan frequently, at least once a week and Katy was looking forward to Bryan's pre-planned visit to New Orleans during spring break.

It was a different Bryan that Katy met at the airport. Previously outgoing and gregarious with an unpredictable sense of humor, this Bryan was sullen, withdrawn and bitter. He had previously told Katy about the cheating scandal and the loss of his job offer, but Katy didn't fully appreciate how deeply the scandal affected him until she saw Bryan in person.

"I'm considering a lawsuit against the school," Bryan said to Katy as they talked in her apartment. "I've worked too hard to get where I am. Those cowards are intent on destroying my livelihood. If it's up to them, I'll never be able to use my law degree.

Katy could tell that Bryan was close to tears. She had never heard him that angry or resentful. This was beyond being merely upset. The experience deeply wounded him. Katy tried to ease the pain.

"It will be ok," she said, fumbling to find adequate words of consolation. "You were a top student before and you're still a top student now. Nothing's changed. The truth will eventually come out."

"But things have changed Katy," Bryan yelled. "And it won't be ok. Can't you see that?"

Katy hesitated for a few seconds. She didn't want to trivialize Bryan's plight, but she also did not want to spend the next three days of Bryan's visit moping around in a funk.

"Bryan, you're only here for a short time," Katy said. "I know this is bothering you and it would bother me too. But this is our first visit since the summer. Can we maybe talk about something else for a little bit?"

Before Bryan could answer, there was a knock on the door.

"Not sure who that could be," said Katy. "I'm not expecting anyone."

Katy looked through the peephole in her front door.

"Oh no," she exclaimed out loud.

"What's wrong?" asked Bryan.

"It's Francois. I don't know why he's here. I haven't spoken to him in months. Quick, in here," she said to Bryan as she escorted him into her bedroom. "Under the bed and don't make a sound."

"Are you kidding?" asked Bryan incredulously as he untangled his arm from Katy's.

"Francois is a bit of a hothead," Katy replied. "It's best if he doesn't know you're here. That will only make things worse. I'll get rid of him as quickly as I can," she said.

Bryan was furious, but he complied. He hurriedly slid on his stomach under Katy's bed as Katy pulled the covers down to the floor to block the view under her bed.

The knocking continued, this time harder than before.

"Coming," yelled Katy as she quickly made her way to the front door and opened it.

"Francois, this is a surprise. I didn't expect to see you. How have you been?" Katy said.

Bryan, now stuffed into a confined space, wished Katy would dispense with the niceties. He heard Francois mutter something as Katy invited him in.

"I was actually on my way out," Katy said to Francois, "so I only have a few minutes."

From his cramped spot under Katy's bed, Bryan could not make out their entire conversation but he did hear Francois ask Katy if there was any chance that they might get back together.

"Francois, we've been over this a hundred times," Katy replied. "It's best we go our separate ways."

Meanwhile, Bryan was getting uncomfortable lying face down under Katy's bed. He quickly realized he should have slid under the bed on his back, if he was going to slide under at all, but he didn't want to create any reverberations now by changing positions. On top of that, he had to use the bathroom.

"Hurry up Katy," he muttered under his breath. "Move it along."

"Francois, I really do have to go," Bryan heard Katy say. "We'll always be friends and I'm sure you will find someone very special. I don't mean to be rude, but you really shouldn't come over here anymore," Katy continued.

Bryan squirmed uncomfortably under Katy's bed. He didn't want to pee all over the carpet beneath her mattress.

"Katy, get on with it," Bryan thought to himself again.

Finally, Bryan heard the front door close. He immediately slid himself out from under the bed and took several quick steps to the bathroom.

Upon exiting a few seconds later, a still steamed Bryan decided he had had enough. The sting from his recent law school trauma remained raw. Now on top of that, he had to suffer the additional humiliation of hiding under a bed to avoid a confrontation with a jealous, ex-boyfriend.

"Katy, I really shouldn't have come here," Bryan said. "This was a big mistake. I thought . . . well hoped, that there might be something between us, something we could build on, but it's just not turning out that way. I didn't come all this way to be parked under a bed. I need to get back to Los Angeles. I'm sorry. Can you please call a cab so I can get a ride to the airport?"

Katy stared at Bryan in disbelief.

"You can't be serious," she said. "You show up here with a 'woe is me' attitude and proceed to pout the entire time you're here. I had no idea Francois was coming over. I haven't spoken to him since last year and he hasn't been to my apartment since before I met you. I'm surprised he even remembered where I live. But Francois is my past, not my future."

"I know what happened to you at school is terribly unfair and I'm very sympathetic. But did you ever even consider that I might be going through some things too? That I might need a shoulder to cry on once in a while?"

Katy stopped. She realized she probably wasn't helping the situation. "You'll bounce back Bryan," she sniveled softly. "We both will, but it takes time, patience and clear thinking. Neither one of us has a lot of that right now."

Bryan was unmoved.

"I'm sorry Katy, I really am. I just have some things I need to work out. Don't worry about the cab, I can get it myself. I just need to go."

"So you're telling me that you came all this way and just like that you're leaving?" Katy replied in astonishment.

Bryan said nothing.

Katy watched stoically as Bryan put his luggage back together and walked toward the door. He tried to give her a hug, but she pushed him away, choosing not to speak as she folded her arms. Katy saw Bryan walk out the door. Then she ran to the window. She watched until Bryan disappeared around the corner. Raindrops had started to fall.

Katy buried her head in her hands. She was too distraught to function. She struggled back over to her couch, thrust herself on it and started a series of neck-jerking gasps, with each breath more pronounced than the previous one.

Chapter 14

A couple of hours later, Katy heard the doorbell ring. Sheepishly, she climbed out of bed and looked through the peep hole. There was Bryan standing in the rain and soaked to the core. Maybe he forgot something Katy thought. In any case, she opened the door. Her tears had dried, but her eyes were still beet red.

Katy didn't know what to say, so she chose levity to make light of the situation.

"Just couldn't do without your sweet old-fashioned southern girl, could you?" she sniffled.

"Something like that," replied Bryan. "That and the fact that the fee to change my airline ticket was $575," he continued with a slight smile.

Katy secretly giggled inside at Bryan's sarcasm. She had a quick flashback to words of advice she received from Nana long ago.

"If you find someone that you can laugh with," Nana once said, "well now then you just might have something."

Katy was not yet ready though to show that her exasperation was melting. The two of them stood silently in the doorway for the next few seconds staring at each other. Then they spoke simultaneously.

"Bryan, I'm sorry," Katy started, as Bryan began talking at the same time.

"You go first," said Katy.

"Katy, I brought a whole lot of baggage with me on this trip and I don't mean just my suitcase. It was really unfair of me to put it all on you. What happened to me at school is not your fault."

Katy smiled through a few emerging tears and opened her arms wide.

"No need to say anything else," she exclaimed. "Now come in from the rain and give me a hug before you catch pneumonia."

Bryan stepped inside. The two shared a long, tight embrace. Neither one wanted to ever let go.

Chapter 15

When Bryan returned from Louisiana he only had a few months of school left before graduation. By this time, the law school had hired an outside consulting firm to prepare a report about the test scandal involving Professor Foster's final exam. The report cleared Bryan, concluding that he had engaged in no wrongdoing.

It was too late. Although Bryan had several offers from other law firms, he had accepted the offer from the Los Angeles District Attorney. He still considered suing, but ultimately decided to move on. Bryan vowed, however, that he would never forget, or forgive, how the law school treated him.

Bryan took and passed the bar exam in July of 1994 and started work with the DA's office the following September. He proved to be a quick study and won several convictions, excelling at oral argument. His courtroom skills were obvious. Bryan was a master at weaving together a series of seemingly unrelated facts, organizing them into a clear, cogent story and persuading judges and juries of the merits of his position.

At about this time, the District Attorney's office was starting to assemble a staff for Case #BA097211, the high profile murder trial of *People of the State of California v. Orenthal James Simpson*. Bryan's work was so impressive that he was briefly considered for a spot on the team. He relished the opportunity. In the end, however, the DA's office opted for more experienced lawyers.

A little over a year later, Bryan decided to visit Katy right after Christmas and spend New Year's in New Orleans. Katy happily agreed to accommodate him, telling Bryan that her extended family was having a celebration on December 30 at Nana Bernard's farmhouse.

Katy picked Bryan up when he arrived in New Orleans on December 28. The two shared a long embrace as Bryan climbed into Katy's car. As they began the drive from the airport into New Orleans, Bryan informed Katy that he had previously called Josephine to tell her he might need a place to stay for a couple of nights so he asked Katy to drive him to the Lafitte complex.

"Bryan Stirling, I will do no such thing. You are staying with me," Katy said, hoping that Bryan was not being overly cautious because of how his last visit to New Orleans went.

"But," Bryan protested, "I already told Josephine I was coming."

"Aunt Jo will understand," said Katy. "I can take you over there to see her tomorrow."

"But Katy," Bryan said again, this time with not quite as much conviction. He very much wanted to stay with Katy, but felt the need to protest just a bit more. "I certainly wouldn't want to disappoint Josephine," he said.

Katy was one step ahead of him and saw through Bryan's strategy.

"We'll see how much he *really* wants to stay at Josephine's," Katy thought to herself.

"Ok," said Katy. "Have it your way. If it's Josephine's you want, then it's Josephine's you'll get," she continued as she pulled sharply over to the left lane to make a U turn and head back in the opposite direction.

"Never mind," said Bryan, realizing he had outsmarted himself. "I accept your offer," as Katy's razor sharp wit and unpredictability, once again on full display, reminded Bryan of why he was so attracted to her.

"I figured you would," said Katy. "There's plenty of room for you to sleep on the couch. After all, a girl can't make everything so convenient for you now can she?" Katy teased, purposely intending to damper Bryan's expectations for the evening.

Bryan just smiled and laughed to himself. He was getting exactly what he bargained for.

Chapter 16

After visiting Josephine the next day, the pair made their way to Nana Bernard's house on December 30 where several dozen members of the Bernard clan had assembled for an afternoon of socializing and dinner.

"It's our annual New Year's Eve's Eve, get together," Katy informed Bryan on the drive to the gathering. "We have it the day before New Year's Eve because everyone scatters to do their own thing on December 31. On New Year's Eve some of my younger cousins will stay out until 5 am on Bourbon Street while most of the older generation will be in bed by nine o'clock. That's why it's easier for the whole family to get together the day before."

After arriving at Nana's farmhouse, Katy led Bryan around the property and proudly introduced him to various family members. Bryan could not help but notice that a number of conversations seemed to flow back and forth in at least three languages, with the dialect often changing in mid-sentence.

"It's a mixture of Creole French, English and Acadian French," said Katy. "It will take some getting used to. I picked it up when I was young. My cousins and I used to serve coffee and beignets to the old folks at family get-togethers. When the adults were sharing salacious gossip, they switched languages if one of children came around."

"Over time I figured it out, but I never let on. I heard all sorts of things, from the local grocer who put expired cans of food at the front of the shelf to sell them, to the deputy getting caught with the police chief's wife, to Mr. Bertrand stealing Ernest Devereaux's hogs, stuff like that. So you better be careful. They might be talking about you. You never know!"

Just then, an older man approached Katy and Bryan with a huge smile on his face. He extended his arm to Bryan for a hand shake as if he and Bryan were old friends. The shake lasted a good fifteen seconds as the man spoke at a rapid pace, while making several gestures with his free arm. Katy provided a brief response but Bryan just listened, smiled and nodded, not having the faintest idea what was being said. Finally the man pointed at Bryan, looked at Katy, patted Bryan on the back and then walked away only to start another conversation with someone else in a different language.

"That's Uncle Maurice," said Katy. "When he heard you were a lawyer he wanted to meet you because his favorite television program is LA Law. He wants to know if all lawyers in Los Angeles are constantly jumping in and out of bed with each other like they show on TV."

"Haven't you heard?" Bryan replied tongue-in-cheek. That's not limited to Los Angeles. Lawyers do that sort of thing everywhere!"

"They better not be," Katy responded, glaring at Bryan.

"Just joking," Bryan replied. "Tell your uncle that lawyers are just like everyone else. Some straight arrows. Some not so straight."

"Anyway, Uncle Maurice likes you and he said I should hold onto you, just in case I ever get into trouble," Katy continued, accenting that last part with a sarcastic eye roll.

"I had to inform him that you're the one who hit the jackpot," Katy opined with a wink.

This particular December 30 featured the added bonus of also being "Gumbo Night," since Nana Bernard decided to serve her specialty dish. Dinner was announced by the ringing of a cast iron, chuck wagon triangle bell like the ones used on the large Texas cattle ranches. The family then gathered in a large circle, held hands and bowed their head while grace was said. After the final "amen," Bryan quickly learned a valuable lesson. One best not be caught flat-footed in the pathway between the serving table and the herd of famished Bernard men who arrived en masse with an overabundance of appetite and attitude, and not necessarily in that order. Nana's gumbo, however, somehow always managed to sooth the most ornery of guests.

After sidestepping the advancing stampede, Bryan took his place in line. The sound effects were classic bayou countryside as playful insults in Louisiana French dialect were exchanged against the background clanking of silverware against porcelain. Bryan started to fix his plate but Katy immediately grabbed it from him and told Bryan to take a seat at the extended dinner table. She would prepare his food for him.

"Don't expect me to do this all the time," Katy said softly so none of her older relatives could hear. "Last time I checked, your hands and feet were in perfectly good working order. But my aunts will be appalled if I let you fix your own plate and will start spreading some not so flattering gossip about me. So just play along. But like I said. Don't get used to it."

Bryan just nodded, unconcerned about who fixed his plate, but silently pleased with the thought that Katy contemplated them having more dinners together.

After they were both seated, Bryan noticed that neither he nor Katy had anything to drink.

"Can I at least go get the punch?" he asked Katy, somewhat facetiously, eyeing a couple of punchbowls on a table in the distance.

"Certainly," replied Katy. "It's excellent punch, citrus I believe. But unless you are prepared for some Louisiana moonshine that will scald your windpipe, I suggest you get our punch from the bowl on the right. Earlier I saw Uncle Norbert and Cousin Felipe emptying their flasks into the other bowl."

Having retrieved the punch, Bryan was ready to sample his first taste of authentic Louisiana gumbo. His face immediately lit up. The savory soup/stew hybrid, accented with generous helpings of okra, crab, Gulf Coast shrimp and andouille sausage, tickled taste buds Bryan didn't know he had. The finished product poured over a bowl of wild rice, topped off with a couple of dashes of hot sauce and combined with a slice or two of warm cornbread brushed with melted honey butter, was the equal of any dish one might find at a five star, downtown New Orleans restaurant.

After dinner, a few of the men hastily created an ad hoc band on the back lawn, with two violinists and one guitarist. They were quickly joined by one of Katy's aunts on the accordion. The music was spirited, if not off beat, and slightly out of tune. Several family members starting dancing spontaneously with Nana Bernard herself grabbing Bryan and taking him for a whirl on the grass. Bryan frantically searched for Katy, hoping for a quick rescue, but she had suddenly disappeared.

When the band finally took a break, an exhausted Bryan again scanned the legion of dinner guests looking for Katy. He could not see her, but Katy was at the rear of the crowd, doubled over in laughter.

Hands on hips, Katy slowly made her way towards Bryan. When he saw her emerging through the sea of unfamiliar but friendly faces, it was if someone had thrown him a much needed lifeline.

"So now you have experienced the *real* Louisiana," Katy said as Bryan caught up with her and she draped her arm over his shoulder. "What do you think?"

Bryan smiled. "I think I want to try some of that moonshine," he said. "And the strings need to be tightened a bit on one of those violins."

"Down here we call them fiddles," came the quick retort.

Chapter 17

Somewhat spent after their evening at the family farm, Katy and Bryan slept in on New Year's Eve morning. They later hit the French Quarter for a couple of hours in the late afternoon, but by nightfall decided to spend a quiet evening at Katy's place.

The pair relaxed, talked and toasted a glass of wine "to us." The two soon became intoxicated, not by the vintage of the spirits or the crackling of the fireworks, but with their deep and longing passion and adoration for each other.

"I guess we won't be out on Bourbon Street until 5 am with some of your cousins," remarked Bryan.

"I guess not," replied Katy.

The rest of the evening was magical with neither one caring about the festivities going on throughout New Orleans. As 1995 turned into 1996 amidst distant refrains of Auld Lang Syne, their focus was elsewhere. Their celebration was private, by invitation only and continued long after the ball dropped in faraway Times Square.

Chapter 18

Shortly after Bryan returned to California, he left the District Attorney's office and accepted a position with Lynn, Ryan & Associates, one of the top environmental defense law firms in Los Angeles. Bryan regularly worked ten to eleven hour days, but the move doubled his salary. Although not a lavish spender, Bryan allowed himself a few luxuries, including a nice condominium near the beach, but he continued to drive the used Toyota Camry he purchased in college.

Ever few months Bryan received a fund-raising letter from Westchester that was mailed to all alumni. He shredded each envelope without ever opening a single one.

Bryan's increased salary afforded him more opportunities for investing some of his earnings. He remembered a couple of discussions he had with his Uncle Carl from Maryland while growing up, about the wisdom of wise investments. Up to this point, Bryan had primarily invested conservatively, mostly in money market accounts and mutual funds. His investment advisor counseled Bryan that he should certainly not become reckless, but that his increased salary allowed him to be a bit more aggressive for the next several years with where he placed his money. Since he was young and had a couple of decades of prime earning years still in front of him, Bryan could afford to take some gambles.

Bryan also had occasional investment discussions with one of his college buddies who was a partner in a Silicon Valley venture capital firm. The friend had previously mentioned to Bryan that he should consider putting some money into emerging technology companies. The risk was high, the friend said, but the potential rewards could be substantial.

Shortly thereafter, the friend informed Bryan that his firm was about to make a series of investments in some promising start-up companies and that the firm was offering a Friends and Family investment pool if Bryan was interested. On a whim, Bryan decided to take a flyer. He committed his entire 1996 investment budget, $15,000, to the pool. If it panned out, great Bryan thought. If it didn't, then the whole venture capital route would be something he was not likely to repeat.

Whether working with the Los Angeles County District Attorney or with an environmental law firm and whether investing in certificates of deposit or venture capital funds, Bryan had one constant. He could not get Katy off of his mind. The two now spoke several times a week and Bryan made frequent trips to New Orleans to see Katy. The more Bryan thought about her, the more he became convinced that Katy was the woman he wanted to marry. Katy still had not been to Los Angeles, but Bryan was cautiously optimistic she would like it, although his one fear was that Katy might not be willing to leave Louisiana at all.

After much contemplation and reflection, Bryan decided that he would propose to Katy on his next trip to Louisiana which Bryan had scheduled for October of 1997. He meticulously planned the evening and scripted out every move. He and Katy would dine at one of New Orleans finest restaurants. Bryan would propose between dinner and dessert and then the newly engaged couple would ride on a horse-drawn carriage through the French Quarter.

Bryan confirmed the dates of his next Louisiana trip with Katy. He was certain Katy had no clue about his intentions. After visits to a number of jewelers, Bryan finally settled on a 1.25 carat, round cut solitaire diamond engagement ring.

As the days inched closer for his visit, Bryan's excitement grew. The year had gone well for him, but he viewed that final "yes" from Katy as the fitting exclamation point.

Chapter 19

Back in New Orleans, Katy continued to progress towards completion of her nursing credential. All was not well, however. Katy's mother had been ill. Worse still, Francine expressed concern to Katy that Jerome was becoming a little too friendly with a couple of petty criminals in the neighborhood. The news did not sit well with Katy, herself a novice in dealing with New Orleans's mean streets.

The simmering uneasiness would soon boil over.

One day after taking the afternoon off from work, Katy decided to pay a visit to her mother. The two of them talked for about an hour.

A short time later, Jerome walked in. Now nineteen, slim and quite handsome, Jerome had grown to nearly six feet tall.

Katy noticed Jerome's snazzy attire, including a brand new designer sweat suit, shiny white leather high-top tennis shoes and a heavy 14 karat gold chain around his neck.

"Where did you get the stylish threads Jerome?" Katy asked. "And weren't you also wearing something brand new the last time I saw you?

"Cut the third degree Katy," answered Jerome. "I'm fine. I'm not looking to start anything with anybody, ok? Just minding my own business. Everything's solid so you need to chill out."

"I want to know where you got that stuff Jerome," said Katy. "Where? And with what money?"

"Am I bothering you?" Don't worry about it ok? I just got it. Don't matter where it came from. I didn't steal it. I can tell you that. So it's really none of your concern," replied an agitated Jerome as he slammed shut a kitchen cabinet and stalked upstairs.

"He's been like that for the last two weeks," Francine said to Katy. "Edgy and always itching for a fight."

"Well I don't like it," said Katy. "Not one bit. Mom there's a lot of bad stuff going on in the streets these days and it's easy to take advantage of kids like Jerome. Buy him some nice things, schmooze him and the next thing you know they think it's Easy Street and they are hooked on that life style. Then the boss just tells them what to do and they do it. And once they're in they can't get out. Jerome can't afford to buy the stuff he's wearing. Where else do you think he got it?"

Francine had a far off look in her eye and just shrugged. Pride, and a twinge of sorrow kept her from acknowledging the obvious.

A few minutes later, Jerome came back down the stairs.

"Did you get a response from those job applications you put in last week?" asked Katy. "I would think a recent high school graduate shouldn't have any trouble finding work in New Orleans."

"Nah," said Jerome sternly, not at all appreciative of where the conversation was going. "Ain't nobody hiring."

"Jerome, did you really put in those applications like you promised or are you just blowing me off?" pressed Katy. "And where did you get that gold chain?"

"Get woke Katy, ok. Just get woke," Jerome fumed. "I'm not doing fast food and I ain't working at a department store. I got bigger plans."

"Let it go Katy," interrupted a resigned Francine. "Please child just let it go."

"I am not letting it go," replied Katy. "Where Jerome? Where did you get the chain? Or should I say, who bought it for you?"

Jerome quietly seethed but said nothing.

"I asked you where you got the gold chain?" Katy demanded. "Are you being bribed into doing stuff you know you have no business being involved in?"

Katy realized she was going over the edge, but it was too late to pull back.

Suddenly Jerome exploded.

"You're going to judge me?" he asked. "Last I checked, you ain't even from here. You didn't grow up here. So you shouldn't have anything to say to me. I told you. I ain't workin' retail for a few dollars a week. That's nuthin' but spare change. Alvarez says I can make a month's worth of fast food cash in one day working for him," said Jerome as he pulled a stack of twenty dollar bills from his pocket.

"Alvarez?" said Katy. "Alvarez Pope?" Katy recognized the name. Pope was the local hoodlum who was rumored to be moving into organized crime and may have been behind some of the extortion threats to small businesses in Treme'. Katy was incredulous that Jerome could be involved with the syndicate that might be extorting Jose.

Jerome then held up the stack of cash and shuffled through it like a Las Vegas blackjack dealer, right in Katy's face.

Katy suddenly slapped upwards right through Jerome's hands, catching him off guard and sending the stack of currency skyward. All six eyes in the room watched as the bills slowly fluttered to the ground like confetti in a ticker tape parade through the heart of Manhattan.

"Go ahead Jerome," said Katy. "Pick 'em up. Pick it all up. That filthy cash you supposedly 'worked' for. It's blood money, isn't it," chided Katy, holding up one of the bills in Jerome's face. "Isn't it?" she demanded.

Jerome stared first at Katy, then at the rest of the twenties, now strewn across the floor. He was fuming but did not want a physical altercation with his sister.

"Where did you get all that money, Jerome?" Katy asked. "And more importantly, what did you have to do to 'earn it'?"

"I ain't saying nothing else," replied Jerome. "You gotta do what ya gotta do to get ahead. I intend to get ahead," Jerome continued before pausing. "And stay ahead. I ain't livin' in these projects the rest of my life."

"You mean nothing to them, Jerome. That's no way to live your life. And when you finally figure out you don't like it, do you think they're just going to let you leave? It doesn't work that way. When they have no more use for you, they'll kick you to the curb like they never knew you. Or worse. They'll make sure you disappear. You know better. You've been taught better."

"Got no other choice," said Jerome.

"That's a lie Jerome," replied Katy "and you know it. There are plenty of other things you can do besides being a lookout for street thugs or a shakedown artist. I heard Mrs. Johnson's son got a job stocking inventory at an uptown warehouse. Seven twenty-five an hour."

"I ain't workin' for no fuckin' seven twenty-five an hour," Jerome lashed out furiously.

"Don't you dare use that type of language in front of your mother," Katy scolded. "You were raised better than that."

"Was I?" responded Jerome. "Like I said, you ain't from around here so you don't know how I was raised. Maybe I was brought up by my friends who were hanging out on the street corner when I got home from school and no one else was there."

Francine hung her head and held back tears.

Jerome had never said it, but he deeply resented the fact that he, unlike Katy was not offered the chance to grow up on Nana Bernard's farm, light years removed from the urban realities of New Orleans' darker side.

"You had opportunities," Jerome continued wistfully. "I didn't. You didn't spend you entire childhood in this hellhole. This is about surviving the streets, something you know nothing about. So don't lecture me. You got no right to tell me how to make a living," Jerome concluded as he finally proceeded to gather the stray cash up off the floor.

Katy sensed the futility of continuing to argue with her brother. She would never simply concede Jerome to the clutches of the inner city, but Katy was at a loss for what to do next. She knew little to nothing about street gangs and even less about crime syndicates. They didn't exist in rural St. Tammany Parish, at least not as far as Katy knew.

As naïve as she might have been, Katy was not willing to stand idly by and watch Jerome disappear into the trap doors of his environment. If intervention was required, then ill-prepared and equally ill-equipped Katy Duvall from the Louisiana countryside was ready to step in.

Chapter 20

The next month went by quickly for Bryan. He talked to Katy frequently on the phone, but gave no hint of his surprise plans. Bryan wanted his proposal to catch Katy completely off guard. As he boarded his nonstop flight from Los Angeles to New Orleans, Bryan doubled checked his carry-on bag to make certain he had everything. Assuring himself that he indeed had his most precious cargo, the ring, Bryan smiled as he took his seat for the three and a half hour flight.

Unlike previous trips where Katy picked Bryan up at the airport, this time Bryan rented a car since he arrived while Katy was at work. After checking in to his room at the Hotel Monteleone, Bryan grabbed a seat at the venue's Carousal Bar, and took a three hundred and sixty degree spin for luck. He then headed up to his room for a short nap. Bryan woke up an hour and a half later, then showered, freshened up and prepared to meet Katy at the restaurant at 6 p.m.

Bryan arrived at 5:57. Katy, who had taken a cab, showed up ten minutes later. She was dressed casually in jeans and a linen blouse to accommodate the warm conditions. Bryan was a bit more formal and wore a pair of navy slacks with a matching jacket.

The two made jokes and engaged in small talk over dinner. Katy told Bryan that she was close to obtaining her nursing certification and also gave him an update on her girlfriends that Bryan had met during their first evening together almost four years earlier.

Bryan then casually mentioned that Tony Ramirez was now a government lawyer, while Rusty was working in his father's legal practice. Rusty was not off to a good start, having missed a couple of court appearances on behalf of his father's wealthy Nevada casino owner clients. Bryan and Katy shared a laugh as they imagined Rusty trying to talk his way out of the crisis he had created for himself.

Then Katy mentioned that she was worried about Jerome's increasing involvement with New Orleans' criminal elements. The mood of the evening dampened a bit with Katy's revelation and it threw Bryan momentarily off stride. He kept waiting for his chance to break into the conversation but Katy, oblivious to Bryan's intentions, continued to bounce from topic to topic.

Finally, Katy paused to catch her breath. Bryan saw a slight opening but he did not want to simply blurt out a proposal without any build-up. Bryan hesitated and waited for a more natural breaking point in the conversation where he could interject with his prepared lead-in line of "Katy, you know there is no woman I've ever met that is quite like you . . ." and then proceed from there.

The night was there for the taking. This was their moment.

And it would slip right through their fingers.

Chapter 21

Just then, Katy's cell phone rang. She could see the call was from her mother.

"Excuse me a second," Katy said to Bryan as she answered the call.

Bryan heard muffled sounds coming from Katy's earpiece. He thought he heard a voice say "Jerome just drove off in a brand new car," but he wasn't sure. But whoever was on the other end of the line was in a panic.

"I know where he lives?" Bryan heard Katy answer. "I found his business card in Jerome's room. Don't worry mom. I'll take care of it."

Bryan then heard more garbled sounds coming from the other end of the phone.

"I will," said Katy. "I promise I will be careful. I'll call you later."

After Katy hung up, Bryan noticed a worried look on her face, one she tried to cover up with a quick smile.

"Bryan, something's come up. I'm afraid I need to leave to run a short errand. What's your hotel? I'll try to drop by later tonight and we can finish our evening with a little more peace and quiet."

Bryan was crestfallen. He couldn't propose now. His best laid plans had somehow gone awry. After gathering himself, Bryan did the next best thing. He volunteered to drive Katy wherever she needed to go.

"My rental car is parked at the garage just around the corner," he said, not completing giving up on proposing later in the evening after the "short errand" was finished.

"Well," said Katy, "if you don't mind, you can drop me off at my place and at least save me the cab fare home."

"No, I'll take you wherever you need to go," said Bryan.

Katy hesitated. "No," she said. "This is probably something I should handle myself."

"Nonsense," replied Bryan. "Seriously, I am happy to do it. I came out here to see you so I've got nothing but time on my hands. Really."

"Well . . . ok," said Katy after a long pause and against her better judgment. "I suppose there's no harm in you being my taxi for the night. I'll make it quick and I'll make sure you get a good tip," she said as she flashed another wink in Bryan's direction.

All of a sudden Bryan felt re-invigorated. Perhaps he could salvage the evening after all.

Part II – Chaos

Chapter 22

Katy guided Bryan through a now darkening New Orleans towards the upscale Gentilly neighborhood.

"Where are we going?" Bryan finally asked.

"Bryan, Jerome is in some trouble," Katy replied. "You remember I told you how worried mom and I were that Jerome is hanging out with gang bangers in the neighborhood. Well, I want to put a stop to it."

"Ok," said Bryan slowly and deliberately, wondering what that had to do with wherever they were going. "So what are you planning to do?" he asked, now starting to feel a bit uneasy.

"I'm going to give the head honcho a piece of my mind," Katy said, "and tell him to back off. That's how we handle things in the country."

Bryan wanted to laugh except that he realized the situation was far too serious to make light of. He believed Katy was deluding herself if she thought she could simply shame an organized crime figure who obviously had some stature, into leaving her brother alone.

"Katy, one thing I know about organized street criminals is that they are merciless," said Bryan. "I sent a number of gang members to jail when I was a prosecutor and I still look over my shoulder every once in a while. Sometimes it's just better to live to fight another day. Are you sure you know what you're doing?"

"Actually, I am not," replied Katy. "But where I come from, if you have a problem with someone, you tell them face to face."

"That might work if the person you're dealing with has some regard for human life," said an incredulous Bryan. "But this is different. These people have no moral code. You expect to just lecture this person and tell him to keep his hands off your brother?"

"I'm sure it won't be that easy," Katy said "and I don't actually know what I am going to say. I just know that Alvarez Pope is behind this and it has to stop. If I don't do it, who will?"

Bryan admired Katy's sense of duty and protective instincts, but he thought her a bit irrational and now feared her actions could get both of them into serious trouble. He had not come to New Orleans to confront a drug kingpin. Bryan reached into his pocket to make sure he still had the ring. It was there, but Bryan was increasingly concerned that his carefully planned evening was not going to end with the magical "yes" from Katy he coveted.

At Katy's instruction, Bryan located the house, Alvarez's house, just off of Wisner Avenue. He parked the car in the half circle driveway.

Katy opened the passenger side door and exited the vehicle. "I'll be right back," she said.

Chapter 23

As Katy approached the front door, she checked her purse to make sure she had her handgun. Katy was adept at handling rifles and shotguns, having accompanied her uncles on several duck hunting forays into the flooded rice ponds of rural Vermilion Parish. She could drop a blue-winged teal at thirty-five yards with a 20 gauge, but was not yet comfortable with a revolver, having only recently purchased one after a series of burglaries in her neighborhood. Katy didn't anticipate trouble, but she wanted to be able to protect herself if the need arose.

She walked up the porch and rang the doorbell. Katy was surprised when Q answered the door. All of a sudden her burst of confidence began to evaporate. Maybe she *was* in over her head. Katy knew Q could be ruthless.

"Well, well, if it isn't little Miss Joan of Arc come to save her people," Q said derisively. "And you remember how the fuck things turned out for Joan don't you?"

"We meet again. X isn't it?" Katy said. "Or was it some other nondescript letter of the alphabet? Z maybe. No, it's Q. That's right, Q.

Funny thing. None of those letters come to mind when I think about you, which isn't often. An 'M' and an 'F' maybe, but not a 'Q'," Katy continued."

Q was not amused by Katy's insinuations.

"If I wasn't a southern gentlemen, I'd tell you to go to hell," Q barked, and then he moved closer to Katy so that he was standing right over her. "Course a pretty thing like you is a lot more useful alive than dead," he snarled with a sinister laugh. "So you might be safe. For now anyway."

Katy stepped slightly back and to the side.

"Well whatever the hell your name is, I didn't come here to waste my time on you. I'm here to see Alvarez. I'd appreciate it if you could let him know he has a visitor." Katy continued, as she took a long diagonal step in an attempt to brush past Q.

Q grabbed Katy's arm, stopping her in her tracks.

"I didn't realize you and Mr. Pope were on a first name basis," he said. "I don't believe you were listed on his schedule for the evening, so I'll have to check. Mr. Pope is a very busy man."

Q left the room and returned a few seconds later. He beckoned for Katy to come forward, then led her into the dining room, past an elongated, rectangular dinner table with eight neatly arranged place settings that included fine Lenox china and Riedel crystal stemware. The living room was adorned with vintage furniture made from North Carolina mahogany. However Alvarez Pope might have earned his money, he was certainly living well.

As they entered the den, stretched out in a recliner with a remote control in his hand to operate the large screen television on the wall, sat

Alvarez Aloysius Pope. He was dressed in a bath robe, pajamas and slippers. Pope folded up the leg rest by pulling his feet towards him, thereby restoring the recliner to its natural sitting position.

Pope was shorter than Katy had imagined, about 5'6". There was nothing imposing about him. He rose from his chair, speaking slowly and deliberately.

"Well, well, well," he said, "so you're the legendary Miss Duvall. Heard a lot about you. The mystical beauty and all that shit. Talk on the street is that you could separate a rich man from his fortune without even half trying."

Pope then eyed Katy up and down. "I believe it," he said, his wry smile revealing a slew of gold and missing teeth. "I certainly wouldn't mind trying to find out. But then we'd never get down to the business of why you're here in the first place, now would we? You came all the way out here. You wanted to see me. What can I do for you? The floor is yours."

Just then Q excused himself from the room. "I'm headed out for the evening," he said to Pope. "Need to check on a few accounts. I'll catch up with you later."

Initially intimidated by her surroundings, Katy quickly gathered herself. She had no interest in an extended conversation with Pope but also was not going to leave without delivering the message that brought her there.

"I'll be brief," said Katy. "Leave Jerome alone. That's it. Just. Leave. Jerome. Alone."

Pope paused for a few seconds. "I'm not certain I know what you are talking about," he said. "I run a legitimate business Ms. Duvall and like most successful businesses, we are always looking for uniquely talented individuals."

"Is that why you had Q shake down El Barrio?" Katy interrupted.

Pope squirmed uncomfortably in his chair, clearly caught off guard by Katy's knowledge of his operations. After a few seconds he spoke.

"It may be possible that sometimes the hired help gets a bit, shall we say, overzealous. But I can assure you, our business always operates within the confines of the law."

"Now I don't know anything about this Jermaine," he continued.

"Jerome," Katy interrupted.

"Yes Jerome, but if he happens to be someone who might work with us now or later, then I would think that would be his decision, not yours. If you don't want a particular friend of yours to accept a job, then you take it up with the friend, not the employer."

"I'm warning you," said Katy her body now slightly quivering as she sprang out of her seat to leave. "Leave Jerome the hell alone."

In an instant, Pope's mood shifted and not for the better.

"Or what?" said Pope. "Or what?" he repeated, his blood starting to boil.

"Look, I tried playing nice," Pope continued, "but the fun and games are over. You're not going to walk into my living room and 'warn' me about anything. Stay out of my business. If we cross paths again, it won't be on your terms. That much I can guarantee. Now take your ass off my property."

Katy started walking backwards in an attempt to reverse her steps. Pope followed.

"I'll let myself out," Katy said as she reached the door, giving Pope one last stare.

Katy tried to slam the front door shut behind her as she exited, but Pope caught it before it closed. His feathers were ruffled by Katy's defiance, having become accustomed to subordinates who catered to his every whim without question. How dare this woman come into his home, uninvited no less, and threaten him.

Pope flung the door open and followed Katy outside onto the driveway. A concerned Bryan looked on from the car.

"Stay the hell away from my house Ms. Duvall," Pope said moving closer to Katy. "Jerome's a grown man. He can make his own decisions."

That last sentence infuriated Katy. Moments earlier Pope had professed not to know who Jerome was.

The two yelled back and forth at each other for another thirty seconds or so as Pope continued to close the distance between them.

Katy's contempt was unmistakable. She wanted Pope to know she was serious and meant business. On impulse when Pope moved to within fifteen feet of her, Katy whipped out her revolver and pointed it in the air. Her eyes seemed to carve a path straight through Pope, who halted his advance.

Pope took another step forward. Katy responded by extending her arm straight up intending to fire a shot skyward. She pulled the trigger. There was no discharge, only a click. Katy pulled the trigger once more, and again the gun clicked but did not fire.

Pope laughed, then resumed his threatening march directly at Katy. Thinking she had loaded her weapon improperly, but still hoping to scare Pope, Katy this time took aim squarely at Pope.

"Stop, or I'll shoot," she warned.

"With what? laughed Pope. "Paper bullets?"

Pope inched closer. He had passed the point of being rational. All of a sudden, Katy had a sickening feeling in her stomach. Her mind flashed back to that long ago meeting with the card reader on that forced trip into the swamp with Eloise. Was this moment to be her second trial by fire as foretold by Clovis?

Gripped with fear, Katy realized there was no time for hesitation. Pope would be upon her in seconds. Someone was going down. That much seemed inevitable.

Katy screamed one last warning. "Stop," but Pope marched forward. The gun was now aimed directly at the chest of the advancing menace. Katy slowly pulled back on the trigger.

"POW." The gun exploded sending a piercing scream through the dark night.

For the next few moments, everything moved in slow motion. A shell-shocked Katy covered her mouth with her hand. Pope stumbled, clutched his chest, stared wide-eyed at Katy and took one final stagger as he collapsed to the ground. He hit the pavement with his eyes wide open, a look of disbelief on his face as his ventricles struggled to keep blood flowing through his body.

Bryan remained in the car, horrified at the nightmarish scene unfolding in front of him. He sat frozen in the front seat, in shock from fear. In an hour's time he had gone from being on the cusp of an engagement, to witnessing a killing carried out by his intended fiancé. It was more than he could absorb.

Bryan's temporary paralysis was instantly curtailed by Katy's desperate plea.

"Don't just sit there," Katy yelled, "help me!" On instinct but still in a stupor, Bryan exited the car. He was almost too stunned to talk, but finally uttered something.

"Katy, we need to get out of here," he said. "Fast. I'll drive, come on let's go."

Chapter 24

The pair hopped into the car as it screeched out of Pope's driveway and down the street.

Bryan immediately lit into Katy.

"How could you bring me here?" he screamed.

"I told you I had to run an errand," Katy said, tears now streaming down her cheeks, "and I also told you I could do it myself."

"What the hell, Katy! I didn't know you were planning on shooting somebody!" Bryan exclaimed.

"I wasn't," Katy said. "He's a piece of filth. I just wanted him to stay away from my brother. Then things got out of hand. You saw it, he rushed me. I was just trying to scare him. I didn't mean for the gun to go off."

"I can't believe you shot him," yelled Bryan, "and now," he continued somewhat under his breath, "I can't believe I am driving you away from the scene."

The situation was dire and getting worse by the minute. All of a sudden, Katy remembered something that caused additional angst.

"We need to go back," said Katy. "Q saw me. He can identify me as being at Pope's residence."

"WHO IN THE HELL IS Q?" Bryan screamed again.

"Bryan, turn around and go back. Or get out and I will go back myself," Katy yelled desperately. "We have to get Pope's body so that no one knows he's dead."

Katy paused for several seconds and then teared up again. "I'm sorry Bryan," she shrieked in agony. "I'm so very, very sorry to have dragged you into this."

Not sure of where he was going anyway, Bryan made a quick U turn on a side street and headed back to Pope's house. He was driving at least 55 miles per hour in a residential zone. In less than a minute and a half, the car swerved sharply back into the driveway it had just exited.

Bryan dimmed the headlights as the car pulled to within feet of Pope's lifeless body. He and Katy exited the car and quickly dragged Pope to the back of the vehicle where they lifted him up.

As Bryan gave one final push to roll Pope into the trunk, a small box tumbled out of his pocket and pirouetted downward. When the box made contact with the pavement, it split open revealing its precious cargo, a stunning diamond ring. The ring came to rest in a pool of Pope's blood, it's brilliance illuminated by the driveway's street lamps.

Katy stared at the ring in disbelief. She had already concluded that her impulsiveness a few minutes before could cost her dearly, perhaps her very freedom. Now Katy realized that the cost had been much greater. She looked at Bryan and started to sob.

Chapter 25

Inundated with fear but recognizing the need to get as far away from Pope's house as quickly as possible, a distraught and frazzled Katy took the wheel with a speechless and bewildered Bryan next to her. No words were spoken for several minutes, as Katy drove in circles around Gentilly while wiping the steady stream of tears that flowed down her cheeks.

Bryan finally broke the silence. "That . . . was for you," he said to Katy, then he lowered his head as his voice sank to a whisper. "It was your engagement ring."

Katy just nodded and continued to weep. She loved Bryan dearly but restating the obvious now was pointless. Once she saw the ring Katy perfectly fit together all the pieces of the puzzle. She figured Bryan hadn't come all the way to New Orleans to propose to Pope.

Bryan tried to change the subject, but his choice of words and good judgment had deserted him.

"Kathryn," he said slowly, "you just killed a man."

"Kathryn?" Katy screamed. "Kathryn? Are you going to be impersonal now? What's next? Ms. Duvall? Nurse Duvall?"

Katy immediately floored the accelerator, swerved hard to the right and cut across several lanes of traffic. A series of oncoming vehicles slammed their brakes and honked their horns as angry motorists glared at the careening Mercury Sable.

One irate driver pulled alongside their car, rolled down his window and yelled "Learn to drive bitch!"

Katy pressed her hand hard down on the horn, then lifted it and pointed it at the man, prominently displaying her extended middle finger in the process.

Clearly shaken and now quivering uncontrollably, Katy proceeded to slowly guide the car to a vacant lot on the outskirts of Camp Leroy Johnson next to the Lakefront Arena at the University of New Orleans.

As the car rolled to a stop, Katy could no longer harness her despair. She realized the full magnitude of the evening's events. Instead of ending up as a fiancé' with a ring that would be the envy of her friends and family, she was now likely a murderer, at the very least a felon. And the person she thought was her soulmate appeared to no longer want any part of her, or at least that is how Katy perceived things.

"Let me make this easy for you Bryan" Katy said softly. "You want to distance yourself from me. That's fine. I understand. I might do the same thing if I were you. Trying to survive and protect your family while living in New Orleans is not your battle."

"Katy, that's not it at all," interjected Bryan.

"Get out of the car," Katy cried, tears running down her cheeks as she continued to tremble.

"Go ahead. Get out. Go back to your flawless life in California. That's what you want, isn't it? Go on and disappear and I'll make sure that your pristine little hands never get dirty."

"Katy, I didn't mean . . ." Bryan started.

"Well what exactly did you mean Bryan?" Katy interrupted as she lunged at Bryan and began pounding on his chest with clenched fists.

"Do you have any idea what it's like to grow up where I was born?" Katy yelled. "DO YOU? Of course you don't. You have no clue," Katy continued, now in full meltdown.

"In your world, you show up, wave your magic wand and everything turns to gold. Well that's not my reality Bryan," screamed Katy. "There's no escape. It's just a matter of when, not if, the streets claim you. Killing folks in New Orleans is not a big deal. Life here is cheap. You can almost get numb to the callousness and that's a shame. It's the hell that scum like Pope have half of the City living under."

"Get out," Katy sniffled. "Get out of the car now. You are either with me or you're not and it's obvious you're not. So get out and I'll handle this on my own. You can catch a cab back to the hotel."

"Katy, I came here to propose to you, so obviously I'm with you," Bryan said.

Katy was not ready to let up.

"Don't worry," Katy continued, as she wiped a new stream of tears from her cheeks. "I'll return the car to you later tonight and you can fly back to California in the morning and just act like nothing ever happened. You never knew 'Kathryn Duvall' and I never knew Mr. Stirling. That's what you want now, isn't it Bryan?" she said.

Bryan stared into space. He couldn't understand why Katy was chastising him. She killed Pope, not him. If he had his way, this night would have been the happiest evening of both of their lives.

Returning to reality, Bryan knew that the smartest thing for him to do was to indeed exit the car as Katy suggested and return to his hotel. He took a deep breath and considered all he was risking if he didn't leave now.

Then he thought about Katy. If only he had been assertive and not allowed their dinner conversation to go off on several tangents. He could have, should have proposed earlier he told himself, right after they sat down. He was certain that the entire evening would have played out differently had he acted more decisively. Maybe it would have worked out. Maybe not. Anything, however, would be better than the predicament the two of them now found themselves in where one and perhaps both of them might end up behind bars.

There was little time for reflection. Bryan opened the car door and started to leave, but then slowly closed it. He could not abandon Katy.

"Drive" said Bryan, climbing back in. "Just drive. We'll figure it out." The car pulled back on to the road as both occupants buckled their seat belts. The vehicle headed south on Franklin Street into the growing and uncertain Louisiana darkness. At that moment, Bryan realized that his life would never be the same again.

Chapter 26

Katy tried to regain her composure as she continued to maneuver the car south out of the City. The tear stains running from the bottom of her eyes, through her cheeks and down to her lower jaw, had begun to dry but they left noticeable tracks, almost like stripes.

As she drove, Katy thought about her own dreams, dreams of getting married, having a family and moving into a nice house on the other side of Lake Pontchartrain back by Nana's house, dreams that now seemed beyond her reach.

Hopping on the freeway, Katy began to plot what to do next. Nothing immediately came to mind. She re-lived the events of the past hour, then quickly fast-forwarded back to the present to deal with the circumstances at hand.

A few minutes later, Katy broke the silence. "Bryan, you saw Pope rush me and then I panicked. You're a lawyer. If I ever get arrested for this, can I claim self-defense?"

Bryan had already been thinking about that possibility.

"You clearly did not intend to shoot him," he said. "You tried to fire twice in the air, but the gun didn't work. So there's a good argument that when you actually shot him, you didn't think the gun was properly loaded. On the other hand, you went to Pope's house, you drew your weapon and your gun fired and killed him. Pope had no weapon. That will make a self-defense claim difficult. You could get off but my bet is that a DA would push for manslaughter conviction, which could mean several years in prison."

Bryan wasn't finished. The circumstances called for him to temper his response to fit the situation and help alleviate Katy's growing trepidation. He couldn't do it. Instead, the courtroom lawyer in him took over.

"Typically," Bryan continued, "the use of deadly force is not justified unless the actor is faced with deadly force himself."

"Bryan, stop it," Katy yelled. "I just wanted a simple answer to what I thought was a simple question. I don't need a legal analysis or a damn law school lecture. I'm your fiance' remember. Or at least I would have been," she continued as her voice trailed off and she started to cry again, now fully regretting that she asked for Bryan's opinion in the first place.

"I was just wondering . . . hoping . . . I guess that . . . well, never mind. It doesn't really matter anymore."

The car kept moving southward deeper into the delta night almost as if Katy had put the vehicle on auto-pilot and programmed it to outrun her troubles.

Suddenly Katy had an idea. She steered the car towards Highway 23, then made a beeline for the west bank of the Mississippi, reuniting with the River at Belle Chase, just south of the English Turn.

Bryan noticed that they were no longer drifting aimlessly as Katy seemed to be driving with a purpose.

"Where are we going?" he asked meekly, more out of resignation than curiosity.

"To a fishing spot my dad used to take me to," Katy responded.

All of a sudden the pair heard sirens in the distance. Katy could see the flashing lights of a rapidly approaching emergency vehicle in her rear view mirror. Her heart sank.

"That's it. It's over," Bryan said. "We're cooked."

As the advancing vehicle closed in, Katy could see it was a Louisiana State Trooper patrol car. It pulled up right behind Katy, then flashed its bright lights. Just then, Katy and Bryan heard a voice on the officer's bullhorn over the blaring sirens.

"Move over," said the patrolman.

Katy hesitated.

"Katy, you heard the man," repeated Bryan, "move over."

Katy guided the car to the right along the highway's shoulder as the patrol cruiser sped by and continued on its journey. She and Bryan simultaneously exhaled a sigh of relief. The troopers were attending to other business.

The police vehicle now thankfully past them, Katy began to tick off the familiar landmarks in her mind as they sped through the suffocating darkness under the watchful gaze of the mighty River to their left. First the town of Live Oak, then Alliance, then a couple of miles later, the Myrtle Grove Marina. As the faint lights of the sleepy town of Davant came into view across the River, Katy pulled off Louisiana 23 and proceeded to navigate through the darkened back roads and gravel trails that she once knew so well.

The irony of the journey was not lost on Katy. Every previous sojourn to this special patch of Louisiana ground had been a fun filled outing with her father in joyful anticipation of the day on the lake that was to come next. This time there was only solemnness and despair.

A mile or so later they reached a location that Katy decided was somewhat close to her father's favorite fishing location. The car stopped. Emotionally and physically drained, Katy and Bryan collapsed into each other's arms and embraced in a hug that lasted a minute or more.

Then, realizing there was precious little time to waste, they pulled Pope's body from the trunk and dragged it through the tall reeds and intertidal marshes. They stopped when they stumbled upon Earl's Bait Shoppe.

"Earl always kept tools in that shed," Katy said to Bryan, "so we need to break in through the back door."

The two of them summoned what little strength they had left and rushed the shed in unison with full force, like battering rams simultaneously crashing into the wall of a colonial fort. On the third try, the lock snapped and the door buckled. With one last push, Katy forced the door open, tripped over the miniature first step and stumbled inside.

Bryan stayed outside. As crickets chirped and bullfrogs croaked, he could hear Katy rummaging around the interior of the shed in total darkness, her collisions into boxes and crates sounding like a demolition derby at the local speedway. Finally, Katy emerged from behind the shattered door with a shovel in hand.

The pair moved quickly and dragged Pope's body from Earl's shack in the direction of the lake.

"We've got to go up," said Katy. "We have to bury him on the highest ground we can find. There's a slight ridge just ahead of us. We'll need to pull him uphill a bit, so it's going to be tougher. "

"Why?" replied Bryan. "Let's just stop right here. It's hard enough dragging him on level ground through all this muck. I can't move another step. Why do we need to go higher?"

"Obviously you don't know anything about burials in southeastern Louisiana," Katy replied.

"You're right about that," Bryan replied sarcastically. "That class in law school on 'The Basics of Louisiana Internment'? I skipped it. I had no idea I'd ever need it."

"Bryan, this is not the time or the place," Katy continued. As distressed as she was, she couldn't help but marvel again at Bryan's attempt at dark humor, especially given the dire circumstances. But matters had gotten far too serious for Katy to acknowledge Bryan's off the cuff remark.

"Come on, pull with me," Katy said. "Let's go."

Finally Katy stopped, figuring that it was too risky to go any further. She concluded that they were far enough away from Earl's shack and high enough to bury Pope's body in a place that would not easily be discovered.

The pair then begun the solemn task of digging a three and a half foot grave. They rolled Pope into it and shoveled the dirt back on top of him, making the scene as inconspicuous as possible. If no one discovered the site in a week or two, the natural conditions and moistness of the soil would result in rapid decomposition.

Depleted and haggard, Katy and Bryan began the somber walk back to the car. When they approached the lake shore, Katy tossed the shovel as far out into the lake as she could.

After reaching the car, Katy resumed her spot in the driver's seat. She turned the key in the ignition, then shifted the gear to reverse in order to back away from the water's edge. The car refused to budge as the rear wheels rotated rapidly in place. The vehicle was stuck in mud.

Katy pressed harder on the accelerator. The engine revved up, raising the decibel level. All of a sudden the car inched to the rear, then sped backwards with a huge thud as the front end bounced hard on the soft earth.

Extricated from their temporary quandary, the pair began the drive back to the City. The bright lights of New Orleans beckoned in the distance and somewhere on Bourbon Street, roisterers were just getting started on an evening of fun and frolic that would last until dawn.

For Katy and Bryan though there would be no celebration. Their eyes met once more only this time there was no joy or anticipation, just a gaze of longing for what might have been. The exhilaration of each of their prior meetings was replaced by fear, desperation and the unspoken truth that the events of this night must never be mentioned again.

Chapter 27

"Sir" the flight attendant admonished. "Sir," she said again to the passenger sitting in first class seat 2B, with his head buried in his hands as his elbows rested on the tray table.

"Sir, please sit back, put your tray table up and bring your seat forward. Sir please. Don't make me remove you from the flight. You must cooperate, we are taxiing toward the runway."

A groggy Bryan slowly looked up and finally complied with the attendant's orders.

"I'm, I'm sorry," he stammered. "I guess I didn't hear you."

"That's quite all right sir," the flight attendant replied as she felt a twinge of sympathy when she noticed the passenger's bloodshot eyes, deep lines on his face and tear stains on his cheeks. "We just want you to be safe. Thank you and have a good flight."

As the jet accelerated down the runway and began to lift off, Bryan took one last look outside. His mind scrambled, he had no idea where he would go from here. Bryan vowed to himself, however, that he would never, ever set foot in Louisiana again.

Chapter 28

Katy couldn't sleep. She tossed and turned in her bed, unable to erase from her mind the events of that October 1997 night a month earlier. As she flung the covers to the floor, the apartment's smoke alarm suddenly went off. Within seconds, Katy detected the aroma of burning metal wafting through the apartment. She rushed to the kitchen to find her teapot ablaze, a hole having been charred through the bottom by the still ignited burner.

Katy grabbed a pot holder, tossed the scorched kettle into the sink and immediately doused it with water from the faucet. The rising steam created a temporary fog that mirrored the one in her head. The teapot was ruined. Katy's frustration had reached its boiling point.

It was not Katy's first major blunder of the past few weeks. A couple of days earlier she had come within inches of flattening a crossing guard as he stepped into the street to escort a group of grade-schoolers across a busy thoroughfare. Later, when the policewoman wrote out the ticket, Katy claimed she never saw the guard or the stop sign he was holding, and only slammed on her brakes when she noticed the kids leave the curb out of the corner of her eye.

Katy's performance at work, usually stellar, was just as dismal. She was easily confused by routine assignments, forgot to note appointment changes from patients and entered information in the wrong files on her computer. Her life was spiraling out of control.

Katy lived in constant fear and paranoia. Each morning she woke up afraid that the New Orleans police were camped outside her door, waiting to slap on the handcuffs as soon as she emerged. She became convinced that every car in her rear view mirror was following her. If she walked past someone wearing dark sunglasses, the person had to be an undercover law enforcement agent, or perhaps an underling of Pope's crime syndicate out for retribution. The anxiety never ceased.

Eventually, Katy's fear led to depression. Then depression became despair when Bryan stopped returning Katy's phone calls. It all added up to repeated sleepless nights, constant angst, no way out and no hope. And now, no Bryan.

Katy thought about simply going to the police and explaining what happened. After all, the shooting was an accident. She fretted about the publicity, however, and wondered whether the police would believe her. Then she remembered what Bryan said about Pope being unarmed. She could not go to the authorities. Not yet anyway. It was simply too risky.

Then, there was the chilling fact that Katy knew Q could place her at the scene. Surely Q must have heard the shot Katy fired if he had still been in the house, Katy thought. At a minimum, Q knew that Katy was at Pope's residence the night that Pope disappeared. Who had he told Katy wondered and what would happen when she ran into Q again?

All roads pointed to checkmate. Paralyzed by fear, Katy's predicament led only to inaction. There was nothing she could do except wallow in her own private prison.

Chapter 29

Bryan lay on his couch staring at the ceiling. He kept hoping against hope that this was all a bad dream. Just then, his phone rang. Bryan had refused to answer it for weeks, partly out of not wanting to speak to anyone and partly out of fear that the caller might be from a Louisiana law enforcement agency. He routinely let the phone ring until it activated his recorded greeting. If the caller decided to leave a message that was fine. If the caller simply hung up, then all the better.

After his greeting ended and the beep sounded, Bryan hoped whoever was calling him this time would hang up but instead he heard a voice. A very familiar voice.

"Bryan, this is Katy. I need to talk to you."

Katy had left a couple of messages before, but Bryan ignored them. He could not bring himself to speak to her yet.

"Bryan, I know you're there. Please answer."

The despair in Katy's voice was palpable. Her desperation was too urgent for Bryan to ignore. He lifted up the receiver.

"Hello Katy," Bryan said softly.

"Bryan, how are you?" Katy replied. "I'm so glad to hear your voice. Do you have a few minutes? We really need to talk."

"Katy, this is not something I want to talk about right now. It's been very difficult for me as I am sure it has been for you. I just need some time to think and sort everything through, that's all."

"Well," said Katy. "I've been thinking about, you know . . . whether it might make sense to just go to the police. But then I back off. I just can't do it. It's very difficult to live with myself. It's very difficult for me to be in New Orleans period."

"There are no easy answers," replied Bryan. "A million things might have gone differently that night but they didn't. None of that helps us now. We are where we are and we can't go back. We've put ourselves into a maze from which there is no escape."

"Well then what are going to do?" said an exasperated Katy, searching for answers that didn't exist.

"I don't know Katy. But I think we should refrain from communicating for a while. For all we know, the police could be recording this very conversation," Bryan concluded, showing that he had become every bit as paranoid as Katy.

"I just can't deal with this anymore," Bryan added. "I know it wasn't your fault, but we have to live with what we've done. And living with what we've done I think means we have to let each other go. At least for now."

"That's your opinion, not mine," replied Katy, "but do what's best for you," she said trying to remain composed. "Isn't that the way things work? I'll manage. Somehow."

"Katy . . . I didn't mean," Bryan started to say before he was interrupted.

"I'm done with rowing upstream," Katy replied. "I understand. You won't have to worry about dodging my calls again."

Neither spoke for the next twenty seconds but it seemed like half an hour.

"Good-by Katy," Bryan finally murmured.

There was no answer. After a few seconds, Bryan heard a click on the other end. The line was dead.

Anguish consumed them both. It would be almost two years before they spoke again.

Chapter 30

May 1998

The following May brought a sweltering spring to New Orleans. By this time, Katy's constant uneasiness had subsided a bit, although the memory of Pope's shooting was never far from her stream of consciousness. As far as Katy knew, Pope's body had not been discovered nor was there any connection made between her and the fact that Pope had not been seen or heard from for months.

Katy did not know it, but the New Orleans police were well aware that Pope had mysteriously vanished from the scene. They were not yet ready to conclude that Pope had been taken out since there were various theories regarding Pope's whereabouts. One rumor had Pope fleeing to Mobile, Alabama to set up shop there after the mob threatened to take over his New Orleans operations. So far, however, there was no confirmation of anything.

Seeking relief from the stifling humidity, Katy started her nightly jog hoping to catch a stiff breeze. After working up a sweat, Katy sensed that she was not alone. She turned around but saw nothing unusual. After dashing a bit further, Katy was certain she detected footsteps. She turned again and this time noticed a hooded figure in athletic running gear trailing about twenty yards to the rear.

Katy accelerated her pace and took a right at the next street, deviating from her usual route. A few seconds later she again glanced behind and saw the runner make the same turn. The gap between them was narrowing.

Anxious, Katy quickened her strides. Always in excellent shape, Katy was now in full gallop. She had recently run a half marathon. If she was being followed, the stalker had better be prepared to match Katy's blistering pace.

Once more, Katy looked over her shoulder. The silhouette behind her was fading in the distance. Katy made one final turn into an alleyway and then shifted into a full out sprint. "Good, I've lost him," she thought to herself, breathing a sigh of relief.

A moment later, a car swerved around the corner and plowed into the alley from the other end, its high beams focused directly on Katy. Startled, Katy turned back and began to flee in the opposite direction. Suddenly the jogger reappeared. Out of breath, he stumbled around the corner and into the alleyway entrance, blocking Katy's only path of escape.

Katy was trapped. To her left was a 10 foot high brick wall but there was no grip to steady her ascent. To her right stood a chain link fence surrounding a storage yard containing dozens of statuary fountains. They were ghastly in the evening light, like giant, marble tombstones. With little time to waste, Katy quickly began to scale the railing, glancing from side to side for any sign of her pursuers. In an instant, two Rottweiler guard dogs emerged from the darkness, weaving their way through the fountains. Eyeing the intruder on the fence, one of them launched an all-out sprint directly at Katy, lunging at her as she escalated upward.

Suddenly Katy was face-to-face with the ferocious canine, now in full attack mode, separated only by the fragile metal strands of the fence. Katy felt the animal's hot breath against her cheeks. She could see rows of pointed teeth in the predator's mouth, mere inches from her. In seconds the other dog joined the fray, ramming itself into the wire mesh and thereby throwing its full weight against Katy. The force of the snarling duo dislodged Katy's fingers from the slick, intertwined links. Flailing backwards, Katy crashed to the concrete below in a crumpled heap.

Groggy, Katy tried to clear her head. Beads of sweat cascaded over her eyelids, blurring her vision and stinging her eyes with salt. As she pulled herself up, Katy heard someone yell, "there she is. Let's go."

In seconds the ground shook with the vibration of approaching feet. The chasers were in hot pursuit and closing in. Moments later Katy found herself looking up into a flashlight pointed at her eyes. She tried to cover her face with her hands but it was no use. Then she heard another voice.

"That's her. Take care of it. Now!"

Still blinded by the light, Katy made out the barrel of a revolver aimed at her temple. Meanwhile, the dogs continued their menacing growls on the other side of the fence, frustrated at being unable to reach their quarry.

Katy heard the gun cock. Acting on instinct and adrenalin, Katy clenched her fists and tried to strike her assailants, but her punches were thrown in vain and hit only air.

"No," Katy screamed. "Noooooooooo!"

Suddenly Katy saw a brilliant flash of orange.

And then . . .

Katy continued punching, but now she was punching the pillow on her bed. She violently ripped off the sheets and jumped out of bed as if leaping from the top floor of a skyscraper. Her palms were damp with perspiration, her pajamas soaking wet. She ran into the bathroom and looked into the mirror. She was a mess, but gratefully all in one piece.

Then Katy frantically searched for something to grab. If she could touch something, feel something, it would prove that she was still alive and that the entire episode was just a bad dream, a nightmare of the worst kind. The first thing that came within Katy's grasp was her stuffed bear, Corduroy. She squeezed him as tight as she could and then sobbed into her nearly destroyed pillow, crying herself to sleep. She held on tight until dawn broke the next morning.

Part III – Matrix

Chapter 31

The City of New Orleans has a famous motto: "laissez les bon temps rouler," or "let the good times roll." When you are in the City, you're expected to enjoy yourself. That's a given. Orleanians take it as a personal affront if you don't. And there are no inhibiting rites of passage or conditions of acceptance. As I was once told by a new acquaintance, "when you are in this city, you're home." His words rang true. In New Orleans, no stranger is a stranger.

This does not mean of course that when you depart New Orleans you will not do so with a lighter wallet. You may well leave the City flat broke and depending upon your choice of vices, in need of a dose or two of penicillin. But you will leave with a full stomach and a smile on your face, yearning for your next visit.

As with most places, there is a flip side to the City's welcoming warmth. In New Orleans, the demons are often camouflaged behind the City's festive exterior, inhabiting the shadows to prey on unsuspecting revelers and natives alike, concealing their deception with elaborate disguises and masks intended to hide their true intentions. It is a matrix of sorts, and by the time the villains have done their dirty work it is usually too late.

Already near rock bottom, Katy Duvall was about to unwittingly enter The Matrix. It would take all of the Louisiana country guile she could muster, and no small amount of courage to get her out of it.

Chapter 32

(June 1999)

Katy scanned the information map located just outside The Shops at Canal Place, searching for the Gucci outlet. She had never shopped there before but had heard from friends that if she wanted to treat herself to an expensive gift, she would find no shortage of choices at Gucci.

If sitting around at home and moping couldn't cure her depression, perhaps a little indulgence in the form of a fancy watch or a sleek pair of shoes would. Katy's search was coming up empty, however. Frustrated and losing patience at the lack of information she needed from the shopping center Directory, Katy turned around and headed for the mall to locate the elusive store herself.

As she stalked towards the mall entrance, Katy nearly stumbled directly into an onlooker who was standing behind her. She regained her balance in the nick of time, avoiding a calamitous tumble.

"Whoa," said the stranger. "That was a quite a tap dancing act." Then after pulling snug his cashmere jacket and straightening his shoulders, he continued. "You must be looking for me," he uttered confidently.

Katy smiled slightly, then pivoted diagonally in an attempt to bypass the man, who was wearing Versace slacks and dark shades. She thought his opening line was a bit lame, but humorous nonetheless.

"I'm Axel Lanier," said the stranger, extending his hand to Katy, who was now two steps past him and rapidly moving in the other direction. "You've probably heard of me. And you are?" Axel asked as Katy quickened her strides away from him.

"Now come on, is that any way to treat a friendly face?" Axel continued.

Katy thought about ignoring him. After all, a Gucci watch beckoned and Katy had no interest in playing "What's My Line?" Problem was, Katy *had* actually heard of Axel Lanier. She slowed her determined march towards the designer accessories ever so slightly.

"Let's start over," said Axel. "Hi, I am Axel Lanier and I'm pleased to meet you."

This time he dropped the aggravating add-on "you've probably heard of me." Axel had a tendency to boast, so any extended communication from him that lacked self-promotion was rare.

"Whom do I have the pleasure of speaking with?"

"I'm Kathryn," said Katy, who by this time had made a half turn towards Axel, with one foot pointing in his direction and the other still lined up with the entrance to The Shops.

"Kathryn?" said Axel.

"Yes, Kathryn," replied Katy, who used her full first name when she felt uncomfortable or wanted to establish a barrier to keep a conversation impersonal. "Kathryn Duvall."

"Well nice meeting you Kathryn Duvall," replied Axel. "Are you going to do some shopping?"

"Maybe," said Katy, "except I can't find Gucci."

Axel let out a loud laugh. "I guess you don't come here often," he said, "but this is your lucky day. Gucci has a small boutique section inside Saks Fifth Avenue. There is no separate Gucci store. That's why you didn't see it on the Directory. Come on, I'll show you."

"Oh" paused Katy, momentarily confused and slightly embarrassed. "Of course, of course," she continued. "I knew that," even though Axel didn't believe for a minute that Katy knew Gucci was located inside Saks and Katy knew that Axel wasn't buying it.

Axel chuckled to himself. His rapid assessment was that the initial coquetry and the flirtations he used with most women were not likely to work with Katy. Still, Axel was fairly confident that Katy would have a hard time ditching him after he had solved the Gucci mystery. That was a good thing he thought, because Katy was indeed stunning. Axel was anxious to continue the conversation.

The two walked inside the mall and headed up to Saks. They made small talk, with Axel doing most of the talking. His tendency to verbalize his self-importance quickly re-emerged.

"My family and I thought about putting in a bid to develop this mall, but we passed on it," he said. "We just didn't think it was a good fit and we knew we had more profitable projects in the pipeline."

Axel didn't realize it, but Katy could care less about how many properties he and his family owned or what "projects were in the pipeline."

Katy's pace accelerated. The sooner she found Gucci, the better she thought, and the quicker she could extricate herself from Axel's musings about his wealth.

Upon arriving at Gucci, Katy started browsing through the women's shoes. Axel was now getting the hint that Katy preferred to shop alone.

After trying on some shoes and some watches, Katy no longer felt compelled to buy anything, especially since the items she liked were outside of her budget.

"Do you see anything you like?" said Axel. "Just let me know. I'm treating. You can treat me next time."

Katy wanted no part of any "next time" with Axel. She surmised that Axel was probably at least fifteen years older than she was. Aside from their age difference, Katy felt uncomfortable with the idea of a complete stranger buying her an expensive gift. Still, those leather loafers she had been eyeing were pretty enticing.

After giving it some thought, Katy said "thank you very much, but I'll have to decline. I appreciate the offer though."

As Katy left Saks and headed in the direction of her car, Axel followed. When Katy reached her car, she turned to Axel.

"It was nice meeting you," she said.

"That's it?" replied Axel. "Well if you going to turn down a gift, then at least you can join me on a date for Saturday night. That is, unless you are already seeing someone and even if you are, you aren't committed to anyone are you?" asked Axel.

Katy hung her head. Axel's question brought back the haunting image of the engagement ring Bryan purchased for her, perched at her feet in a pool of blood, Pope's blood. The emotions were still raw and powerful. She almost teared up, but collected herself.

"I have an event to attend on Saturday but no one to go with," continued Axel. You wouldn't say no to me twice, would you?" he asked.

"What event?" said Katy, brushing back a tear or two.

"You'll see," said Axel. "I'll take that as a 'yes.' It's a formal dinner. Where do you live and I will pick you up at 6:30."

Katy hesitated. She really wasn't interested but then thought that an evening away from her self-imposed confinement might do her some good. She gave Axel her cell phone number and address and agreed to the Saturday evening engagement.

"I'll see you then Kathryn," said Axel.

"You can call me 'Katy'," Kathryn replied.

As Katy drove home, she tried to remember where she heard the name Axel Lanier, but kept drawing a blank. Then, when Katy pulled into the parking space at her apartment, it came to her. Of course. Axel was the President of Lanier Properties, one of New Orleans' largest, family-owned businesses. Lanier Properties was the landlord and developer of several apartment housing complexes.

The man she had just met was one of New Orleans' high rollers.

Chapter 33

The Lanier family fortune that Axel inherited was built through hard work, bold decisions, impeccable timing and a dash of pure, dumb luck. In the late 1700's, Axel's great, great, great grandmother of Native American, Spanish and African descent, became the mistress of a prominent French naval officer, who made regular pit stops in New Orleans from his patrols on the Gulf Coast. More than a hundred years later in the 1920s, one of the descendants of their union Pierre Lanier, Axel's grandfather, would be appointed Chief Inspector of the Port of New Orleans.

Like his brothers and sisters, Pierre was worldly and educated. His fair skin, straight hair and blue-green eyes made him stand out as the most European-looking among the Laniers of his generation. Because he passed for white most of his adult life, Pierre found himself presented with economic opportunities not afforded to his siblings and seventeen first cousins. He took full advantage of them.

Pierre's business acumen was extraordinary. He was frugal with his earnings, figuring that if he were ever exposed as being part black and thereby cut off from work that paid the salary he had become accustomed to, his savings would enable him to maintain his standard of living. When the Great Depression hit, Pierre used his accumulated nest egg to purchase about a dozen parcels of raw land in the New Orleans area at huge discounts from panicked landowners desperate to sell.

For years Pierre resisted the suggestions of family members, many of whom were eager to benefit from his acuity, who urged him to liquidate his properties and cash in. When the national economy boomed during World War II, the value of Pierre's holdings skyrocketed. He then sold off several parcels for substantial profits, while still retaining land in some undeveloped parts of Orleans Parish.

Pierre's dealings created the Lanier real estate empire that was eventually passed down to subsequent generations. His legacy as a shrewd and cunning businessman, already substantial, was permanently secured.

The words ultimately spoken about his grandson would not be nearly as charitable.

Chapter 34

The limousine arrived promptly at 6:30 p.m. just as Axel promised. Katy opened her door to be greeted by a fully uniformed chauffeur. Determined that her attire would fit the occasion, Katy was clad in the only long evening dress she owned, off-white with a long split up the side of her leg. She wore a sapphire necklace that was a college graduation gift from her father.

Axel emerged from the vehicle, presented Katy with a dozen roses and then opened the door for her. As Katy entered the back seat of the limousine and sat down, she noticed a bottle of Dom Perignon in a bucket of ice directly in front of her, resting on a plate with oysters on the half shell surrounded by sliced sourdough bread.

Katy was not used to such opulence. Axel poured her a glass of champagne as the limousine made its way through the Garden District towards downtown. "Are you still refusing to tell me where we are going?" Katy asked.

"It's a surprise," said Axel. "But you will know soon enough."

Finally, the limousine stopped and parked outside of the World War II museum. Katy had been there on a number of prior occasions. This time, however, the two made their way to the museum's banquet hall which was normally off limits to the public.

Axel strode in with Katy on his arm, clad in a $4,000 navy suit, custom made and tailored by Zegna of Italy. The pair was escorted to the front of the dining hall and seated at one of the reserved banquet tables.

Katy noticed a program at each place setting. The cover of the program read "1999 New Orleans Veterans of Foreign Wars Annual Community Awards Gala Banquet." Katy started to open the program, but Axel gently placed his hand over hers to keep the inside of the program hidden from her view. Axel motioned with his hand and gestured with his eyes for her to wait.

The ceremony proceeded with the introduction of various dignitaries complete with the recognition of their career milestones and accomplishments. A few veterans received distinguished service awards for their combat service, including one 78 year old man who had been run over by a tank in Aix, France north of Marseille during World War II.

As the ceremony reached its climax, a local retired colonel stepped to the podium to announce The Person of Year. After some introductory remarks, the colonel continued with his speech.

"This individual has demonstrated an exemplary dedication to veterans by providing apartments for 47 formerly homeless veterans in just the past year alone. Ladies and gentlemen, I present to you our Person of the Year, Axel Lanier."

The crowd cheered loudly and stood as one in raucous applause. Axel acknowledged the salutations, kissed Katy on the cheek, and rose from his seat to take his place at the podium for his acceptance speech. It contained more self-serving braggadocio which made Katy cringe.

After the dinner concluded, Axel introduced Katy to several of the luminaries in attendance. Katy was not accustomed to attending formal events or mingling with the "who's who" of New Orleans society, but she moved easily and gracefully among the local socialites.

One of the attendees, a particular handsome gentlemen who appeared to be about thirty-five years old, approached Axel and Katy.

He extended his hand to Katy, held her fingertips in his palm, and lightly kissed the top of her hand as he bowed slightly on one knee.

"Lanier, you've outdone yourself," the man said to Axel as he continued to gaze at Katy.

At that point, Axel felt compelled to introduce the stranger to Katy although he otherwise would have rather not.

"Katy, this is Augustine Perilloux. His friends call him Gus. I won't tell you what I call him," Axel laughed. "Gus owns Perilloux Realty, one of Lanier's chief competitors. You could say Gus and I are adversaries. Friendly adversaries of course."

"Adversaries indeed," Perilloux muttered. "Pleased to meet you Katy," he said. "Yes, somehow Axel always seems to outmaneuver me at the last minute for the prime construction deals. Now he's got the prettiest lady in the building on his arm. If I didn't know better, and I do, I'd swear Axel must be living right."

Then Gus whispered in Katy's ear, but loud enough so Axel could hear him.

"If you ever get tired of this old guy, just give me a ring," he said as he winked at Katy and walked away.

"Son of a bitch," Axel muttered to Katy as soon as Perilloux was out of earshot. "Gus wants to play with the big boys but he doesn't have the stones to do it. All hat, no cattle as they say in Texas."

Katy found the whole episode amusing. Perilloux was suave and debonair, but clearly had an ax to grind with Axel. Axel seemed perturbed by Perilloux's insinuations about his character and didn't appreciate the not so subtle flirtations with his date. And there sat Katy on the big stage, unwittingly in the middle of a tug-of-war between prominent New Orleans real estate developers.

After another hour or so of hobnobbing, Katy and Axel prepared to leave. Axel shook several hands on his way out. While he was doing so, Gus managed to locate Katy. He slipped her one of his business cards while Axel was looking the other way. Katy glanced briefly at the card which contained Gus' business address and contact information, then turned it over. There was writing on the back of the card but Katy had to look closer to make it out.

"I was serious," it said, under which was drawn a smiling face and Gus' scribbled signature.

After Katy glanced at the card, she looked up and turned to Gus, but he had vanished into the crowd. Just then Axel appeared and wrapped his hand around hers. With her other hand, Katy quickly slipped Gus's business card into her purse, but Axel noticed.

"What was that?" he said.

"Oh nothing," said Katy, who quickly changed the subject.

"I had no idea you were so dedicated to helping homeless veterans," Katy said. "You should be proud. I'm impressed with the work you and your family are doing in our community."

Katy didn't know Axel well but from what little she had seen, she correctly deduced that Axel's focus could be shifted by steering any conversation no matter the subject, to an alternative topic that heaped praise and flattery on him. Her tactics proved successful.

"The Laniers are committed to enhancing the lives of the good people of New Orleans," Axel boasted, puffing out his chest and forgetting all about the card that Katy had placed in her handbag. "We're just doing our part."

As the limousine cruised through a moonlit New Orleans, Katy leaned back on the head rest and closed her eyes. "There are some things about this Axel guy I'm not sure about," she thought to herself, "but he's got some good qualities. Perhaps I should not have pre-judged him. I'm going to keep an open mind."

Those types of thoughts had things moving in just the direction that Axel hoped.

Chapter 35

Katy didn't know it, but her "chance" meeting with Axel Lanier at the Canal Place shopping center was not by chance at all. Axel first spotted Katy years earlier when she and her mother came to clean the Lanier family mansion one summer weekend in the mid-1980s when Katy was sixteen. Axel, who had just assumed control of Lanier Properties at the time, was thirty-seven, married and happened to be at the house that day when Katy and Francine arrived to vacuum, dust and mop. Always one with an eye for beautiful women, Axel could not help but notice the shapely teenager scrubbing the kitchen stove.

"Who are the cleaning people?" Axel casually asked his mother Mercedes, trying to seem uninterested yet at the same time very interested. Mercedes informed Axel that they were "Francine Bernard and her daughter Kathryn from one of New Orleans public housing projects, I don't know which one. All I know is that they do a much better job cleaning the house than the last people we had in here from the other side of the tracks."

From that time forward, Axel never forgot "Kathryn" the cleaning lady's daughter, but he had no idea what became of her or that Kathryn's last name was Duvall, not Bernard.

Meanwhile in the years after first seeing Katy, Axel continued his determined path of steering Lanier Properties to greater heights of financial success following his father's retirement. Axel believed his father was too nice when running the company and had been unwilling to make tough decisions when tough decisions were required. Axel had no such problem.

He methodically worked his way up the family hierarchy, pushing aside anyone who got in his way. His objectives were not complicated. Axel wanted to amass as much wealth as possible and was willing to consider any intriguing opportunity that presented itself. As a result, he dabbled in several outside business ventures along the way, some of them legal, many of them not. He made a number of acquaintances, a few friends and a legion of enemies.

Veering from the ethical business practices that guided his grandfather and father, Axel was governed by a conscious that was exclusively his own. If there were dollars to be made, he was willing to consider just about anything.

It was this mindset that led Axel to a late-1980s meeting with Alvarez Pope. Pope, a small-time drug dealer at the time, was crafting his vision of a mini-crime syndicate in New Orleans that he would orchestrate. Pope envisioned himself as a sort of bayou Godfather who would create an operation positioned to capitalize on the New Orleans street trade in drugs, prostitution, small firearm sales and business extortion.

The big city crime organizations were not paying attention to New Orleans Pope thought, and if he could establish a foothold and build a local infrastructure, he might be able to ward off larger enterprises who showed up later. Pope was convinced no one knew the pulse of the New Orleans streets like he did. He had the vision and the blueprint, but he lacked the capital.

Hearing from a mutual friend that Axel Lanier regularly invested in "off the books" ventures of questionable legality, Pope finagled his way into a meeting with Axel. Initially annoyed by Pope's pushiness, but then intrigued by Pope's vision and determination, Axel cut a deal with Pope. Axel would advance $25,000 to Pope to help Pope jump start his business. In return, Axel demanded 10% of all future profits from Pope's enterprise, in perpetuity.

Pope wasn't crazy about the idea of having Axel around as a permanent partner, but he was desperate and knew no one else would offer him that kind of money. Convinced that the financing would propel him to his goal of becoming kingpin of the New Orleans streets, Pope agreed to Axel's terms. If Axel became a problem, Pope would figure out how to deal with that when the time came. Pope's vision came to fruition several years later when the proceeds of his organization's illicit activity began rolling in.

Axel's 10% share of Pope's income soon doubled and then tripled his original investment. His decision to finance Pope had paid off handsomely. Unlike the profits from Lanier Properties which were split among several family members, Pope's quarterly payments to Axel were Axel's and Axel's alone.

The additional income did not sit idly by. Among Axel's many vices were two houses, a number of condominiums sprinkled throughout the City and a cabin a couple of hours outside of New Orleans that he used for liaisons with his collection of mistresses. Axel also relished fancy vacations to exotic, tropical destinations, especially those with casinos. He gambled late into the night, pursued as many women (attached and unattached) as he could and generally wanted everyone to know how wealthy and important he was. His cut of Pope's profits came in quite handy.

Axel somehow managed to keep his private life from adversely impacting his public persona. As the Chief Executive Officer of Lanier Properties, Axel was the face of a distinguished New Orleans family business that made significant contributions to local charities for decades. A long-time member of the local Chamber of Commerce, Axel was frequently recognized at New Orleans civic events. His Person of the Year award from the Veterans Association was merely another feather in his cap and an additional opportunity for public adulation.

Few knew or suspected that Axel's hands were all over a burgeoning organized crime syndicate that was seeking to rule the New Orleans underworld.

Chapter 36

Shortly after Pope was shot in the confrontation with Katy, Q who as a senior lieutenant to Pope knew all about the Pope-Axel arrangement, called Axel to give him the details.

"Got some news for you that hasn't hit the street yet," said Q, "so brace yourself, but it's something I think you need to know about. Alvarez was taken out a couple of days ago."

"He was blasted by some crazy woman," Q continued. "She shot him right in his own driveway. Then I saw her and someone else drive off with his body."

"That can't be true," said a disbelieving Axel.

"Seriously. No joke," replied Q.

"Do you know who she was?" asked Axel, now somewhat shaken but still wondering if Q was telling the truth.

"Someone named Katy Duvall," replied Q. "From the 6th Ward. Fine as hell too. She crossed me a couple of times before. Came out to Pope's yelling and screaming about something going on with her brother so she and Alvarez got into it big time. I saw the shit unfold right in front of me. Alvarez told her to get the hell off his property, then walked away. The bitch shot him right in the back," Q continued, lying about what actually happened.

"Can you believe it? Smoked him in cold blood."

Pope had been lining Axel's pockets for years, but Axel had no lasting affinity for him. He also had no desire to become directly involved in the day-to-day operations of Pope's enterprise. All Axel wanted was to keep receiving his periodic payoffs. If Pope was out of the picture, the organization might well crumble without him. That possibility worried Axel who wanted to preserve his profit share from Pope's operations at all costs. Pope's death, if Q's words were true, could place all of that in jeopardy.

Q sensed what Axel was thinking. He had heard Pope lament on numerous occasions about having to pay Axel. As far as Pope was concerned, Axel had already received back his original investment many times over. Pope believed that was more than fair. He complained about it every time he made another payment.

Not at all certain how things would play out and himself somewhat worried about his future without Pope, Q sought to reassure Axel until he could determine his next move.

"We'll have to figure out how to keep this shit going," Q said to Axel regarding Pope's business, "but rest assured, you will keep getting your cut."

Axel's anxiety momentarily subsided. If Q knew about his deal with Pope and was willing to continue the arrangement then that would be an acceptable result. Axel decided to adopt a wait and see approach. If the payments continued to be made timely and in the amounts expected, Axel could live with that.

There was something else about what Q said though that struck a chord.

"Katy Duvall from the 6th Ward," Axel thought to himself. "Katy Duvall from the 6th Ward. Hmmmm. I wonder."

Axel decided that he needed to learn more about this Katy Duvall. He immediately retained New Orleans' most covert private eye to compile as much information on Katy as possible.

Before Axel hung up, he had one more question for Q.

"Say, did you tell the police or anyone else about that little gunfight at the OK Corral?" he asked.

"Hell no," replied Q. "The last thing I need is for the cops to be out snooping around. You and I are the only ones who know."

"Good," replied Axel. "Let's keep it that way," as he tried to figure out how he could use this newfound information to his advantage.

A week later after news of Pope's disappearance finally hit the local newspapers, the detective Axel hired presented him with a thorough dossier on Katy Duvall.

Axel flipped through the pages. "Grew up in Lafitte," it read, "then moved to St. Tammany Parish to live with her grandmother when she was ten or eleven. Returned to New Orleans after high school. Graduated from Southern University. Single. Currently pursuing a nursing credential at Loyola University."

Axel took a deep breath and hesitated before turning to the last page. Slowly and deliberately he flipped it over. The page revealed a full color face shot of Katy. The image detailed her appealing smile, a few freckles on her cheeks, shoulder length, reddish-brown hair slightly curled at the bottom and an almost imperceptible small dimple in the middle of her chin.

Axel was certain it was the cleaning lady's daughter he had first observed more than a decade earlier. He decided he had to have her. And armed with this new information from Q, Axel was confident that he possessed the goods to get it done.

Chapter 37

After hearing of Pope's demise and learning that the shooter, this Katy Duvall, was the teenager he had first eyed years before, Axel devised a plan. He would pursue Katy with the intent of making her his own.

Axel had plenty of women. That was not the point. But he had never forgotten about Katy. He always figured he might run into her one night at a club or party. In New Orleans, everyone knew everybody else. And if there was someone you didn't know, you likely knew their cousin. The City was very intimate in that way. But Axel and Katy's paths never crossed.

Now here was Katy, front and center, severely compromised and ready to be conquered. Axel's curious interest had already turned to lust and lust was rapidly mushrooming into obsession. His several mistresses notwithstanding, Axel now shifted his focus to Katy. He was willing to do anything to get her.

So Axel began tracking Katy's movements, learned her patterns and habits, then pretended to run into her by accident at the mall. After their "chance" meeting, Axel invited Katy to the Veterans Gala where Axel knew he would be receiving an award. He had carefully choreographed each of these steps to impress Katy and to convince her that in addition to his considerable wealth, he was also one of New Orleans' finest citizens.

The ducks were lined up and falling into place. Axel's plan seemed to be working. If Axel had his way, Katy would be his after realizing how fortunate she was to be pursued by one of New Orleans wealthiest, and most eligible bachelors.

And if that didn't work, Axel had a back-up plan, this one much more sinister. He would lean on his ace in the hole to get his way; the fact that he knew Katy's most intimate secret about the life-changing evening when she gunned down Alvarez Pope in his driveway.

Chapter 38

Axel and Katy saw each other frequently over the next few weeks, all part of Axel's plan to put on a full court press. Their whirlwind of activities included dining at New Orleans finest restaurants, attending a couple of lavish parties and even making an appearance at the New Orleans Opera (which Katy didn't know existed). Axel was pulling out all of the stops. He was so consumed with flaunting his wealth, boasting about his accomplishments and introducing Katy into his exclusive social circles that he failed to recognize or appreciate that these things meant little to her. The path to Katy's affections required a different approach.

It's not that Katy didn't enjoy occasional extravagance, but having a glass of wine and a casual meal at Cochon Butcher in the Warehouse District, going to the movies, shooting a couple games of billiards or spending a quiet evening at home and engaging in meaningful conversation once in a while would have suited her just fine. Katy had little interest in trying to be seen or in acting famous as a means of becoming famous.

There was one thing that Axel got right though. As determined as he was to spare no expense to wine and dine Katy and expose her to the side of him he wanted her to see, he was just as careful to obscure "the real Axel" side of his life from Katy. He certainly didn't want Katy to know about his multiple affairs (which continued), at least not before he was able to get Katy to commit to him.

And technically Axel was not yet a bachelor at all. He and his wife Theresa had been separated for more than two years and just about everyone assumed they were divorced. Theresa, however, had not yet signed the papers, having had a change of heart at the last minute when she discovered some assets that Axel had previously hidden. If Axel really wants to get rid of me Theresa thought, it's going to cost him a lot more than he has on the table right now.

Above all else though, Axel took great pains to shield Katy from his numerous and sordid professional dealings. He dare not let Katy learn about his secret arrangement with first Pope and now Q. The deal that continued to line Axel's pockets with the illicit profits from the street crime rampant throughout New Orleans' poorest neighborhoods.

Chapter 39

Mercedes Lanier was constantly sticking her nose in her childrens' business. Thus, when she found out that her oldest son Axel was dating someone, she needed to know more details. Mercedes pushed Axel to bring his new girlfriend to the Lanier house so that she could size her up.

This made Axel nervous. He didn't want Katy's memory of her previous visit to clean the Lanier mansion over a decade ago, to be rekindled. If that happened, then Katy might start putting two and two together. Axel took some solace in the fact that the kitchen had been redone, the furniture reconfigured and the house painted a different color inside and out since Katy was last there, but there was still the chance that Katy might recognize the residence.

Then there was Mercedes. Always one who sought to control everything and everybody within her grasp, Mercedes' firm grip on her family and the lives of her children was slipping. Her loss of influence appeared to coincide with a recent display of schizophrenic tendencies and more than one close relative was convinced that Mercedes was losing her mind. Yes, there was a possibility that Mercedes might recognize Katy if Axel brought her over but Axel was more concerned that Mercedes might say or do something off color. Axel knew his mother was a wild card. Any visit with Katy must be handled with extreme caution.

After constant pressure from Mercedes, Axel finally relented. He would bring Katy to the house to meet his mother, but told himself that he would keep the visit short and hope for the best. Katy accepted Axel's invitation to meet Mercedes in the home where Axel grew up.

The next Saturday, Axel brought Katy to the family estate in the Audobon District. The house was immaculate Katy thought to herself as she stepped onto marbled tiles and entered the foyer. Katy could see in front of her an antebellum-style, broad staircase that wound its way upwards around an open area just behind the entry way, as it disappeared upstairs.

Katy had heard of the great New Orleans estates, maybe even driven past a couple, but the instances were few and far between when Katy had been inside a house as stately as this one. And yet the house for some strange reason, just like the walkway, seemed eerily familiar. Katy could not help but think she had been there before, but concluded she must be imagining things.

Just then, a woman who looked to be in her seventies, floated out of the kitchen. She wore a silver necklace with a large, sparkling, pink gem around her neck. Her right wrist was adorned with jeweled bracelets and on her left wrist she wore a Swiss watch, by Tiffany & Co.

"Katy, meet my mother, Mercedes Lanier," Axel said proudly.

"Well, any friend of my Axel's is a friend a mine," said Mercedes as she extended her hand to Katy.

"Pleased to meet you ma'am," said Katy, still somewhat intimidated by the entire setting.

Mercedes led Katy and Axel into the living room where they all sat down.

"Axel, you run along," Mercedes said, "so Katy and I can get to know each other a little better." Axel fretted over leaving the two of them alone but Mercedes insisted.

"Now Katy dear, where are you from?" Mercedes asked, wasting no time getting straight to the point after Axel left the room.

This was the moment that Katy had dreaded. She was not ready to explain her life history to a complete stranger, especially one who seemed all too willing to pry.

"I grew up in Treme' in the 6th Ward," a tepid Katy replied.

Mercedes paused. Parts of the Treme' neighborhood were quite respectable. The entire area itself was legendary in the history of New Orleans as the birthplace of jazz and the first community in the South where free non-whites could openly buy property. Ok, so far so good, thought Mercedes.

Then Katy added defiantly, "In Lafitte."

Mercedes turned stone-faced. She was well aware of Axel's philandering, playboy history. Surely she thought though that Axel knew better than to bring a girl from the projects into her house. Mercedes quickly made up her mind that Axel could do better.

"Oh," Mercedes said. "Well where did you go to college and what type of work do you do?" she asked, anticipating that Katy would be both uneducated and unemployed.

Katy felt like she was being interrogated and didn't much like it.

"I'm a medical assistant downtown," Katy replied. "I work for Dr. Stonewall Curry, one of the finest physicians in New Orleans. I'm sure you have heard of him haven't you?"

Mercedes said nothing and the two sat opposite each other for another half a minute in complete, uncomfortable silence. Mercedes Lanier pegged Katy for a gold digger and instantly formulated in her mind how Axel and Katy got together. Katy had no doubt targeted her son, flaunted herself in front of him to get his attention, and then manipulated Axel to her advantage.

Finally Mercedes spoke. "Well how did you and Axel meet?" she asked, fully expecting Katy to lie about having set her sights on Axel as a potential meal ticket.

Katy sensed where the line of questioning was going, so she preempted the notion that she had chased Axel.

"Actually, I didn't meet Axel," Katy replied. "Axel saw me and introduced himself while I was doing some shopping at Canal Place." Katy was going to further add that Axel tried to entice her by offering to buy expensive gifts, but figured that part was better left unsaid. She had made her point. Better to leave it at that.

Then Mercedes moved over towards Katy's side of the couch.

"Come closer dear," Mercedes said. "I want to tell you a secret." Katy hesitated, then reluctantly complied and slid over a bit in Mercedes' direction. When she got within a foot and a half of Axel's mother, Mercedes suddenly reach out and grabbed Katy's wrist, drawing her even closer.

Katy pulled back, but Mercedes held firm. Mercedes then leaned over and whispered menacingly into Katy's ear.

"He'll *never* love you like he loves me. Just you remember that."

Startled, Katy yanked her arm free of Mercedes' grip causing Mercedes' fingernails to pierce Katy's skin. Katy hastily retreated to the far corner of the couch. As she began to rise from the sofa, Axel reappeared.

"Well, I need to get home," said Katy, standing up from the couch, ready to sprint to the front door. "I have to transcribe some records for Dr. Curry this weekend."

By this time though, Axel had gotten comfortable that Katy had no recollection of her prior housecleaning visit to the Lanier mansion. True to form, he shifted back into his customary mode of self-aggrandizement having no idea what had just transpired.

"Just a few more minutes Katy," he said. "I want to show you a couple of things. Did you know that this house was built in 1915. It has six bedrooms, six full baths, two half baths and is almost 8,500 square feet. The master bedroom is 1,350 square feet by itself."

Katy glared at him and motioned towards the car outside.

"But," said Axel.

"Axel, I need to leave," Katy repeated sternly, and Axel could tell that she meant it. "Now."

"It was nice meeting you Mrs. Lanier," said Katy. You have a lovely home."

Axel kissed his mother and then he and Katy exited the house and walked back to Axel's car.

"I guess that didn't go so well," Axel remarked as he opened the car door for Katy.

"That's an understatement," replied Katy. "I won't be back."

The Cayenne Matrix

Chapter 40

Katy and Axel continued to see each other on a regular basis. The more Axel was around Katy, the greater his obsession. He had to have her. Axel was convinced his plan was working. There was no way Katy could do better than him, he told himself. Surely, any woman would jump at the chance to be with Axel Lanier.

From Katy's standpoint, however, the jury was still out. Her interest in Axel piqued at the Veterans Gala and the needle hadn't moved much since then. Yes, Katy was impressed by Axel's apparent philanthropy and community consciousness. She also realized that Axel could make her financial worries a thing of the past, possibly for life. There was no trivializing that.

But Katy wasn't out for money. She craved an emotional connection and so far wasn't getting that from Axel. The two of them rarely laughed together and the things Katy thought humorous didn't register or matter to Axel. Katy also found Axel to be frequently superficial and she was convinced that there were times when he simply wasn't telling the truth. Her instincts told her that Axel was probably not right for her.

Then there was that surreal encounter on the couch with a partially deranged Mercedes. That certainly was not helping Axel's cause. He should have known better than to expose Katy to his mother. Things were beginning to point to the conclusion that it might be time for Katy to cut the chord with Axel.

Meanwhile, Katy's thoughts regularly drifted back to Bryan. She missed what they had. The two of them didn't communicate any more, but Katy remembered the way they were before the events that changed everything. She could kick herself for having insisted on confronting Pope that evening. The cost had been far too great.

Still, Katy understood that the way she wanted things to be was no longer the way things were. If having Bryan in her life again was now just a pipe dream, Katy knew that she would have to move on, for her own sanity if nothing else. That ship had probably sailed. Katy was just not quite ready to admit it yet.

Chapter 41

Katy woke up one Monday morning with a new determination. Today was the day she would end her relationship with Axel. The more she pondered it, the more convinced she became that it was the right thing to do. The thought itself was liberating. It was time for her to move on. Axel was a grown man. He would be fine Katy told herself. It was best for them to part and go their separate ways.

Katy called Axel and asked him to meet her for lunch so they could talk. Axel told Katy that he had meetings all morning and was too busy, but perhaps they could have lunch the next day. Not wanting to prolong things and anxious to act while she had the nerve, Katy showed up anyway at Axel's office, unannounced. Upon arriving, the receptionist told her that Axel was in a meeting.

"I'll wait," said Katy.

In a few seconds, the door to Axel's office flung open as a man who appeared to be in his late sixties stormed out. He had a gray goatee and a long, stringy ponytail pulled together from thin strands of hair on both sides of his head that surrounded a crowning bald spot. His camouflaged jeans jacket was open in the front revealing a white tank top t-shirt. In the middle of his chest was a tattoo of an American eagle. A shoulder patch on the jacket read "51st Airborne, 2nd Battalion, Vietnam."

The man turned on his way out and shouted back into Axel's office, pointing a finger in the direction of whoever was in there.

"I'm not leaving my apartment," he screamed. "I've shed too much blood, sweat and tears for this country to be evicted by the likes of you. If you want me out, you can come try to throw me out yourself. Fuckin' leech! I know all about you. Just remember that Axel. I even know where the hell you live."

The office fell silent as the man left, slamming the front door behind him.

Axel then emerged from his office and saw Katy sitting next to the front desk.

"I thought I told you I didn't have time for lunch today," he barked, embarrassed by the scene that had just unfolded and the fact that his entire staff had witnessed it.

"Axel, I need to talk to you," Katy said tepidly, now fearful of making a bad situation worse.

"Alright," said Axel. "Come in." He knew that all eyes were on him and that he needed to lower the tension level now permeating the premises.

"What was that all about?" Katy asked quietly as she sat down across from Axel.

"Nothing," Axel replied. "Just a disgruntled tenant that's all. They expect you to do everything for them these days. It's not my fault his freezer went out and flooded the floor. Anyway, I'm sorry you had to witness that. Now what was it you wanted to talk to me about?"

Axel had no clue what was coming.

"Axel," Katy said ready to get straight to the point despite the circumstances. "I've really enjoyed spending time with you. It's been nice to be exposed to some things I've never done before. And I sincerely appreciate your interest in me. But I think we both know we're just sort of killing time and spinning our wheels. Our lives are really headed in opposite directions. I just think it would be best if . . ."

Axel cut her off.

"Katy, what are you trying to say?" Axel asked abruptly, as he ceased shuffling the papers in front of him. He certainly did not agree that their lives were headed in opposite directions, especially since he was trying to merge them together.

"Katy, are you trying to break-up with me?"

"Well, um, I would not exactly put it that way," said Katy, wanting to be polite and not exactly in agreement that there was even enough of a commitment to be breaking up from. "But I think we should just cool it for a while," she continued. "You know, maybe see other people, experience different things. It would be good for both of us. We can still be good friends of course."

Axel's demeanor quickly changed.

"Good friends? Good friends," he repeated, beginning to chastise Katy. "Katy, do you know how fortunate you are to have me interested in you? Do you know how many women would gladly switch places with you at the drop of a hat?"

"Axel, I do," Katy said, knowing full well that is what Axel expected to hear.

"Well let me tell you," he interrupted. "Plenty. Think of all of the benefits of being with someone like me. Anyplace in the world you want to go, you can go. Anything you want to buy, you're free to get it. You can meet famous people. No worries, no cares, nothing. Everything you could possibly want is at your fingertips. I can deliver New Orleans to you on a silver platter."

Then Axel crossed into an area that he probably should have avoided.

"I would think that would mean something to someone who came from where you came from."

Katy fumed inside at the slight, but stayed calm. She did not want to get sidetracked from the purpose of her visit, but so far things were not going as planned. She just wanted the conversation, and the relationship to end, but she had underestimated Axel's obsession with her.

"Axel, I know this isn't easy," she said.

"Isn't easy?" Axel exclaimed. "What do you mean it isn't easy?" He couldn't believe he was being patronized by a girl from the housing projects.

Axel was agitated. He already considered himself to be groveling and he didn't like it. He should have backed off, but he let his frustration and over-anxiousness get the best of him. He was about to play his trump card way too soon.

"Look Katy, you're never going to find anyone like me. That much should be obvious. And you know what else? We can look out for your best interests. My family has some connections with the New Orleans police department. We can protect you."

Katy paused. She was taken aback by what Axel said. Where did *that* come from, this business about police protection? The words sent a sickening chill down Katy's spine. At the beginning of their discussion, Katy was annoyed. Now she was terrified. Finally she responded.

"Axel, what makes you think I need to be protected from the police?" Katy inquired.

"Not saying you do," replied Axel realizing he had gone too far and now trying to backtrack. "But if you ever did, we've got you covered," he said with a wink.

"Axel, what are you talking about?" Katy demanded. Katy slowly twisted in her chair. She could not believe the words coming out of Axel's mouth. It just couldn't be. She shook her head from side to side.

Then it dawned upon her. "Axel knew," Katy thought to herself. He knew her deepest, darkest secrets. He had to know what had happened between her and Pope. What other explanation could there be for his talk of "police protection?"

"Axel, are you?" then she stopped and began to tremble. "Axel, are you trying to blackmail me?" Katy asked slowly.

"Blackmail? Of course not," replied Axel. "There is nothing in your past I know about that you could be blackmailed for." Then after a long pause, he pointedly added, "is there?"

"Katy look," Axel continued. "We're a great fit. We can be a New Orleans power couple. And not just any power couple. *The* power couple. There's no need to change a good thing. I'm not blackmailing you. Just looking out for your best interests. That's all. Let's just continue to see each other and see how things play out. And any skeletons that might be in the closet from our pasts, well those will just remain our little secret. Ok?"

Katy felt as if she were freefalling in a bottomless pit. Her soul and body ached. Now she was certain. Axel knew all about the events at Pope's house and intended to hold what Katy had done over her head to get what he wanted. But how could he know? And what connection, if any, did Axel have to Alvarez Pope?

Chapter 42

Axel finally had the control over Katy that he was accustomed to exercising over everyone else. He preferred not to view Katy as being coerced into doing something she didn't want to do. Instead, Axel convinced himself that his actions were for Katy's own good. She would eventually realize the benefits of being paired with him and then would be happy about it, appreciative of the lifestyle that only he could provide.

He was certain that Katy would figure all of this out in time and then move past any lingering resentment over his methods.

Axel considered it a minor miracle that he had even found Katy. He had long since given up the hope of fulfilling the fantasy he imagined the first time he saw her. Now that Axel had Katy enveloped in his clutches, he did not intend to let go.

The relationship would be exclusive, from Katy's side at least, and would leave Axel free to prance around New Orleans with Katy on his arm whenever he wanted. Whatever Axel desired, attendance at social events, an evening out on the town, or sex, Katy would provide. And when Axel didn't want to be bothered or have time for Katy, he would carry on his business without her.

And if Katy ever rebelled, Axel held the ultimate leverage. As far as he was concerned, Katy would be in no position to deny his desires. Ever.

Katy's misery provided a stark contrast to Axel's elation. Where Axel was free to come and go as he pleased, Katy was for all intents and purposes detained, languishing in a box to which Axel held the only key. Unable to devise a way out of her confinement and fearful of her past deeds being exposed, Katy reluctantly complied with all of Axel's wishes.

The burdens of Katy's new existence were many. The rewards few. Contrary to Axel's beliefs, Katy found no joy in the benefits Axel perceived he was providing. Most of all Katy dreaded their moments of intimacy. Whenever Katy heard from Axel early in the day that he would be "stopping by" later that evening, Katy knew what that meant. She quivered as Axel's hands, cold to the touch, first massaged her shoulders then worked their way across the rest of her body.

Katy came to know what to expect and what was expected of her. She tolerated Axel's advances and endured his indulgences, but that didn't make things any easier. She had become in every sense of the word, a "mistress," and a captive one at that.

Axel held a hammer over her and Katy knew it.

Chapter 43

When it came to his business ethos, Axel remained as cutthroat as ever. He had recently created great angst among the Lanier family members when they learned that he had ousted their long-time development partner Burgess Petty.

Petty's connection to Lanier Properties dated back to an alliance with Axel's father that began decades earlier at a time when business collaboration between white and black-owned businesses in New Orleans was taboo. But Petty paid no attention to racial stereotypes. He was willing to work with anyone. And so at great risk to his business and the safety of his family, Petty and his company Petty Construction entered into a joint venture with Lanier Properties. The two family owned-organizations had frequently worked together ever since, with Lanier Properties retaining Petty Construction to undertake the building of the apartment complexes that Lanier would later manage.

After years of running the business, Axel became convinced that Lanier Properties should be getting a larger share of the joint profits than the current 50/50 split with Petty. So Axel devised a plan to freeze Petty out of project control, something his father would never have condoned.

While Petty was away on a month-long vacation, Axel took advantage of a reciprocal Power of Attorney arrangement that he and Petty had granted to each other years earlier for use in an emergency. Long forgotten by Petty, Axel used the agreement to execute and file legal documents with the Louisiana Secretary of State that changed the control structure of their various business ventures. Sole decision-making authority was now vested with Lanier Properties, essentially cutting off Petty's role in partnership management. It was a new low, even for Axel.

Going forward, Axel was free to hire whoever he wanted for project construction or force Petty to take a smaller profit share. Upon returning from vacation and discovering Axel's treachery, Petty was furious. He filed a lawsuit, but the documentation he signed years early was valid. The suit was dismissed.

In the meantime, Axel began cutting side deals with other contractors, increasing the pressure on Petty Construction to completely sell out its partnership interest to Lanier Properties for Axel's low-ball offer.

Distraught and nearly broke from a lack of work and mounting legal costs, a disconsolate Burgess Petty sold his half of the business to Axel for a fraction of its worth. Petty was never the same. His son August quietly seethed. August vowed that what the Louisiana Circuit Court declined to do by judicial decree, he would accomplish with his .22 caliber rifle and a few rounds of hollow point ammo.

August bided his time but resolved that when the opportunity arose to fix his sights on Axel, he would be ready to act.

Chapter 44

Axel Lanier's treachery did not stop with Lanier Properties, his secret investment in Pope's crime syndicate or his undercutting of Burgess Petty. Axel also had business interests at the State Capital in Baton Rouge.

Several years earlier Axel had forged an unlikely alliance with Guidry Monroe, a Louisiana state senator from Shreveport. The pair had become acquainted through their fathers who served in the military together. Monroe's family had accumulated significant wealth when a natural gas deposit was discovered on family property, but Monroe squandered a good chunk of his share of the family fortune on bad investments and lavish automobiles.

Upon being appointed to the state legislature's Commerce Committee, Monroe was given oversight to the bidding process for state residential construction and housing projects. Once Monroe was elevated to Committee Chairman, Axel approached him with a proposal. If Monroe would tip off Axel on the value of competing sealed bids, Axel would provide Monroe with a handsome kickback on any contracts that the Committee ultimately awarded to Lanier Properties.

Monroe agreed, although neither man trusted the other. For several years, the two implemented their surreptitious plan. Monroe illegally opened sealed bids, then placed phone calls to Axel to inform him of the bid values. Subsequently, Lanier Properties would submit a contract bid that undercut the other bids. The Committee then awarded the contract to Lanier Properties.

Later, after having won a contract, attorneys for Lanier Properties would attempt to identify errors in the original contract proposal that might justify a price increase. Monroe brought the revision requests to the Committee floor for consideration, then pushed through as many of them as he could. When Lanier Properties received the additional funds for the contract modification, Axel cut a nice check to Monroe for his trouble.

The clandestine agreement was executed like clockwork. And just to further shroud their back room deal, every once in a while Axel and Monroe were careful to orchestrate things so that Lanier Properties was the losing bidder. The "intentional lose" strategy covered their tracks. Axel didn't get every valuable government contract but he made sure that Lanier Properties obtained the ones he really wanted.

Chapter 45

Katy struggled to deal with her new found reality. It was bad enough that her attempt to call it quits with Axel had been blocked from the start. Now, if Axel had his way, he and Katy would become so intertwined that it would be impossible for her to separate herself from him.

Katy shuddered at the possibility that this new, unforeseen dimension might become the status quo. She was already stressed with the daily burden of living with what she had done in those few treacherous moments in Pope's driveway. They would haunt her forever. The addition of a controlling Axel to the mix who could hold her past deeds over her head to get whatever he wanted, was frightening.

Ever resourceful, Katy plotted how she might escape her predicament. Going to the police remained an option. But she wouldn't do that without talking to Bryan first and she and Bryan had not communicated in well over a year. She missed Bryan constantly anyway, but his absence in tough times made things much worse.

Another approach was to consider confronting Axel. But that might mean taking on the entire Lanier machine and who knows where that would lead and what the outcome might be. Katy imagined that standing up to Axel could plunge her deeper into the abyss and if an unhinged Mercedes got involved, there was no telling where things might lead. Katy could see herself left holding the bag for a whole host of misdeeds she had nothing to do with.

Emotionally exhausted and with few good options, Katy found herself at a crossroads. She knew it was time to act but the forks in the road were all clouded with uncertainty.

Axel, however, was one step ahead of Katy. He did not equivocate on his next steps or on what needed to be done. Having been alerted to Katy's desire to cut ties with him, Axel had readjusted his thinking. If he expected to retain his grip on her, Axel knew his response must be swift and decisive. He had to keep the pressure on and not allow Katy any wiggle room to defy his wishes.

Axel quickly revised his plan of action on the fly. He had a surprise in store for Katy that would ratchet up the intensity on her and leave

Katy even more tightly bound to him than she was currently. Axel's next move would make things exponentially worse.

Chapter 46

One day while at work, Katy received a text from Axel. It said simply "Free tonight?" Katy didn't answer, knowing that Axel would show up anyway, probably around 8:15 as was his custom.

After arriving home from work, Katy fixed herself dinner, put on her nightgown and awaited the ring of her doorbell. Resigned to another torturous evening, this time Katy partially undressed herself, figuring that might speed up the process and hasten Axel's departure. She had a movie to watch at 9 and wanted Axel to be long gone by then.

Axel steered his late model Maserati sedan into the parking lot of Katy's apartment complex right around eight o'clock. Two well-dressed passengers were in the car with him. As Axel turned a corner in the lot, a black cat suddenly flashed across his path. Axel slammed on his brakes, then felt a slight bump on his rear fender.

He stopped his car, turned off the ignition and immediately jumped out of the front seat. The door on the driver's side of the vehicle behind him slowly opened.

"You need to watch where you're going," Axel yelled towards the car that had hit him, rushing to check for any damage to the back end of his vehicle.

"I'm . . . I'm sorry," replied the muscular driver who was about six feet tall and couldn't have been much more than thirty years old. "I didn't expect you to make such a sudden stop. I guess I wasn't paying close enough attention."

"You most certainly were not," scolded Axel.

"Lucky for you there appears to be no damage. Any blemish on this car would surely cost more to fix than your annual salary," Axel admonished having no idea how much money the other driver made. "Well, I guess there's no harm. But be more careful next time."

"I will sir," replied the man. "And again, my sincerest apologies."

Axel hopped back in his car and continued slowly ahead until he found a parking space directly adjacent to Katy's building. He had important business to attend to and didn't like being thrown off schedule by a careless tailgater.

A few moments later Katy heard a knock on her door. Expecting Axel only, Katy opened the door without even checking to see who it was, wearing her bathrobe over her pajamas. She found herself face-to-face with not only Axel but also with two other men clad in expensive suits, both holding briefcases.

Axel asked if the three of them could enter. "I'm not really decent," Katy hesitated, "but yes, come in." Axel clearly wasn't there for an intimate encounter with Katy, so perhaps the visit would be brief Katy thought to herself.

As the four of them sat in the living room, Katy wondered what was going on not having expected Axel to bring others with him. The momentary silence only deepened her suspicions. She would not have to wait long to find out.

Axel then proceeded to introduce the other two men, identifying them as Lanier family attorneys.

"I informed our lawyers of our engagement," Axel said, "and our attorneys think it's a good idea for you to sign a prenuptial agreement before we tie the knot. It's for your own protection."

Katy's jaw dropped. She was stunned. Engagement? What engagement? What could Axel possibly be talking about? The two of them had never discussed marriage. Katy considered it a major concession on her part to even continue seeing him. And as far as Katy knew, Axel's divorce with Theresa had not been finalized, not that it would have made any difference. Katy would not willingly marry Axel under the best of circumstances.

"I'm sure you'll find everything in order," Axel continued with a straight face as one of the men handed the documents, packaged neatly in a leather binder, to Katy.

Katy felt herself simmering to a slow boil. She knew that Axel had brought his attorneys along to intimidate her and to minimize the possibility of a confrontation when he sprung the false narrative about their engagement. Another power play by a man who seemingly held all the cards.

As Katy snatched the binder from one of the attorneys, her eyes remained fixated on Axel. How could he, she thought. As angry as she was, Katy kept her composure. When the attorney handed her a pen to sign the agreement though, Katy protested.

"As Axel's legal team, I'm sure you two have obviously drafted and reviewed these documents on behalf of your client. I'll need some time for my attorney to look them over as well. It's only fair that everyone have their own legal counsel. I think that's reasonable. Don't you Axel?" said Katy, continuing to stare daggers at him.

"Uh . . . well of course," said Axel sheepishly. "Yes, of course," chagrined that Katy was not gullible enough to sign the prenuptial agreement on the spot.

"Now if you gentlemen have nothing further to discuss, I really need to get to bed," Katy continued as she opened the front door and motioned for her guests to leave. "I'll get back to you all in a few days."

Axel was the last one to exit.

"This is for your own good," he whispered to Katy on his way out the door. "After all, a husband can't be forced to testify against his wife, now can he?" Axel smiled.

Another veiled threat.

"And besides. I'm a free man. Theresa signed the papers today. The divorce is final."

"Son of a. . . .", Katy shouted and then stopped, as she slammed the door behind him not caring at all if Axel's attorneys heard her.

Katy had long thought her situation couldn't possibly get any worse. She was wrong. She had underestimated Axel. He was even more cunning and ruthless than she had given him credit for. Katy decided to play along with the marriage charade, at least temporarily. If she balked, she couldn't be certain that Axel would not follow through on his threat to expose her secret.

Once again, Katy harkened back to that fateful reading of the tarot cards and The Three of Swords that Clovis had drawn. Three swords for three trials. First there was her traumatic encounter with Cassandra that eventually forced her to move away from her mother and brother. Then, there was the horror of shooting, killing and burying Alvarez Pope. That event was bad enough by itself, but it also led to her separation from Bryan. Finally, it now appeared that Katy was going to be saddled with Axel Lanier for better or for worse, for the foreseeable future. Perhaps Axel was indeed destined to become the third trial that Clovis had predicted; the box from which she could not escape.

But there was something inside Katy that was not quite ready to accept the fate that had been assigned to her by a mere deck of cards. She would not simply roll over. Axel must be dealt with. But how?

Chapter 47

Once Katy came to grips with what accepting Axel's "proposal" meant, she sullenly communicated the engagement news to family and friends. Those members of Katy's family who were impressed by status were elated, thrilled to learn that one of their own was marrying into the upper echelons of New Orleans society.

Katy still had one more phone call to make. She needed to tell Bryan. Katy was not resigned to marrying Axel but she didn't have a clear path to break free. Not yet. Still, Katy needed to hear Bryan's voice again and she wanted to let him know what was going on. Especially now that Katy was convinced that there were others who were aware of what happened at Pope's house that night.

As she dialed the 310 Los Angeles area code, Katy's hands trembled and her throat parched.

The phone rang twice and then Katy heard a familiar voice on the other end of the line. "Hello," the voice said.

"Hello Bryan, this is Katy. How are you?"

"Hi Katy," Bryan said cautiously. "This is a bit unexpected. I'm . . . doing . . . fine." Bryan hadn't spoken to Katy in close to two years although he thought about her all of the time. He worried that her call might bring additional bad news about the black cloud that seemed to be permanently fixated over both of their heads.

"I'm . . . um . . . ok," said Katy, barely holding herself together.

Given her emotions, Katy decided that she needed to break the news to Bryan as quickly as possible for her own sake. There was no need for an extended dissertation.

Katy took a deep breath.

"Bryan, I called to tell you that I am getting married," Katy blurted out.

There was a long pause on the other end of the line. As the silence deepened, Katy held back the tears.

"Well," said Bryan slowly. "That's certainly a surprise. I know we don't talk anymore but I was kind of hoping in the back of my mind that eventually, you know, if things ever blew over maybe you and I . . ." then he stopped short. "Congratulations Katy. That's all I can say. Congratulations."

Bryan had no interest in hearing all of the wedding details but he didn't want to simply hang up on her. So just to make conversation, Bryan asked "so when is the big day?"

"No date yet," replied Katy, "but it will be a few months. If the wedding happens at all that is."

That last sentence didn't quite make sense to Bryan. Why would Katy call him to tell him she was getting married, then immediately cast doubt on whether or not the wedding was going to take place. Strange Bryan thought, but he chose not to seek clarification.

"I'm sure you'll make a lovely bride Katy, and some lucky man will be very happy. I wish you all the best," he said.

"Bryan, there's something I need to tell you and it's very important that we stay in touch," Katy fumbled. She was distracted from the message she intended to deliver about Axel's knowledge of Pope's shooting, and instead had become worried about the tone of finality she was hearing from Bryan. Might this be the last time they ever spoke?

"I'm sure we'll talk again at some point down the road," said Bryan, as he tried to process the abrupt end of their prior relationship. "But the past can't be undone. I just wish that night had turned out differently but things happen for a reason. It just wasn't meant to be I guess. There's really too much water under the bridge at this point to go back. Maybe our paths will cross again someday, but if not, I really wish you the best and hope you will be very happy."

More silence. The conversation had veered off track and Katy couldn't steer it back to where she wanted to go but there was so much more she wanted to say. How much she missed Bryan. How her life had been in shambles living under the realization of what she had done. The constant fear, paranoia and sleepless nights that had left her unable to function. And now, being blackmailed into marrying a man for whom she had little, if any feelings. Even worse, that man knew Katy's darkest secrets and perhaps Bryan's too.

If she didn't pour it all out now in front of Bryan, there was no telling when, or if she would ever get the chance. Katy took a deep breath. She prepared to bare her soul.

"Bryan," she said, but he interjected before she could finish.

"I was actually in the middle of something when you called," Bryan replied, cutting the conversation short, "so I have to run. Congratulations again and I hope everything works out."

"Good-by Katy," Bryan said, but he continued to hold the phone in his hand. He wanted to say something else. Katy waited on the other end of the line at a loss for words. Ten seconds passed, then twenty.

Finally Katy heard a click, then a dial tone. Her nightmare continued.

Chapter 48

A month later, a miserable Katy was half asleep in her lounge chair watching a Law & Order rerun when her phone rang.

"Hello," she said.

"Hi Katy, this is your cousin Myra Fontenot. Do you remember me?"

"I, I'm not sure," said a still groggy Katy. "Myra, hmmm, that does sound familiar," said Katy now sitting up. "I do remember. Didn't we hang out on the playgrounds when we were kids? Of course. Hi Myra, how are you? How's your mom? I haven't spoken to you in years."

"I'm doing ok," answered Myra.

There was a long pause.

"Myra, can I help you?" said Katy.

"Katy, I don't know how to say this and I am not even sure I should be calling you. But I heard from my mother that you are engaged to Axel Lanier."

Katy paused and took a deep breath. She did not like discussing anything about Axel, much less her pending nuptials.

"Yes," Katy finally said slowly, not particularly happy at having to again acknowledge her engagement to Axel. "Myra, what is it? Is there something wrong?"

Myra hesitated.

"Katy my family . . . me, Guillon and our three kids, we're really having a tough time making ends meet. And, I'm sorry this is really not your concern, but we just received an eviction notice from our landlord. We have no place to go."

Katy paused. She wasn't sure where this conversation was headed or what Myra expected from her. Surely Myra was not going to ask to move her family into Katy's one bedroom apartment.

"Myra, I'm very sorry to hear that," Katy said. "Is there anything I can do to help? Why are you being evicted?"

"A month ago our heater stopped working. It was early November so it wasn't really cold yet. But now the place is freezing. That's when we filed a second complaint with our landlord. And Guillon, he's been on disability ever since he returned from the Gulf War in Kuwait, is struggling to find work. We've been in this place for less than a year. I just don't understand it."

Katy still wasn't sure what Myra was expecting from her.

Finally, Katy said something.

"Myra, I'd like to help but I just don't know . . . "

"Katy, our landlord is Lanier Properties," Myra interrupted. "We have thirty days to move out. I was just wondering . . . hoping really, if you might be able to speak with someone at Lanier. Maybe even Axel perhaps, and find out what's going on or if we can have a little more time to find another place."

Now Katy understood. Still, she didn't think she could help her cousin.

"I'm really not involved in Lanier Properties at all," Katy said, "so I don't think there is much I can do."

Katy hesitated. She could feel the despair in Myra's voice, even over the phone. It was clear Myra was in desperate need of hope, no matter how thin the thread.

Katy wanted to help. She really did. But at the moment, Katy was every bit as defeated as Myra and didn't have the will to step in.

"I'm sorry Myra," Katy repeated, "but there really is nothing I can do."

Chapter 49

After Katy hung up the phone, she stumbled around her apartment in a daze. A childhood friend, no worse than that, a relative had just requested help and Katy had meekly declined. That was not like her. Shuffling from room to room, Katy wandered aimlessly in circles, completely losing track of time. Finally, she stopped in front of the full length mirror. She took a long look at herself, staring at her quivering reflection. She was unrecognizable. Katy wondered who she had become.

Angry, frustrated and disappointed in herself, Katy grabbed a nearby flower pot and flung it at the mirror as hard as she could, hoping to eviscerate the imposter staring back at her. The pot struck its intended target dead center, sending cracks in every direction that permeated to the mirror's edge. The symbolism of the shattered mirror was fitting. It provided the perfect reflection of Katy's fractured soul.

Katy's spunk, spontaneity and fun loving nature had all but disappeared. Her signature qualities had exited the premises, hot on the heels of her feistiness and determination. The lethargy permeated every aspect of Katy's very existence. At work, she was listless. Outside of work, Katy had reduced her social outings to the bare minimum.

No more weekend trips to the Farmer's Market to purchase fresh fruits and vegetables and converse with the local growers about their methods of harvesting produce. No more volunteer shifts at the senior citizens home where twice a month, Katy and three women in their eighties engaged in a high spirited card game of whist. Katy had simply left her cohorts high and dry.

Worse still, Katy had abandoned her family. She had not been to Nana's farmhouse in weeks and had ceased all contact with her mother and her brother. "Who am I?" Katy thought. She didn't have a good answer. All she knew was that whoever or whatever she was, it was just a mere shell of her former self.

Axel had sought to overwhelm her with his power, connections and prestige. And right now Axel was winning. Katy hated the thought that his manipulations and heavy-handiness might actually steal her life from her.

Katy resolved to do better. If Axel was her third trial by fire as predicted by Clovis and she was going down, she was going to go down swinging.

Chapter 50

Katy wasn't sure what she believed anymore. But she knew where she wanted and needed to go. After reflecting a bit more, Katy walked outside, started her car and drove straight to St. Louis Cathedral. She needed a quiet place to reset things. Katy entered the sanctuary, sat in one of the rear pews and then sank to her knees. Tears started to flow down her cheeks. She lowered her head and sobbed softly for several minutes.

Finally, she spoke in a barely audible whisper.

"Lord, I know I'm not perfect. But please help me to stand up to my adversaries," Katy said, making the sign of the cross over her chest. "I just want the strength to fight back."

Then Katy walked out of the Cathedral determined to take back her life. Her self-imposed pity party was over.

Chapter 51

An empowered Katy knew exactly where she wanted to go next. She had to visit Jose and see how he was doing. Katy had not dined at The Barrio in months. She wondered how Jose was faring. After her initial confrontation with Q at Jose's restaurant years earlier over Q's strong-arm tactics, the criminal elements had backed off for a period of time. Katy had heard through the grapevine though that Jose was having trouble again. She wanted to catch up with her old friend, grab an appetizing meal and find out what was going on.

When Katy arrived, however, she was bitterly disappointed. The restaurant's doors were padlocked and chained. An "Equipment For Sale by Owner" sign hung out front.

"Sangsue meprisable," an enraged Katy said to herself which was French for "despicable bloodsuckers." She feared what might have become of Jose and made a mental note to find out. Resolution of Jose's plight was now on her checklist.

Meanwhile, there was still Myra. Despite her earlier reluctance to get involved, perhaps Katy could help. A week earlier Katy was too distraught about her own dire straits to be of any assistance. But now she was invigorated. Katy was needed. She mattered again. And that by itself was a great feeling. After Katy returned home, she decided to give Myra a call.

Chapter 52

Myra answered the phone with an apathetic and downcast "hello."

"Myra, this is Katy," said Katy with renewed energy and enthusiasm. "I thought about what you said. I can't promise you anything, but I'll look into your eviction and help in any way I can."

The gesture, simple though it was, turned out to be enough.

"Thank you, thank you," replied Myra, who Katy could tell was on the verge of a breakdown. "You don't know how much this means to us. I'll be forever grateful for anything you can do."

After Katy hung up, she thought more about her earlier conversation with Myra. She was puzzled. How could Lanier Properties evict a member of the Armed Forces and his family? There had to be some mistake. Hadn't Axel been recognized and praised for his efforts to find housing for veterans? That's what won him the Person of the Year Award. Everyone knew that. They damn near held a coronation ceremony for him at the Veterans Gala that would have made Queen

Elizabeth proud. That award certainly did not square with the circumstances Myra described.

Where was the disconnect? Maybe there was just an innocent oversight by a billing clerk or apartment manager, Katy thought. Or could there be another explanation? Katy made up her mind to find out.

Chapter 53

Determined not to live the rest of her life under Axel's thumb, Katy wondered how she might tip the scales back in her favor. Axel knew Katy's secrets. It was time for her to discover some of his. Katy was certain Axel couldn't possibly be squeaky clean.

Katy had also come to some conclusions about her engagement to Axel. She had not yet figured a way out, but it was time to end the charade, consequences be damned. Axel Lanier would no longer dictate her every move. But first she had to help Myra.

Unbeknownst to Axel, Katy had secretly made a duplicate key for the Lanier Properties offices. She had also memorized the combination to the office's file room, having observed one of the secretaries enter it one day when she stopped by to see Axel. Armed with the means to gain entry to the office and desperate to examine the company's private records to dig up any dirt on Axel she could, Katy waited impatiently for an opportunity to strike.

She would not have to wait long. A few days later when Axel told her he would be meeting late into the evening with city council members to discuss a new development project, Katy drove to the Lanier Properties building after hours. She parked around the corner, then walked briskly to the office. After a quick glance up and down the block to make sure she wasn't being followed, Katy unlocked the front door with her spare key. Entering the office, Katy then made her way through the dark hallways to the file room guided only by her flashlight.

After punching in the combination and opening the file room door, Katy started perusing through the dozens of boxes stacked in the file room cabinets. She wasn't sure where to start and didn't know exactly what she was looking for. The boxes were heavy, about twenty-five pounds each so it was a chore to move them around, even for someone as fit as Katy. She opened the boxes one-by-one, undertook a brief examination of the contents and then moved on to the next box.

After about twenty minutes, Katy finally stumbled upon a box marked "Confidential." She opened the top and began sifting through the folders. The box contained at least a dozen files, but Katy zeroed in on two that appeared to be promising; one was marked "Vet Housing," and the other "Baton Rouge." Peering nervously over her shoulder, Katy took out her mini-camera and began rapidly snapping photographs of as many documents from the two files as she could, including one newspaper article about a new bill passed by the Louisiana legislature.

Suddenly Katy heard a click. Startled, she froze in her tracks. *Someone had opened the front door.* Katy turned off her flashlight and hopped outside of the file room. She heard chatter and footsteps as her eyes struggled to adjust to the darkness. After a few seconds, Katy was able to make out furniture silhouettes across the office as she searched for a hiding place.

Spotting what looked to be a large desk in the far corner, Katy quietly tip-toed across the room in the dark and then crawled into the desk's open, recessed chair space. Packing herself into the opening to become as compact as possible, Katy folded her arms and legs and squeezed herself all the way back in the vacant cavity up against the wall.

Then Katy detected the footsteps coming towards her. She was certain that her pounding chest would give her away. She could not tell how many people were approaching. The footsteps abruptly stopped. Then Katy heard the faint giggles of a man and a woman.

The unseen visitors continued through the office now headed in the direction of the desk where Katy lay still as a church mouse. The footsteps grew louder and now Katy could actually make out two pairs of four legs just inches in front of her. Lewis and Clark could not have led the intruders any more directly to Katy's location. Still, it was nearly dark and the pair didn't notice Katy right beneath them as they reclined on top of the desk.

Then Katy heard a voice, *Axel's* voice.

"I'm ready for dessert right now," he said, as Katy detected a slurring and slight stutter in his speech. "Not wanting to wait any longer."

"So this is his late night city council meeting," Katy thought. She was not upset though. Any time that Axel spent with other women just meant there was less time for him to spend with her.

"You're funny Axel," replied the husky female voice. "Don't be a naughty lover. You only get the appetizer now. The main course and dessert come later. We'll be more comfortable at my place anyway. I promise you won't be disappointed," she teased.

Katy heard them both laugh again and this time the laughter was followed by the "clink" of two wine glasses touching each other.

"Come on Axel, you've got the papers you said you needed to pick up. Are you sure there is no one else here? I'm ready to leave. This place is starting to give me the creeps," said the woman, suddenly feeling that there was something not quite right.

Katy twitched ever so delicately and silently wound herself even tighter. She could see Axel's legs shuffling closer to the woman as the pair got up off the desk.

"I want you," Axel said clumsily, clearly having imbibed way too much of whatever had been his evening's choice of elixir.

Axel leaned forward again but the woman had moved slightly to the side. There was nothing to break Axel's momentum except thin air. He stumbled nearly to the ground, his scattering feet barely missing Katy who was far enough back in the crawl space to be just outside the reach of Axel's aimless flailing.

Katy held her breath. Her cheeks were ready to explode but she dared not exhale.

The woman picked Axel up. "Let's go Axel," she said with a tone of increasing aggravation. Katy began to breathe normally. This time she heard only one set of footsteps, but the steps were accompanied by a sound that reminded Katy of her uncles dragging hundred pound sacks of flour across the wooden floor at Nana Bernard's storage shed.

The pattern of stilted steps and the tugging of dead weight faded in the distance as the pair moved further away from Katy. Then Katy heard a loud sigh. There was exasperation in the husky voice as it exclaimed "I should have known this evening was going to be a huge disappointment."

"Welcome to the club," Katy thought, struggling mightily to restrain herself from snickering.

Finally, the office's front door opened and closed. Katy remained motionless for another two or three minutes. She eventually determined that the coast was clear. She considered opening more boxes to snap some additional pictures, but thought better of it. There was no need to further press her luck. It was time to get out.

Returning to the file room to conceal her evening's work, Katy rearranged the boxes back to their original configuration as best she could. She then waited a couple of more minutes until she heard a car start outside and drive off. Breathing a sigh of relief and somewhat traumatized but still undiscovered, Katy left the building and drove back to her apartment.

Chapter 54

Axel had his hands in too many cookie jars to notice anything Katy might be up to. Any move that might strengthen control over his business empire he considered fair game. The ruthless search for opportunities to tighten the screws on every aspect of his money making operations left

Axel clueless as to what was going on right beneath his nose. It was simply unthinkable that he might somehow be outfoxed by Katy.

Thinking that Katy was completely on board with the new life that Axel had scripted for her, Axel scheduled a dinner with Katy. They would review the lavish wedding Axel had planned.

Meanwhile, Katy was anxious to get her photographs developed and blown up so she could examine the confidential Lanier documents in more detail. She intended to review each picture with a fine-toothed comb, probing for any hint of a scandal. The time to turn the tables on Axel was now. Katy knew there would be no second chance.

Chapter 55

Guidry Monroe was agitated. Axel Lanier had not fully paid him the normal "commission" he was accustomed to receiving for his most recent leak of confidential bid information that helped Lanier Properties obtain a coveted contract.

Within the last month, Monroe had begun to wonder about the wisdom of continuing his illicit business arrangement with Axel. It was creating too much risk for him. If he was going to get stiffed and then have to chase Axel for payment, the entire kickback scheme became less and less appealing.

There was a reason for Axel's slowness to pay. He had now figured out on his own how to properly bid the contracts that Lanier Properties had to have, without Monroe's help. In Axel's mind, there was little value in continuing to pay Monroe for inside information. Axel might as well pocket the hefty payments himself if he could get the contracts anyway. It was time to cut Monroe loose just as Axel had previously discarded Burgess Petty.

One afternoon as Axel sat in his office, the phone rang. Since his assistant was out for lunch, Axel picked it up. He was less than pleased when he recognized the caller's voice.

"Lanier, this is Guidry here. I have some information regarding a new contract in New Orleans that might interest you. A youth center. It's going to be big."

"About that," said Axel. "I think I've got it covered Guidry." Then because he was just a little curious and because Axel knew the contract for the New Orleans Youth Center would indeed be lucrative, Axel decided to hedge his bets. "Since I have you on the line though, I'm willing to listen. Go ahead. Tell me what you got."

"Not so fast," replied Monroe. "You still owe me a hundred and fifty grand from our last little transaction. When can I expect to see it?"

There was a long pause from Axel.

"Look Monroe," exclaimed an agitated Axel, "the fact of the matter is I got that last contract on my own. You told me nothing I didn't already know. So the way I see it, I don't actually owe you much of anything. But because I'm an honest businessman, I'm willing to split the difference with you. And I've been thinking. It's probably best for both of us to consider this relationship over. It was fun while it lasted. It made us both a hell of a lot of dough, but it's time to move on," concluded Axel as he hung up the phone.

Monroe was stunned. He didn't mind that their uncomfortable pairing was at an end. He did mind that Axel still owed him one hundred and fifty thousand dollars and wanted to settle it for seventy-five.

Monroe determined that Axel was going to pay and pay in full. And if Axel didn't pay, there would be consequences. Yes sir. If Axel Lanier thought he had heard the last of Guidry Monroe he was sadly mistaken.

Chapter 56

Finally, the pictures were ready. Katy couldn't wait to examine them.

"I'm going to figure out what that weasel's up to," she told herself.

Katy examined the blown up photos with a magnifying glass. Initially she was stumped by what she saw. Then the pieces of the puzzle started to fall into place after she read the newspaper article from Axel's files. It described a new law, the Veterans Assistance Act, approved by the Louisiana legislature. The Act provided for stipends to landlords who rented to military veterans. The government would pay half the veteran's rent and then give the landlord an additional $20,000 bonus if the veteran remained in the apartment for at least six months.

Now, with an understanding of the program, Katy gave the documents a second look. She quickly determined that Lanier Properties was a frequent participant in the government initiative. Katy also recalled Myra's story about the sudden eviction notice her family received. Then there was that chaotic scene in the Lanier offices where the Vietnam veteran all but threatened to dismember Axel if Axel tried to remove him from his apartment.

And then it all came together. Suddenly, everything made sense. The Laniers had gotten greedy. They were double dipping.

Katy cracked the code. She unmasked the scheme. After a veteran tenant reached the six month occupancy period thus earning Lanier Properties the $20,000 bonus, the Laniers looked for an opportunity to dump the veteran they had just brought in. If a rent payment was late or the apartment needed a repair and the tenant failed to complete the paperwork required by law, the Laniers would send an eviction notice.

Since there was always a waiting list of homeless veterans seeking to enter the program, the plan worked to a tee. In essence, the Laniers were recycling their tenants, bringing in new ones to replace those just evicted, and thereby re-starting the six month period for earning another $20,000 on the same apartment.

This was not what the Louisiana legislature intended when it passed the law, but Axel found a loophole and took full advantage of it. The veterans organizations that were so enamored with Axel and Lanier Properties, had not yet caught on to the full extent of Axel's duplicity. Instead of calling him out, they praised him. To Axel, the Person of the Year award wrapped his entire master plan up in a tidy gift box with a neat little bow on top.

But Axel Lanier had not counted on having to deal with Katy Duvall.

Chapter 57

Katy nervously awaited her dinner date with Axel to review the wedding plans. Axel showed up at the restaurant fifteen minutes late. After ordering a cocktail, he started flipping through some contracts, barely pausing to look up at Katy.

Sitting across the table from Axel, Katy pulled out a black and white picture from her purse. The picture was worn around the edges and showed a women in her thirties with her three children. She slid the picture over in front of Axel.

"Who's that?" said Axel.

"Myra Fontenot," replied Katy.

"Ok," said Axel. "Are you ready to order?"

Katy was not amused.

"Myra is my cousin," Katy said pointedly. "Her husband is in the Army. They live at one of your properties, Evangeline Gardens I believe. Myra just received an eviction notice. She says they've always paid rent on time. Then the heater broke, they complained about it and right after that they received a certified letter from Lanier Properties. Myra says your signature was on the letter. But you wouldn't do something like that because Lanier Properties takes excellent care of their veteran tenants. So I know there must be some mistake. Right?"

Axel attempted to brush off Katy's concerns.

"I'm certain there is an innocent explanation," Axel said. "Undoubtedly a mix-up somewhere. We have several hundred tenants. I don't remember the circumstances for each one, but I'll look into it later this week."

Then Axel quickly changed the subject, although he spoke dispassionately as if conversing with a hired wedding planner and not his fiancé.

"We really need to decide on the wine goblets for the reception tables," Axel said continuing to focus on the paperwork in front of him, having already dismissed Katy's concerns about Myra from his mind.

"I was thinking we get top of the line crystal, maybe Zwiesel, that's from Bavaria you know, or Waterford. The glasses should be frosted, with our names engraved and etched into each one. 'Axel and Katy.' What do you think?"

"I think there's not going to be a wedding," Katy replied quickly.

Axel suddenly looked up from the documentation that had occupied his attention.

"What did you say?" Axel asked incredulously.

"I said there isn't going to be a wedding, at least not one involving me," Katy replied. "I'm not marrying you. No way in hell. It's not happening."

"Well. . . ." said Axel, "that's quite a surprise. Of course you know . . ." and then Katy cut him off.

"The only thing I know," continued Katy "is that I am not marrying you. Not unless of course you want the details about how Lanier Properties deals with military vets to be published in all of the local newspapers and broadcast on every television station. You're familiar with how that little scheme works aren't you Axel? Of course you are. You probably designed it."

"You know, where Lanier Properties has this revolving door of tenants who served their country in the military, many of them disabled. They come in, Lanier Properties makes $20,000. Then you search for an excuse to throw them out. If you find it, they're on the street, replaced by another needy veteran which earns you more money. Isn't that the Lanier blueprint Axel? Isn't that what happened to Myra and her family?"

Axel paused.

"That's right Axel," said Katy, "I know all about it. My lawyer knows about it too. And if anything should suddenly happen to me, my bank has instructions to open my safe deposit box and mail copies of the contents to media outlets throughout New Orleans."

Katy had come prepared. She knew it was foolhardy to battle the Laniers with only an open hand when they were playing with clenched, iron fists.

"So here's the deal Axel," Katy continued. "First, the wedding is off. Second, there will be no more late night visits to satisfy your urges just because you feel the need. Third, I won't say anything else about your filthy laundry, although you might want to consider changing a few things about your disgusting business practices. And whatever you know about me, well, that goes no further than you."

Axel sat in stunned silence. It never occurred to him that Katy, the cleaning lady's daughter, had the intellect or the grit to take him down. She certainly had his full attention now.

"Oh and one other thing," Katy said sliding the same photograph she showed Axel minutes before of Myra and her family, back across the table into Axel's pile of paperwork.

"You're not going to evict Myra's family. Instead, you're going to upgrade them from a two-bedroom to a three-bedroom. And they will pay no rent for forty-eight months."

Axel swallowed hard. The jig was up and he knew it. Still, he could not live with himself if he permitted the Lanier Empire to be brought to its knees by the likes of Katy Duvall. Backed into a corner, Axel concluded it would be best to retreat now and regroup later. He would need to go back to the drawing board to figure Katy out. In the meantime, he had to cut the best deal he could.

"Twenty-four months," he replied, trying to carve out the most favorable surrender terms possible.

"Thirty-six months," said Katy.

"Agreed," replied Axel.

Chapter 58

Katy had solved the riddle of the documents in Axel's "Vet Housing" file. She was still not certain about the story to be told from the paperwork in the "Baton Rouge" file. Katy noticed that the pages contained several scribbled dollar amounts in different places, some of them next to the letters "LBS."

At this point Katy strongly considered leaving well enough alone. After all, her primary objective was to boot Axel out of her life, hopefully for good. On that score, mission accomplished. But Katy was curious.

"You never know what information might come in handy on a rainy day," she thought. So she decided to take Gus Perilloux up on his offer of assistance made at the Veterans Gala. She pulled out Gus' business card and dialed his number.

"Hello Mr. Perilloux," Katy said softly when Gus answered. "This is Katy Duvall. You probably don't remember me but . . ."

"Oh I remember you," interrupted an intrigued Gus. "How are you?"

"I'm fine. I only have a couple of minutes. I want to talk to you about something very important. But first I need to know that this discussion will remain confidential," Katy said sternly.

Gus hesitated. He hadn't spoken to Katy since he overtly flirted with her at the Veterans Gala.

"Katy, please call me Gus," he said. "Of course. This conversation goes no further than me."

"Ok Mister . . . well, Gus," Katy said as she took a deep breath.

Katy then asked Perilloux about his suspicions regarding Axel's ability to repeatedly obtain the most coveted government contracts for Lanier Properties.

"Not that I can prove anything of course," said Perilloux, "but Axel has to be getting inside help from somewhere. He just has to. I can't tell you how many times I was certain I had a contract locked up but the award comes out and it's the same old story. Lanier Properties. They always manage to underbid me by two, three thousand dollars. If it happened once, ok, I could see that. But numerous times losing out by a lousy twenty-five hundred dollars. And huge contracts too. Come on."

"Well," said Katy, "I have some documentation that might interest you. I'm not sure it's helpful, but you might want to take a look."

Gus' interest was suddenly piqued. Katy had his undivided attention.

"Katy, what did you say?" Gus responded cautiously, seeking to confirm whether Katy actually said what he thought he just heard.

"Never mind," said Katy, beginning to regret she had made the phone call. "It's not important. I shouldn't have called you."

"No, no, no," said Gus. "I would be happy to look at whatever you have. It's just that . . . well, you know, with you and Axel being engaged, I guess I didn't think . . ." and then he stopped. Gus realized he was talking himself out of information that might be useful to him. Besides, even if whatever Katy wanted to show him wasn't relevant to the Lanier Properties operations, seeing Katy again alone and without Axel might be worthwhile. That by itself was reason enough to continue the discussion.

"Can you stop by our offices about 5:30 this evening," Gus continued. "Almost everyone should be gone home by then and we can talk privately."

All of a sudden Katy had doubts. As much as she loathed Axel, she wasn't completely comfortable with showing copies of Axel's private documents to a competitor. Then again, Katy knew that if she didn't cut off the head of the snake it might come back to bite her. The Laniers were merciless that way.

Katy decided that she was too invested in the process of exploiting Axel's vulnerabilities to turn back now. Any additional ammunition she could acquire might well prove useful in the days ahead. And Gus just might be the person who could help her.

"5:30 it is," said Katy firmly. "I'll see you then."

Chapter 59

Gus Perilloux was waiting for Katy at the reception desk when Katy entered the Perilloux Realty premises at 5:30. He showed her into his spacious office which overlooked downtown New Orleans with the winding Mississippi River in the background, then closed the door. Gus pulled up a chair in front of his desk for Katy to sit in, then walked behind the desk and reclined in his own chair. Katy was just as attractive as he remembered.

"So what is this about some information you discovered?" Gus asked curiously.

"Just a few things I picked up," said Katy pulling out several of the photos she had taken of Axel's documents and then handing them to Gus. "I'm not sure who this G Monroe is," she said "or what all this means. And why all the references to pounds?"

Gus carefully reviewed the handwritten notes on the pages.

"Katy, if you don't mind my asking, why are you bringing this to me?" he said.

"I can't answer that question right now," replied Katy, "but I've got my reasons. Let's just say that you made an accusation against Axel. I don't know what to believe, but I want to know the truth." Then somewhat impatiently she pressed Gus. "Do you see anything here that might be important?"

Gus continued to examine the photos. He got up from his chair and slowly walked over to the couch that was in the corner of his office and motioned for Katy to follow him.

"Katy, these are notes of conversations with Guidry Monroe, the chairman of the state legislature's Commerce Committee. The Committee is responsible for awarding government contracts to contractors like me. And like your fiancé'. And 'LBS' doesn't mean pounds, it means 'lowest bid submitted.' If I had to guess, I'd say the person who scribbled these notes was getting information from Monroe about sealed contract bids. That would be illegal of course."

"Whoever took these notes," said Gus, firmly believing that the writing was Axel's, "had a huge advantage over the rest of us in the bid submission process. Probably insurmountable. Monroe looks like he is on the take and whoever received this information would owe him big time."

Katy knew the handwriting was Axel's.

Gus then raised his eyebrows and handed the papers back to Katy. As far as he was concerned, this was proof that Axel and Monroe had conspired to undermine the bidding process for state contracts. And they had done it brazenly and to the detriment of Perilloux Realty and others.

Gus didn't know what he was going to do about it. If he really wanted to nail Axel, the easiest thing would be to make copies of the notes in Katy's photos and hand them over to the police, but Gus didn't want to do that since Katy had come to him in confidence. Besides, Gus was involved in a number of shady ventures of his own. There was no need to unnecessarily cast attention on himself. He would have to give his next move some thought.

Gus then turned his attention to something else he had been eyeing. He inched closer to Katy and put his arm around her, as if to comfort her. Handsome and successful, Gus viewed himself as a commodity. Plenty of women had made fools of themselves chasing him in the past. Katy was something to be conquered and what better way to start exacting revenge against Axel than to seduce his fiancé'.

Gus assumed that Katy was attracted to him. But then Gus assumed that *all* women were attracted to him. After all, hadn't Katy returned his flirtations at the Veterans Gala? He drew Katy closer to him and looked directly into her eyes. Katy stopped fidgeting with her paperwork, somewhat surprised by the sudden absence of conversation and the new direction the meeting was taking.

The two moved closer and Gus began to caress Katy's shoulder. His tactics had worked plenty of times in the past. He was confident they would be successful again.

Then he and Katy kissed as Gus continued to gently massage Katy's back and shoulders. Katy felt a sudden sense of excitement from her embrace with Gus. She had not come to his office expecting them to wind up in each other's arms, but Katy found Gus smooth and stimulating, although not irresistible. This level of attention from a younger, handsome man was a welcome departure from the coolness and indifference she had felt lately when with Axel. For a brief instance, Katy felt liberated. She sensed herself gradually acquiescing to the sensuousness of the moment.

Gus began to lift up Katy's blouse.

"Gus . . . Gus," said Katy taking a couple of deep breaths and trying to compose herself. "I can't," she said. "I can't."

"Why not?" whispered Gus as he ran his fingers through Katy's hair and tried to kiss her again. "I want you and you want me. It doesn't need to be any more complicated than that. And no one will ever know."

"I just can't," said Katy, readjusting her blouse as she gently pushed Gus away. "I really should leave now," Katy continued as she gathered her belongings, put them back in her purse and stood up from her relaxed position on the couch.

"You've been very helpful. Thank you so much. I'll show myself out."

Katy straightened her blouse, brushed her hair and walked briskly to the door.

"Anytime Katy, anytime," replied a frustrated Gus. "And if you ever change your mind, let me know. My offer still stands. I'd take you off Axel's hands any day."

Chapter 60

A week later Gus Perilloux worked late into the night. He was putting the finishing touches on a contract bid he was preparing for submission to the Louisiana legislature. The contract was for the construction of the New Orleans Youth Center, complete with retail shops, restaurants and an apartment complex. It was by far the most lucrative deal Perilloux Realty had ever bid on.

Perilloux carefully reviewed each page and every sentence of his submission. Perilloux Realty had fallen on hard times and Gus knew this contract was critical to the survival of his company. If his bid was unsuccessful, significant layoffs of some long time employees and family members would follow. Conversely, if the bid was accepted, the contract would put the company in the black for years to come. It was a potential game changer and could make Perilloux a very wealthy man.

Perilloux had done his homework. He had a good idea where most of his competitors stood. He knew how much their suppliers would charge for materials. He had calculated down to the penny what subcontracting costs would be and where some of the other contractors might cut corners by using non-union labor. He had figured out everyone else's desired profit margin.

What he couldn't counter, however, was the story told by the scribbles, dollar signs and figures on the pieces of paper that Katy showed him. No matter how much Perilloux planned, the bottom line was that he was playing with one hand tied behind his back. If indeed Axel Lanier was getting inside help from Guidry Monroe, which Perilloux fully suspected to be the case, there was nothing he could do. As far as Perilloux knew, Axel continued to have an ace in the hole. No amount of planning and calculated bidding or cost cutting, could change that. It had become clear to Perilloux that he was simply banging his head up against a brick wall.

Frustrated and angry, Perilloux suddenly ripped his proposal into a thousand pieces. What was the use of submitting it? It wouldn't matter. As he tossed the shreds of his carefully constructed bid in the trash can, an uncontrollable rage came over Perilloux. He had come to the realization that Axel Lanier was destroying his livelihood. And Axel Lanier would pay.

Chapter 61

Axel's confrontation with Katy left him badly shaken. He was used to dictating terms to everyone else, not the other way around. Nevertheless, many things were still trending in Axel's favor. His company was about to be awarded one of the richest construction contracts in Louisiana history. Cash was rolling in by the truck load. And Axel had ridded himself of Guidry, his "mole" in the State Capital who he now found useless.

But the dream of marrying and then controlling his trophy wife had been shattered and with it, the notion that Axel was invincible. Axel was not used to retreating with his tail between his legs and he didn't much like it. Still, he resolved that Katy had not heard the last from him. Suffering from a crisis in confidence and needing a weekend getaway, Axel retreated to familiarity, his cabin in the woods, taking time to arrange for one of his occasional female companions to join him. Little did Axel know that the party was about to come to a crashing end.

After arriving at the cabin, an exhausted Axel reclined on the couch. He noticed that the room seemed uncommonly warm and he quickly fell into a deep slumber. A short time later Axel awoke, coughing and gasping for air. Barely able to breath, he struggled to lift himself off the couch. His stomach unsettled, he staggered forward. Axel knew he needed to reach the front door, but he saw two doors. In fact Axel saw two of everything as the entire room spun around him. On the verge of passing out and severely weakened, Axel finally grabbed the door knob, but it had been jammed from the outside and wouldn't move.

Summoning the last ounce of his fading strength and frantically seeking breathable air, Axel finally got the door to budge. The opening door startled someone sitting on the front porch. Before Axel could escape, the figure, who was wearing a gas mask, leapt out of the chair, kicked Axel in the groin and immediately shoved him back inside. Slamming the door shut, the intruder barricaded it again, this time more forcefully than before. Axel tumbled to the floor, the noxious gases now completely encircling him. He thought he recognized the steely eyes of his attacker through the mask, but his consciousness was rapidly fading.

Axel tried to scream for help, but was only able to manage a series of muffled coughs. "You . . . won't . . . get away . . . with this," he hacked, covering his mouth in an attempt to preserve whatever precious little oxygen remained. "Let me out!" Axel wheezed one final time as he again reached for the door before finally lapsing into unconsciousness as he succumbed to the toxins that filled the room.

In the surrounding clearing, the still calmness of the bayou wilderness was interrupted by the commotion emanating from the cabin. Two inca doves perched on the branch of a Tupelo tree about thirty feet away instinctively thrust themselves upward into open air, having become momentarily confused by the shock waves proceeding from the slamming door and the brief struggle that preceded it.

About ten minutes later, Axel's date for the weekend entered the cabin with her private key after removing a wedge that had been slipped under the door to keep it shut. She immediately began to feel queasy, then discovered Axel lying motionless on the floor. She quickly dialed 9-1-1, then covered her face. Struggling, she then dragged Axel out the front door onto the porch.

Chapter 62

Katy showed no emotion when informed of the assault on Axel. She remained composed, then sat in her apartment staring at the walls surrounding her for nearly an hour. At that point, a few tears finally rolled down Katy's cheeks. Minutes later, the tears had become a deluge.

Katy cried not for Axel, but for herself. On one hand there was relief. From the way things sounded, Axel would no longer be an impediment to her daily existence anytime soon. That much was certain. But as much as Katy despised him, she had no desire to see Axel physically harmed.

And where precisely did all this leave Katy? What would become of all of her plans for the future, plans she had dreamt about from the time of those carefree days spent on her grandmother's farm. Could that simple innocence ever be restored? Could she recapture the love she lost? Could her life ever return to what it once was? And even if things somehow got better going forward, it could all be undone at the drop of a hat if Pope's body was discovered and Katy's dreadful secret unraveled.

There were no easy answers to Katy's questions. She was determined to keep moving forward but hope was becoming elusive.

Chapter 63

A couple of days later there was a knock on Katy's apartment door. Katy was surprised to find two New Orleans police officers standing in her entry way.

"Ma'am, I'm Officer Marshall," one of them said "and this is my partner Officer Teague. We'd like to express our sympathy for the unfortunate circumstances regarding your fiancé'. We have a few questions for you. May we come in?

"Absolutely," said Katy. "How can I help you gentlemen?"

"I'll be brief ma'am," said Marshall. "We're just tying up some loose ends regarding Mr. Lanier. Routine police work, that's all."

"I understand," said Katy, "but I really don't have any information for you."

"Well," continued Marshall. "You might start by telling us where you were the day your fiancé was attacked inside his cabin."

"I was here by myself. Why do you ask?" Katy replied. "And I thought Axel was overcome by gases from a faulty heater. What makes you think he was attacked?"

"We'll get to that in a minute, ma'am. Can anyone substantiate that you were at home?" Marshall inquired.

"No, not really," Katy said. "Officer, are you . . . am I . . . am I a suspect? I guess I don't really have an alibi. I never thought I'd need one."

"Not at this time ma'am, but if you don't mind me saying, I would have expected you to be a little more . . . well, distraught."

"If you gentlemen expected to see me in mourning," Katy said, "well you've come to the wrong place. I'm not sure that I was going to actually marry Axel anyway but I certainly wouldn't wish what happened to him on my worst enemy."

"Just the same ma'am," Marshall pressed, "we took a look at footage from the security camera at Lanier Properties from a few weeks back. Seemed to be someone who looks like you entering the building after hours when no one else was there."

It was Teague's turn to chime in.

"Then, about twenty-five minutes later, the tape shows your fiancé' going into the office." Teague paused. "With another woman. A short time after that, your fiancé' and his companion left. But you didn't leave until later."

"Which means," added Marshall, "that you were in the building when Mr. Lanier and his friend arrived."

"So you see our problem ma'am," concluded Teague as the two of them continued their tag-team interrogation of Katy. "The way we figure it, your fiancé and his companion surprised you when they came in. It wouldn't be unreasonable to infer that you became infuriated when you saw Mr. Lanier with a lady friend so you started planning his demise. As the saying goes, 'hell hath no fury like a woman scorned.' A couple of weeks later you saw an opportunity to get even and the next thing you know 'poof,' Mr. Lanier just happens to meet with an untimely 'accident'."

Marshall then accepted the final baton pass from Teague. "I have to hand it to you . . . uh, what I mean of course is hand it to whoever did this. The plan was very clever. Pumping carbon monoxide from a generator into the house furnace so that it overwhelmed your fiancé shortly after he arrived and making it look like an accident. Only the plan didn't quite work. Too bad Mr. Lanier lost consciousness again right after they got him to the hospital. The doctors think he was trying to identify his assailant right before he slipped into the coma."

The whole thing sounded so ridiculous to Katy, she wanted to laugh. Except she realized the officers were serious.

"Well if that's what suffices for good police work these days," she said "then New Orleans is in far worse shape than I thought. Yes, I was in the building when Axel and his 'friend' came in. So what? I didn't try to kill him. I would have no reason to and besides he wasn't worth it. If I was going to get rid of Axel, I would have waited to try until after I married him. At least then I might have gotten something out of it."

"Axel had enough enemies to start a small platoon and he acquired most of them before he met me. That's where you might want to start looking. Don't expect me to do your homework for you officers," Katy chided.

Marshall nodded but he was not ready to give up. "Yes ma'am, I understand. Just one more thing. The would-be killer made a big mistake. The cleaning service confirmed that several hand-carved board games and a set of dominos is missing from the cabin. Seems that your fiancé' had a rare set of very expensive gold-plated dominos that he purchased somewhere in the Caribbean. Whoever gassed his house couldn't resist keeping their hands off 'em. Otherwise we might never have suspected foul play. Do you mind if we look around. When we find Axel's expensive play things, we likely will have also found his attacker."

"You can look all you want," said Katy. "I have no extravagant games or dominos here." Katy had never been to Axel's cabin but often wondered about the level of opulence Axel surrounded himself with when he left town on his weekend soirees. She knew Axel owned a jade chess set and had a fetish for collecting other exquisitely-crafted games, so she was not surprised that he might have outfitted the cabin with expensive toys and exotic amusements.

The officers proceeded to undertake a quick search of Katy's apartment. They did not find what they were looking for.

"We may want to talk to you again," said Marshall, "so don't plan on leaving the state. And just so you know, if Mr. Lanier does not survive then of course we will be looking for a murderer. You might want to think about that."

Marshall let his words percolate for a bit, but Katy showed no reaction.

Then he continued. "Thank you ma'am. We'll let ourselves out."

As the two police officers strolled back to the car, Marshall remarked to his partner, "if I were a betting man, I'd say she didn't do it. If she did, she would have been crying up a storm and would already have a perfect alibi. That woman's got too much contempt to be hiding something."

After the officers left, Katy thought about the irony of their visit. In the last few years she had been proposed to twice, well she never actually had been proposed to at all, and been associated with two horrific crimes. She was suspected in the one that she had nothing to do with and remained completely off law enforcement's radar screen in the one she committed.

Chapter 64

The Lanier clan gathered around the grim-faced physician standing next to Axel's hospital bed. Dr. Winston then proceeded to provide an update on Axel's condition. It was bleak. The carbon monoxide that was ingested into Axel's system had caused some involuntary flexing of the limbs which could be an indication of severe brain damage, Winston explained. There was no telling when, or if, Axel would come out of the coma and what condition he would be in if he did.

"He might be fine," Winston opined, "or he might be a vegetable."

It was unclear if Mercedes Lanier, who had finished her fourth glass of wine just before Dr. Winston entered the room, fully comprehended the prognosis.

"All we can do now is wait," the doctor said as he left the room, "and keep pumping oxygen into his bloodstream."

"And pray," yelled Mercedes to the roomful of somber heads nodding in agreement.

A few minutes later, Mercedes became agitated. Her condition had been worsening by the day, even before Axel's misfortune. Looking for someone to blame, she first went after the hospital staff. Accusing the nurses of not doing their job despite their constant attentiveness, Mercedes began piling blankets on top of a comatose Axel. Stunned relatives tried to calm her down, then quickly removed the pile of covers that Mercedes had stacked on Axel's chest.

After a brief period of calm, paranoia soon set in. Mercedes was convinced that she was being patronized and not taken seriously by the others who were there. Friends and family now seemed to her like an encampment of enemies surrounding both her and Axel. She must defend him. Springing into action, Mercedes suddenly slammed her wine glass against the sink near Axel's bed, spraying razor sharp fragments across the room. A large piece came to rest on the plastic tubing that was funneling oxygen to Axel's brain.

"Which one of you poisoned my Axel?" Mercedes demanded, as she stalked around the room holding the shattered goblet by the stem. Not recognizing her own children, she thrust the jagged edges of the broken chalice within inches of the face of each person she confronted, staring them down with bloodshot eyes. For the next few moments no one dared challenge the suddenly weaponized, half-crazed matriarch.

Axel's sister Margeaux then bowed her head. She had been ousted by Axel years earlier in his purge of Lanier Properties' top management and had been looking for work ever since. Instead of praying for Axel's recovery though, Margeaux secretly prayed for his demise and then added that she wouldn't mind it all that much if Mercedes soon followed him.

After a few more intense seconds, order was restored when two of Mercedes' sons wrestled the lethal remnants of the goblet from her hand and strapped their sobbing mother into a chair.

"Axel's going to be just fine mom," one of them whispered softly as Mercedes first struggled, then passed out. "You just wait and see."

Chapter 65

Katy never heard anything else from the police in the months following the attack on Axel. As time passed, her mind wandered back to the time when she and Bryan were together. Katy wanted to call him, but could never quite get up the nerve. At this point who knew if Bryan would even be bothered with her. So Katy decided to contact Bryan through a method that would permit him to decide if he wanted to speak to her or not. She took out a pen and piece of paper and started to compose a letter.

"Dear Bryan," she wrote. "I hope you are doing well. A lot has happened since we last talked, but first things first. I did not get married. It's a long story, but maybe we can discuss it someday. The reason I am writing is because I still have strong feelings for you. I hope we can be friends one day but I would completely understand if you never want to speak to me again. That's probably what I deserve. It would mean the world to me though if you and I could talk once in a while, just like we used to. Please call me anytime. (504) 821-9328. Love you, Katy."

Katy sealed the letter, applied the proper postage and mailed it off. She had no idea if she would ever hear from Bryan again.

Chapter 66

Eugene Carson was ready to make his final mail drop of the day. Carson had been on the delivery force for 26 years and was among the most decorated letter carriers in Los Angeles, having been recognized by his union, the American Letter Carriers Association for dedicated service, a 99% plus attendance rating and participation in fund-raising activities for local food banks. Carson had also received the Postmaster General Hero Award for his extraordinary efforts in completing delivery services to elderly and shut-in residents. He was the best the postal service had to offer.

As Carson prepared to make his final deliveries in the Marina del Rey section of Los Angeles to wrap up his day, his mail truck stalled when he tried to start it. Once more he turned the key in the ignition. The truck started with a loud bang. Moments later Carson smelled smoke.

In seconds the truck was on fire. The larger mail trucks had fire extinguishers, but Carson's smaller version did not. The fire spread rapidly. Carson leapt from the vehicle, crawled around to the rear, opened the back door and began tossing package and letters out of the truck as fast as he could.

Within a minute, the truck was completely engulfed in flames, the intense heat melting the cab area and forcing Carson to retreat from the vehicle altogether. He had managed to save 95% of the truck's cargo, but a few letters were consumed by the inferno.

All that was left of one envelope was a stamped postmark from Metarie, Louisiana. The remainder of the letter and envelope were destroyed.

The cause of the fire was officially listed as mechanical failure. Residents who did not receive their mail that day were requested to contact the postal service for anything they had been expecting that was missing.

Bryan Stirling later learned that a credit card bill scheduled to be delivered to him in that day's mail, never arrived. He did, however, receive the quarterly fundraising request from Westchester Law School and promptly shredded it, as was his custom. Other than that, nothing else was missing as far as he knew.

None of the residents from Carson's final delivery stops were expecting anything mailed from the greater New Orleans area. Thus, the almost completely burned letter with the Metarie postmark was never identified or claimed.

Chapter 67

Bryan struggled to accept the fact that Katy had married someone else. He and Katy would be forever linked, of that he was certain, but not for the reasons he had hoped.

Although Katy's phone call left him distraught, the rest of 1999 and the years that would follow went well for Bryan. Everything he touched turned to gold. In August of 1999, Bryan received some totally unexpected news. The $15,000 venture capital investment he made a couple of years earlier, paid off in a way Bryan could not have imagined. Half of the funds had been applied to acquire equity interests in Silicon Valley start-up companies that were now on life support and going nowhere. Thus, the first $7,500 of Bryan's investment was a total loss.

The other $7,500, however had been used to purchase stock of Cerent, a company whose technology made it easier for wireless communications carriers to transmit data over long distances. With internet usage and e-mail accounts now proliferating across the country, Cerent all of a sudden became a hot target for larger e-commerce businesses. The company was eventually acquired by Cisco Systems for several billion dollars, netting its venture capital investors, including Bryan, a return of 238 to 1. Bryan's $7,500 investment had mushroomed into a payoff of nearly $1.8 million.

Bryan's legal career was also coming up aces. He won 90% of his cases and was in high demand. In 2001, a rival firm made him a lucrative offer to jump ship. Bryan leveraged the offer in his negotiations with

Lynn, Ryan. After intense discussions, Bryan emerged with a partnership position after just five years with the firm, something almost unheard of. He was now pulling down an annual salary in the high six figures. That, plus his earlier venture capital homerun made Bryan, now in his early thirties, financially secure. It also made him a highly coveted bachelor.

Eventually Bryan started dating again and ultimately ended up in a serious relationship with Tamara Harper, a childhood friend. Joyce Harper, Tamara's mother, had for years engineered subtle (and not so subtle) behind-the-scenes maneuvers to get Tamara and Bryan together. Her surreptitious efforts finally paid off.

After nearly a year of seeing each other on an exclusive basis, the two announced their engagement much to the delight of an increasingly impatient Joyce Harper. The wedding was set for the summer of 2002. Joyce Harper mailed out the invitations before the ink on them had dried. Bryan did not bother to inform Katy. He was over her.

Or so he thought.

Chapter 68

The words rolled perfunctorily off Bryan's lips, as if by rote, uttered in lockstep and following the minister's lead.

"To love and to honor," "forsaking all others," "till death do us part," he repeated. Bryan said what he was expected to say, but his words lacked emotion or conviction.

After the minister pronounced the couple husband and wife, an apprehensive Joyce Harper immediately dotted the "i's," crossed the "t's" and signed the marriage certificate as *both* Witness 1 and Witness 2. And with that, the deed was done.

Bryan thought he would be excited. He believed this would be one of the happiest days of his life. He loved Tamara, that much he knew. But try as he might, Bryan could not put Katy out of his mind when reciting his wedding vows. It was not the ideal way to begin a marriage.

The blissful stage lasted about two weeks. Then reality set in. Bryan quickly returned to being totally absorbed in his work. He paid superficial attention to his marital obligations. He simply did not or would not give his all to the relationship.

Tamara tried everything to grab and hold Bryan's attention. She planned elaborate parties on his birthday, surprised him with weekend getaways and bought tickets for jazz concerts featuring his favorite artists. Nothing worked.

Eventually, a frustrated and exasperated Tamara, who frequently drew the attention of other men, began to see one of them socially. At about the same time, Tamara stopped attending the couple's counseling sessions. The praise lavished on her by other suitors filled the void created by her husband's indifference. She gave Bryan the option of choosing which one of them would move out. Tamara filed for divorce in January 2003.

Chapter 69

In the fall of 2003, Bogalusa Oil & Gas one of Bryan's largest clients, was investigated by the Federal Trade Commission for price fixing on spot market sales of crude oil. Bryan's partners urged him to travel to Louisiana for the document review needed to prepare the defense of Bogalusa. Bryan, wanting no part of Louisiana, offered to send his top senior associate instead. He reluctantly changed his mind after a meeting with his managing partner. Upon arriving at Bogalusa's headquarters in Port Allen just across the Mississippi River from Baton Rouge, Bryan toured the refinery, met with Bogalusa management and plotted strategy for assisting his client in the government inquiry.

There was a lot on the line. Bogalusa was facing several million dollars in fines if found culpable, a sum that could cripple the company going forward. Top executives insisted that Bryan handle the case. They were willing to pay whatever it took for a successful defense. Bryan's law firm partners reminded him of the case's importance. He could expect a hefty bonus at year's end if he was able to quash the government's contentions.

The FTC requested hundreds of documents from Bogalusa that government lawyers wanted to examine for any additional evidence to support their case. At his client's instruction, Bryan carefully reviewed the documents before turning them over. He found nothing incriminating. If anything, Bryan believed that the evidence supported Bogalusa's position. Based on his evaluation, Bryan now felt that the case against Bogalusa was weak. He was confident he would be able to show that no price fixing or illegal manipulation of the oil market had occurred.

Ever pedantic, Bryan noticed one innocuous footnote at the bottom of one of the last pages of the documents he examined. The notation simply said "Operation HS Blackwater." Bryan didn't think it was particularly significant, but he wanted to make sure before forwarding the report to the government with the rest of the package.

He asked one of the Bogalusa managers what the comment pertained to, but the manager didn't know and referred him to the refinery's technical staff. After speaking with several staff members, Bryan had come up empty. No one seemed to know what the reference meant.

As Bryan was closing up his briefcase and getting ready to head back to the hotel for the evening, he heard a knock on the conference room door. "Come in," he said, without bothering to look up.

The door slowly opened. A young man no older than twenty-five peered nervously over his shoulder, then quickly stepped into the room and drew the shade to block the view into the room from the hallway.

"My name is Daryl Ander . . .," then the man stopped in mid-sentence. "Actually, my name is Al. I'm a chemist at the refinery, a Level III," he said softly. "Please don't ask me my last name. I have some information for you, but it's strictly off the record. I heard you were inquiring about what 'Operation HS Blackwater' means," Al said.

"I . . . I was directed to write those words. I can't tell you by whom. The words refer to hydrogen sulfide, a by-product of the oil refining process. It's highly toxic. Normally, HS is disposed of by shipping it off to a sulfur recycling plant."

The man now calling himself Al stopped and reflexively twitched his hands. He took a deep breath.

"In this case though, the company didn't want to incur the cost of recycling, so we dumped it into the Mississippi. Hundreds of gallons of the stuff."

Bryan looked up. Al, Daryl or whoever he was, did not waver. "Can you . . . can you prove what you are saying?" Bryan responded slowly. "That's a pretty serious accusation. Who would have ordered this?"

"I really have to go," said Al, trying to slip out of the door as covertly as he came in. "Remember, we never talked and you didn't hear this from me."

Before Bryan left for the hotel that evening, he pulled out his copy of Bogalusa's personnel roll. The list revealed a junior chemist named Daryl Anderson.

When Bryan arrived back at the Bogalusa offices the next day, Friday morning, he faced a dilemma. He decided to call a meeting of Bogalusa's management team, which included the individuals responsible for hiring Bryan's law firm.

Bryan quickly explained the problem and passed copies of the sheet of paper referencing "Operation HS Blackwater" around the room for all to see.

"I have information," he said, "that this notation refers to the dumping of hydrogen sulfide into the Mississippi River. Would anyone like to confirm or refute that assertion?"

One manager spoke up. "I don't see how this has anything to do with price fixing," he said, "which is what we hired you to look into."

Then Bogalusa's President chimed in. "Was this document requested by the government?" he said.

"Yes," replied Bryan.

"Well, as our lawyer," the President continued, "can't you just make it go away. They asked for what, 2,452 pages of documents. So if you give them 2,451 pages, who's going to notice? You represent us. We pay you. We have a right to presume that our high priced legal team will protect us." The President paused. "Don't we?"

Bryan looked around the room. Every head at the table nodded in agreement with the President's statement. Bryan would have to decide what to do, but his client's expectations had been made crystal clear.

Chapter 70

An exasperated Bryan returned to his hotel room later that evening. The way things were looking, he was going to have to spend the weekend and another few days in Baton Rouge to get to the bottom of what Bogalusa may have done.

By Tuesday of the second week, Bryan still had not finalized his response to the government's document request. His frustration was growing. He was ready and able to defend the government's charges. There was no issue there. But now his client was insinuating that he needed to act to protect their interests in a manner that was borderline unethical. The stress consumed him.

Then on a whim, Bryan thought about calling Katy. He had not spoken to her since Katy told him she was engaged. Almost four years had passed since then. But Bryan needed a mental break from the strain of the case and Katy was only 100 miles down the interstate. Why not call her?

On the other hand, the mere thought of contacting Katy caused Bryan to break out in a sweat. After going back and forth, he entered the New Orleans area code into his phone, then stopped dialing. What if Katy recognized his number and refused to answer? After all, Bryan had acted rudely when Katy called to tell him she was engaged. What if she wanted nothing to do with him? Awash in doubt, Bryan terminated the call before it could be completed.

Then he mulled it over for another half hour. He again decided to make the call. He couldn't keep his fingers steady though and had to start over three times after hitting incorrect phone buttons. Finally, Bryan punched in the right numbers. He heard the line ringing on the other end. His palms were wet, his stomach churned and he nervously tapped his feet. Part of Bryan wanted Katy to answer. The other part secretly hoped that she had changed her phone number and that his efforts to reach her would be futile.

Katy answered the phone. Much to Bryan's surprise she seemed happy to hear from him. Bryan told Katy that he was in Baton Rouge working on a case and that he would be flying back to California on Sunday morning.

"Well you can't come to Louisiana and not visit New Orleans," Katy said. Then she added, "and you can't visit New Orleans and not see me."

Bryan paused. He was calling merely to say hello. He had not expected an invitation to visit. Would Katy's husband approve, he wondered? Or maybe Bryan was just getting ahead of himself. For all he knew, Katy was just being hospitable to an old friend. Then Bryan got chills all over his body. He remembered how his last trip to New Orleans turned out.

Bryan suddenly realized that while he was playing out all of these scenarios in his head, Katy was on the other end of the line waiting for a response. He forced himself to say something.

"Katy, I am tied up in Baton Rouge and probably can't get to New Orleans until around mid-day on Saturday," he said.

"Perfect," replied Katy. "I have no Saturday plans, so I am free for dinner if you are available."

"Fine Katy . . . that's fine," Bryan said slowly, being somewhat confused and surprised all at the same time and not knowing what else to say. "I'll see you on Saturday then for dinner."

After hanging up the phone, Bryan found himself starting to get a little excited about seeing Katy again after all these years. He had also figured out a "band-aid" solution to his dilemma regarding the FTC's Bogalusa document request. Bryan determined that he had to provide the FTC with the page that included the hydrogen sulfide reference. The federal government had requested certain information and part of what they requested appeared on that page. There was no way around that short of blatant non-compliance.

But there was an exception in the request that permitted Bogalusa to block out certain "proprietary information regarding the company's business operations unrelated to price fixing." Bryan concluded that the dumping of hydrogen sulfide into the Mississippi River was part of Bogalusa's business operations and thus satisfied the definition of information that could be redacted.

The dumping was illegal, yes. But it was also technically unrelated to the government's price fixing inquiry. As a result, Bryan included the page in question in his submission to the FTC, but blacked out the reference to "Operation HS Blackwater."

The redacted language would likely draw the attention of FTC lawyers. Bryan also knew that his intended course of action would not make his client happy. Bogalusa management preferred that he not turn over the page with the suspect reference at all. Bryan knew that he could not ethically comply with Bogalusa's wishes. He would turn over the page to the government in redacted form. If the FTC later requested more information, then that would just open up another can of worms. Bryan decided that he would fight that battle when and if he had to. His solution was far from perfect and under the circumstances, probably a bit of an ethical stretch. But given the situation, it was the best he could do.

Chapter 71

Katy arrived for work on Friday morning a nervous wreck, filled with the anticipation of seeing Bryan the next day. Usually reliable, Katy neglected to pass numerous messages from patients on to Dr. Curry, misfiled several documents and dropped a pitcher of water that scattered sharp glass fragments all over a common hallway shared with other offices, soaking the hallway's entry carpet and inundating it with pieces of broken glass.

By this time, Curry was wondering if his office would make it to the end of the day without being set ablaze. He suggested that Katy might want to take the rest of the afternoon off. Katy balked, but Curry insisted. The very existence of his medical practice was at stake. Curry had to act. He would gladly pay Katy for the entire day. He sent her home at 1:30 p.m., exhaling in relief as she walked out the door.

Chapter 72

The journey east on Interstate 10 from Baton Rouge to New Orleans brought back memories to Bryan of a similar drive he made 10 years earlier with Tony and Rusty, his fellow volunteers in the Mississippi summer legal program. At that time, the aspiring lawyers had the world at their fingertips and the future possibilities seemed limitless. None of them had a care in the world. "My how things have changed," Bryan thought, reflecting on the past.

The drive itself was impressive. Bryan had forgotten how scenic it was. Long stretches of the interstate wound its way through a corridor surrounded by intense shrubbery on both sides, disguising streams and bayous mere yards from the road. Then there were a series of antebellum sugar plantations whose manicured grounds were punctuated with long moss hanging from historic oaks. Finally, elevated bridges navigated travelers above murky swampland for miles at a time, with fishermen clad in chest high waders casting their lines into bass-filled ponds, visible far below. "Sportsman's Paradise" indeed Bryan confirmed as he saw those words etched on one Louisiana license plate after another.

Eventually Bryan arrived in New Orleans. He checked into his hotel and nervously awaited his evening dinner with Katy. He had no idea what to expect. A couple of hours later Bryan approached the front door of the French Quarter restaurant where he was to meet Katy, with a great deal of trepidation. He didn't know how he would feel when he saw her. Katy was excited, but apprehensive. She was already seated when Bryan arrived. As Bryan sat down, he couldn't help but notice how gorgeous Katy still was.

"She hasn't lost a thing," he thought to himself.

Their initial exchange was reserved and guarded, each trying to figure out what the other was thinking. After some small talk about work and their extended families, Bryan told Katy that he had moved from Los Angeles to the Bay Area to help develop his law firm's Northern California practice. That seemed to break the ice.

"So whatever happened to your friends that were with you when we first met?" said Katy, feeling a little more comfortable as she tried to advance the conversation.

Glad that she had given him an opening to talk about something that was not so serious, Bryan relaxed a bit. He told Katy that Tony had risen through the ranks and was now California's Assistant Attorney General.

Rusty on the other hand, had been forced to close the legal practice he inherited from his father. He had since relocated to the Nevada high desert community of Pahrump, where he operated a convenience store under an assumed name, convinced that his former clients had hired hit squads to take him out.

Katy smiled as Bryan told the story. She remarked that nothing involving Rusty surprised her. Her familiar giggles started to put Bryan at ease and lightened the atmosphere. Neither one of them acknowledged the waiter standing beside them who was now engaged in a theatrical, and well-rehearsed presentation of the evening's dinner specials.

Katy stopped him in mid-performance, remaining focused on Bryan. "We'll have a shrimp cocktail," she said, waiving the waiter away.

After the crestfallen waiter retreated, the conversation hit one of those awkward speed bumps of complete silence. The chit-chat topics were all exhausted. The elephant in the room was becoming a mastodon.

Bryan noticed that Katy was not wearing a wedding ring. Katy noticed that Bryan was. Katy was the first to broach the subject.

"So I see that you are now married," she said, cutting to the chase.

"Well, yes," said Bryan. "Her name is Tamara." Bryan then hesitated for a few seconds. He was not telling Katy the whole truth. He would get back to Tamara, but at the moment Katy had given him an opening to inquire about her status. He decided to be just as direct as she had been.

"Married life certainly appears to be treating you well," he said.

Katy had a quizzical look on her face.

"Bryan, you do realize I am not married, don't you?" Katy replied.

"How would I know that?" Bryan said. "The last time we spoke before a couple of days ago, you called to tell me about your engagement."

"I broke off my engagement," said Katy "and unfortunately a short time after that my former fiancé' met with some tragic circumstances.

Someone tried to gas him to death. They didn't succeed but he's been in a coma for a while. I sent you a letter because I was too embarrassed to call you. When I didn't hear from you, I just assumed you had no interest in talking to me anymore."

"I never received a letter," said Bryan, now very interested in every word falling from Katy's lips. "I had no idea. I just assumed all of this time that, well that you . . ." His voice trailed off.

"And as it turns out, you're the one who tied the knot," said Katy.

"Well, not exactly," replied Bryan. "I mean I did but . . . gosh, this is embarrassing. I just had this vision in my head of you being happily married all this time. Katy I'll be honest. My life's a mess. I'm miserable and didn't want you to know, so I thought I would just wear my ring and pretend that everything was fine with me too. The truth is, I got married a little over a year ago. I'm not proud to say that I wasn't the world's best husband. I'm currently separated. My divorce becomes final next month."

There was a long pause.

"Bryan," Katy said. "You really didn't need to make up a story for my benefit. No pretenses necessary with me. I'm not one for casting stones of judgment, you know that. Life happens to all of us. And I'm sorry to hear that you're getting divorced," even though Katy was not really sorry at all. "So what happened?"

"It's a long story," said Bryan. "But Tamara and I didn't get off to a good start."

"Well," said Katy, "no need to go into details now. Let's just enjoy the short time we have together. You've got me for the rest of the evening."

Katy had a way with words that always knocked Bryan a little off kilter. What did "you've got me for the rest of the evening," mean? Was Katy secretly flirting with him or was this just her natural, unpretentious charm, innocently conveyed without any hidden motives? The answer was anyone's guess, but it reminded Bryan of how Katy was always able to captivate him in the past. He found himself wanting more.

Soon, the two were talking like they had never been apart. True, the events of that night long ago when they ended up burying Pope in the Plaquemines Parish swamps had not been forgotten. But for the next hour they turned back the clock and conversed nonstop like wide-eyed fourth graders on the first day of school, anxious to share the details of summer vacation. Not a word was spoken about Pope, Q, Axel, Tamara or any of the other trials and tribulations they had each endured since they last spent an evening together. They exited the restaurant giddy and capricious, not having eaten a single thing.

Bryan walked Katy back to her car. The small talk between them continued for several minutes, meandering in a variety of directions as they each struggled with trying to figure out how to part. Neither one of them wanted this to be the final time they saw each other. Eventually Bryan said good night, extended his arms out to hug Katy and reached over to kiss her on the cheek.

As he planted a soft peck and his mouth retreated from her skin, Katy pulled him back. Their lips met and stayed softly locked for several moist seconds, neither wanting to be the first to break away. As the kiss reached its climax and their lips separated, Bryan next found himself nibbling on Katy's ear, while Katy repeatedly pecked on his neck. The hot and heaviness was approaching a full boil. They stopped only upon the sound of approaching footsteps.

Finally, they separated, but only slightly. Bryan kissed his finger and then gently applied it to Katy's lips. Katy sighed wistfully, momentarily stunned by the events of the evening.

"I didn't think I would ever see you again," she said. "And now this." She paused again.

"To be continued?" Katy asked hopefully.

"Just tell me when and where," Bryan replied.

Chapter 73

Katy could not stop twitching her fingers as she waited to board her flight to Oakland. She was on her way to visit Bryan who had invited her to California after their recent dinner in New Orleans. Before Katy would have been hesitant to leave New Orleans. Now, she couldn't wait to go. It was her first trip to California and Katy wasn't sure what to expect, but she was anxious to rekindle the relationship with Bryan if at all possible. Ditching Louisiana for all or part of her two weeks of vacation might do her some good.

Bryan couldn't wait to see Katy again. Their New Orleans "dinner" date revealed many obstacles the two of them needed to navigate, he knew that. But the excitement of having re-established contact with her energized him and helped make some of the past pains and disappointments a distant memory. Their passionate exchange at Katy's car when they parted had only served to heighten Bryan's anticipation.

After Katy landed, Bryan took her to dinner in Jack London Square. Later the two of them retired to Bryan's high rise condominium in Emeryville for the evening. Katy was astounded by the view. Looking west, she had clear sight lines to the Bay Bridge, the Golden Gate Bridge and downtown San Francisco. When lit up at dusk, the juxtaposition of the Bay, islands, bridges, the San Francisco skyline and the Pacific Ocean in the distance was spectacular. It was unlike anything Katy had ever seen before.

Katy quickly adapted to the Bay Area vibe. She spent a day shopping in Union Square in San Francisco, strolled along Fisherman's Wharf and then caught a ferry to Alcatraz. One evening Bryan took her to one of his favorite restaurants, Angeline's Kitchen in Berkeley. The food and the atmosphere reminded Katy of being home in New Orleans.

Katy also loved being around Bryan day after day. The two thoroughly enjoyed each other's company and the discovery of being a couple again. They intentionally side-stepped any discussion about the events at Pope's house for almost all of Katy's visit. One thing Bryan couldn't resist, however, was bringing up their prior discussion about Clovis, the tarot card reader.

The conversation started one evening after Bryan anxiously awaited Katy's opinion of the jambalaya he had prepared for her.

"Well, what do you think?" he said, gaining confidence after noticing that Katy continued eating after her first bite.

"It's pretty good," replied Katy. "You must have been practicing. It's almost like home."

"So do I get my Louisiana chef certificate now"? Bryan inquired.

"Not so fast," Katy replied. "I said 'almost.' But you're on the right track. We can work with it," she chuckled.

Bryan just smiled. Then he said, "Hey Katy, I have a word for you."

"Oh really. What's the word?" replied Katy.

"Superstition," said Bryan.

"What?" Katy responded.

"Superstition," Bryan again repeated. "I figured out that Superstition is the song you were talking about the first time we met when you explained your experience with the tarot cards. I think the precise lyrics are 'when you believe in things you don't understand, then you suffer.' The song is by Stevie Wonder. First recorded on his Talking Book album, which in my opinion is one of his best."

"You're right," Katy replied. "That's it. Of course. That's it."

Then they laughed and finished the chorus in unison.

"Superstition ain't the way . . . nah, nah, nah!"

"That was fun," Katy said. "You should know though that I'm long past letting what Clovis had to say impact my life anymore. These days I'm more worried about having to suffer from the things I *do* understand, never mind the things I don't understand."

Katy paused. Their mood, gleeful for a moment in time, was shifting to sullen as they pondered the topic that had been avoided up until now.

"Bryan, I'm not convinced we're out of the woods," Katy continued in a cadence that was barely above a whisper.

Bryan laughed nervously as Katy leaned her head on his shoulder. He gently massaged her back, ran his fingers through her hair and planted a soft kiss on her neck. Though the words remained unspoken, he knew full well what Katy was referring to. Neither one had the appetite to continue the discussion at that point, however, so Katy's observation went unanswered.

Their progression towards tackling the taboo topic would have to be gradual, not sudden. It was too overwhelming to absorb at one sitting.

A couple of nights later, Bryan asked about Katy's brother Jerome. As Katy explained, Jerome eventually severed ties with New Orleans and Pope's organization.

"Once he found out that those people meant business and weren't playing around, he decided he had enough. Jerome moved across the Lake to Madisonville near Nana's farm, enrolled in electricians school and just started his apprenticeship." Katy remarked how good she felt about where Jerome was in his life.

"Too bad he couldn't figure all that out earlier. He might have spared a bunch of people a lot of trouble," smirked Bryan, immediately regretting that last comment.

Katy stared at Bryan in disbelief.

"I'm sorry," he said. "I meant . . ."

"I know what you meant," said Katy.

The mention of Jerome raised the looming specter of Alvarez Pope and that unforgettable night that turned both of their worlds upside down. If Katy and Bryan had any hope of reigniting their relationship, it was not a topic that could be swept under the rug forever.

Chapter 74

On the evening before Katy was scheduled to return to New Orleans, she and Bryan reclined on the sofa and shared a glass of wine. They had reached one of those awkward moments of silence where both knew what needed to be discussed, but neither was anxious to take the lead.

Finally, Katy broke the muzzled impasse.

"Bryan," Katy said slowly and deliberately, "I need to tell you something."

"Ok," replied Bryan tepidly. "Fire away." He had his doubts as to whether he was ready for what was coming.

"When I told you I was getting married," Katy said, "I didn't get the chance to tell you that Axel, my fiancé if that's what you want to call him, had been making some not so subtle insinuations."

"Like what?" replied Bryan.

"Well," continued Katy, "like 'you better agree to what I want, otherwise I will expose some secrets that you may not want revealed.'"

"Katy, are you saying you were blackmailed?" asked Bryan, now becoming more concerned than he already was. "Do you think Axel was aware of what happened at Pope's house?"

"He never said so directly," replied Katy, "but Axel certainly gave the impression, on more than one occasion, that he knew all about it. And that he would use it if I didn't agree to give him everything he wanted. Plus, we already know for certain that one of Pope's syndicate members answered the door when I rang the bell. So it's almost a given that there are people out there running around who know what we did."

Bryan squirmed uncomfortably. Nothing Katy said was totally surprising. For years though, he had just tried to put that evening as far in the back of his mind as possible. Having it presented to him front and center again immediately brought back gut-wrenching memories.

"I'm thinking about just going to the police and explaining to them exactly what happened," Katy continued. "I shouldn't be guilty of anything. Neither should you. The entire shooting was an accident. I just want the weight of that night to be lifted from my shoulders. I don't want to live under this cloud anymore. What occurred should be out in the open, once and for all. And at that point whatever happens, happens."

Bryan hesitated. Pope's shooting was not something he ever discussed. At times, Bryan had convinced himself that he was never even involved at all. There was risk in Katy's suggestion, not just to her, but also to him. He could still be charged as an accessory to murder and now with the passage of time, Bryan had even more to lose than he did when the event occurred.

"I don't know Katy," Bryan said. "I just don't. Part of me says just let sleeping dogs lie. Another part of me wants everything brought to light because I know we didn't do anything wrong and we should be cleared. But coming forward at this point and admitting what we've done . . . well, I'm not sure. It could backfire. A lot of attention will be focused on both of us and we can't guarantee that our explanation of what took place will be believed. Things could easily be twisted around and misconstrued into something different than what actually happened."

The entire discussion was making Bryan nauseous. It wasn't doing Katy much good either. She began to hyperventilate. Katy quickly changed the subject.

"So, I told you a little about my so-called engagement. Are you up to talking about your marriage?" she asked.

Bryan said nothing for several seconds. He took a deep breath. Finally Bryan spoke.

"Katy, you were always Plan A," he said, causing Katy to blush inside. Those words, even under these circumstances, warmed her heart since Katy never expected to hear anything like that from Bryan again.

Bryan continued.

"I just didn't know how to restart things because of how suddenly and shockingly everything ended. Then, after you called me and it became apparent that Plan A was out of reach, I moved on to Plan B. I needed someone to help ease the pain. Looking back on it, that really was not fair to Tamara. Lots of people have to settle for less than what they really want, but I should have reflected a bit and waited to make sure I was ready for what I was getting into. It was just a case of meeting the wrong person at what I thought was the right time. It only led to resentment on her part and regrets on mine."

Intrigued by Bryan's answer, Katy pressed on.

"Do you think there would be regrets if instead of meeting the wrong person at the right time, you met the right person at the wrong time?" she asked.

Bryan looked puzzled. He had not previously considered Katy's question. Finally he replied. "Probably not. Meeting the right person at the wrong time sounds only like a recipe for enduring heartache."

"I agree," said Katy. Once more, she pondered what to say next.

"Bryan, do you think it's possible to meet the right person at the right time, twice? I mean suppose you met the right person and for whatever reason things didn't work out and then you became reacquainted with that person again years later. Do you think that could work?"

"I think you're not disguising your thoughts very well," Bryan laughed. "But perhaps we will get a chance to find out."

Bryan then put down his wine glass and reached over and gave Katy a brief kiss, followed by a second and a third. He dimmed the lamp as they looked out over the water, the sun now having set beneath the ocean, it's hazy orange aftermath creating a portrait against the sky. The rotating lamp atop the Alcatraz lighthouse was visible in the distance, with the silhouette of the Golden Gate Bridge on the horizon beyond that.

Bryan planted a series of kisses on Katy's neck as he ran his fingers through her soft hair. Katy reciprocated, massaging Bryan's back and shoulders but her emotions were bittersweet. Her heart, numbed by what might have been, a relationship that had missed its prime and the sparkling diamond she never got, ached for all she had lost. Overcome by the moment, Katy shed tears of pain for the times that never were. But there were also tears of joy from the realization that suddenly, out of nowhere, there might be a chance for a new beginning with Bryan. Maybe it wasn't too late after all.

Bryan sensed the same thing. Instantly, the two became exhilarated by the prospect of recapturing what should never have been lost, their anticipation cautiously tempered by the stinging defeats of the past. They held on tight as if to ward off the unseen forces that had repeatedly kept them apart.

Soon their fears subsided. Relaxed, they focused only on each other, oblivious to the hundreds of commuters traversing the bridge in the picture frame that was Bryan's window. As downtown San Francisco twinkled in the distance, their feelings for each other, thwarted for years, were slowly and passionately unleashed. To Katy, the night was timeless. It symbolized one of the thousands she had once hoped to spend by Bryan's side.

The moment was fleeting and Katy feared that if she let go the feeling would never be recaptured. Experience had taught her how suddenly bliss could slip through her grasp and vanish in the night, never to return. This time though, Katy's grip was firm. She would not easily relinquish what had eluded her for years.

Eventually dawn broke. Soon it would be time to leave. Katy dreaded the thought. But she knew she had to open her fist and let the dove fly. She could only hope that it would soon return.

After Katy left for New Orleans, Bryan noticed that a certain emptiness had enveloped his condominium. He realized what was happening. He missed Katy. Her presence, her energy, Katy being Katy. Just having her around made the day brighter, his daily routine more meaningful. Bryan smiled. The feeling was back. After all these years, Bryan's intuitions confirmed what he knew all along. Katy completed the circle.

Chapter 75

As Bryan had previously explained to Katy, Tony Ramirez, Bryan's law school friend and fellow Mississippi poverty center volunteer had gone on to a highly successful legal career and was now second in command at the state Attorney General's Office. Tony and Bryan kept in touch regularly. At the end of 2004, a retiring judge created an opening on the bench of the California Supreme Court. Ramirez immediately called the Lieutenant Governor who was compiling a list of names to submit to the Governor for consideration to fill the vacated seat.

Tony enthusiastically recommended Bryan. "He's a brilliant lawyer," Tony said "and his character is beyond reproach. Young, tons of energy, a real star. You won't do any better." A short time later, the Governor reviewed the profiles of the potential nominees. Bryan topped the list.

After some vetting, Bryan emerged as the top candidate. The Governor personally called Tony to get his input. Tony again sang Bryan's praises.

"You won't regret it," Tony promised. "Bryan is top notch. He will make you look good. History will look back on his nomination as a brilliant selection on your part. He might even be appointed one day to the United States Supreme Court."

A few weeks later, the Governor signed off on Tony's recommendation. He intended to select Bryan to fill the vacancy on the California Supreme Court.

Bryan was in his office at the law firm when his phone rang. The voice on the other line was a familiar and welcome one. It was Tony Ramirez.

"Are you sitting down?" said Tony, "because I've got some wonderful news for you."

"Actually I'm standing up," laughed Bryan. "My doctor says it's healthier for me to stand at work, so I am trying it out. Go ahead. Give me what you got!"

"Well," said Tony slowly, "the Governor on my recommendation is going to nominate you to fill the vacant seat on the California Supreme Court. And I might add, you would be the youngest member in the Court's history!"

There was a prolonged silence on the other end of the line.

"Tony, I'm . . . I'm speechless" said Bryan. "That's fantastic. I don't quite know what to say."

"Say you'll accept," said Tony. "That would be a good start."

"It will certainly be hard to turn down," countered Bryan. "It's just an amazing opportunity. And a great honor. But give me a couple of days to think about it."

"That's fine," said Tony. "But I'll anticipate hearing something positive from you soon."

All of a sudden Bryan had a lot on his plate. He immediately called Katy to tell her the news.

"I'm so excited for you Bryan," she said. Then laughing Katy added, "does this mean you'll be making more trips or fewer trips to New Orleans?"

"I haven't accepted yet," said Bryan, "but I am seriously considering it. It may mean that you'll just have to come out to California more often."

"Fine by me," said Katy, who by this time had allowed herself to dream that her newly revived relationship with Bryan might actually exceed occasional liaisons in California and Louisiana.

"Where do I sign. And let me know when you've booked my next flight!" Katy continued enthusiastically.

There was no more talk of perhaps turning themselves in to the Louisiana authorities. Still, Bryan realized that becoming a California Supreme Court justice would subject him to far more scrutiny than he ever received as a partner in a national law firm. He also knew that accepting the position would necessitate a large pay cut.

Nevertheless, Bryan was financially set so the money wasn't a huge deal. Maybe this was a good time to reset things and slow his life down a bit. He could always return to private practice if things didn't work out, but he would probably never again have the opportunity to sit on the state's highest court.

Bryan decided to accept the nomination. What would Westchester Law School think of him now?

Chapter 76

Bryan invited Katy to the swearing-in ceremony, but Katy's mother had been hospitalized after a fall so with much regret, Katy declined and was unable to attend.

Before the ceremony, Bryan was required to review the California Code of Judicial Ethics as part of the approval process for all new California judges. He shuddered when he reached Canon 3D(3), "Disciplinary Responsibilities." It read partly as follows:

"A judge shall promptly report in writing to the Commission . . . when he or she is charged . . . with any crime in the United States . . . including all misdemeanors involving violence . . . A judge also shall promptly report in writing upon conviction of such crimes."

Chills went up Bryan's spine as he was reminded once again of that October 1997 evening. Bryan remembered driving Katy to Pope's mansion, the struggle between Pope and Katy in the driveway and finally Katy firing the fatal shot.

Then, as if it were happening all over again, Bryan recalled helping Katy drag Pope's body to the back of the rental car, lift Pope up and then roll him into the trunk. All followed by the long, frantic drive through the dead of night to dispose of Pope's body in the remote Plaquemines Parish swamps.

Bryan stared at the words on the document in front of him. How could he in good conscience accept this prestigious judgeship knowing he had participated in a murder?

He immediately began the process of self-serving rationalization. Under the strict language of Canon 3D(3), Bryan argued to himself, he had no obligation to report anything because he had not been charged with a crime, much less convicted of anything. Thus, Bryan was technically not in violation of the wording of the ethics rules, although he clearly had run afoul of the spirit of the rules by, well, actually participating in a killing and disposing of a body. At a minimum, he was likely an accessory to murder.

Sweating profusely, Bryan set the ethics rules aside for a moment. He needed to contemplate one more time whether he could look himself in the mirror if he accepted the position being offered to him. Could he faithfully execute the duties of the office he was about to assume?

Part IV – Reckoning

Chapter 77

(August 13, 2005, near the Gulf of Guinea of the west coast of Africa, 6,313 miles from New Orleans.)

The scorching breezes that originated in the Sahara Desert twisted high in the atmosphere and formed a loosely connected mass of hot, swirling gusts. As the gusts intensified, they coalesced and began circling in a counterclockwise direction.

The infant storm was pushed west across the Atlantic Ocean by trade winds that centuries earlier brought freedom seekers and explorers from the European continent, eager to discover the wonders of the New

World. This time though the winds were escorting the most unwelcome of guests.

Ten days later the winds from Africa intersected with a tropical depression over the lower reaches of the Bahamas. As the system intensified, it harvested millions of kilowatts of energy from the warm ocean waters below, creating a gigantic spiral of vicious thunderstorms. Its formation now complete, an unleashed and unapologetic Katrina barreled its way through the Gulf of Mexico darkness like a runaway locomotive, with a bullseye on Louisiana.

Chapter 78

New Orleans, Louisiana, August 29, 2005

Most of New Orleans sits below sea level at the bottom of a "bowl" with Lake Pontchartrain on one side and the Mississippi River on the other. The city is protected from these bodies of water by a series of levees and canals, supported by flood walls designed to keep New Orleans safe from storm overflow in the event of a tropical storm or hurricane.

The steel piles that anchored the flood walls, however, only extended seventeen feet into the soil. Additional depth was needed to provide stability in the event of a major flood. The deficiency proved critical when Katrina passed slightly to the east of New Orleans heading northwest. This trajectory, occurring at the worst possible time, high tide, enabled a bulked-up, highly energized Katrina to push water from Lake Pontchartrain back into New Orleans and send it cascading over the flood walls.

By the time Katrina hit New Orleans, much of the city had been evacuated. Hundreds of displaced residents were packed into Superdome. Katrina's winds promptly blew a gaping hole in the roof. Thousands more fled to Houston. Many never returned.

The State of Louisiana suffered over 1,500 deaths from Katrina, with most of the fatalities in New Orleans occurring from drowning among elderly residents in Lakeview and the Lower Ninth Ward. The Lafitte Housing Project where Katy grew up, was destroyed. Subsequent studies revealed that if the steel pilings had been driven to a depth of 30-40 feet through the soft clay and into more sturdier sand (as had been recommended by some engineers), the flood walls would likely have held.

Katrina unearthed a number of New Orleans' most tawdry secrets. It also unearthed the body of Alvarez Pope.

Chapter 79

Katrina initially made landfall in Louisiana at Buras, south of New Orleans in Plaquemines Parish at 6:10 a.m. on August 29, 2005. The hurricane's force knocked Buras' landmark water tower from its moorings and caused the iconic powder blue and white storage tank to crash to earth.

Although much less publicized, Plaquemines Parish was hit harder than New Orleans with more than 90% of its area being impacted by Katrina's storm surge and winds. Entire blocks of houses lay crumbled together like piles of kindling. Neighborhoods were unrecognizable and property and livestock were swept away as thousands of residents lost power for months.

Days after Katrina left Louisiana in tatters, local farmer Jonathan Delacroix made a gruesome discovery on his farmland a few hundred feet from the shores of Lake Hermitage. Emerging from the muddy soil was the crown of a human skull. A startled Delacroix hastily dialed 9-1-1 and summoned the police who said they would be on the scene as soon as they could.

"Alright," said a still shaken Delacroix, "but hurry. And you might want to bring the Coroner with you."

Chapter 80

Esmerelda Cortez gently opened the tiny bottle of eye shadow, curiously examined its contents and then practiced using the application brush by lightly stroking it into thin air. She was a complete novice at putting on makeup, but the slight possibility that she might become more glamorous and appealing to her husband was worth the effort.

Esmerelda blinked several times as she struggled to keep one eye open while a trembling hand brushed eye shadow on the closed lid of the other. She squinted to make sense of the cloudy images in front of her, clear proof of erosion to her mirror's silver backing from prolonged exposure to the Louisiana humidity.

After successfully applying the purple eye shadow, Esmerelda smiled as she opened a new case of bright, crimson lipstick. She had picked the rouge out herself at the local department store, making her selection based solely on the lipstick's name, Paris Nights. In doing so, Esmerelda ignored the advice of the assistant at the store's makeup counter who recommended something a little softer that might work better with Esmerelda's skin color and choice of shadow.

Years earlier, Esmerelda's grandmother told her that the family was descended from a second cousin of Marie Antoinette. It was a white lie, but Esmerelda desperately wanted to believe it. She embraced the notion that her heritage included French royalty. As a result, Esmerelda had been partial to anything having to do with France ever since. No, Paris Nights it would be and that was that.

Distressed by the realization that her best days were behind her, Esmerelda was making one last ditched effort to win back the affections of her husband, Marteen Cortez, a twenty-five year veteran of the New Orleans Police Department. Theirs was a tempestuous relationship, mostly because of Marteen, but he remained the only man Esmerelda ever loved. They had been together since their junior year in high school, a year in which Marteen won the Louisiana state high school wrestling championship and Esmerelda was named third runner-up homecoming princess, a designation created to placate Esmerelda's father who was the school's largest donor.

They married two years after graduating from high school, with Marteen's proposal coming a week after learning of a substantial inheritance Esmerelda would receive from her grandfather on her wedding day. Now, after thirty-two years of marriage, Esmerelda felt their union crumbling. She had long suspected Marteen of cheating on her, but had no proof until a recent police operation went awry.

The elaborate sting was designed to catch and publicly embarrass the affluent high roller customers who fueled New Orleans' sophisticated call girl trade, including Wall Street investment bankers and Miami Beach shipping magnates. The operation was a colossal failure.

Doomed from the start, the plan started to unravel when a cruise line owner recognized one of the "new girls" as a police woman. After confirming his suspicions with a local pimp who was anxious to eliminate the competition to his business from the police sting, word then spread like wildfire throughout the community of call girl patrons. In an instant, the big spenders looking for action on the New Orleans streets quickly retreated to dealing only with familiar faces.

Thus, the only "John" the mission netted was Marteen who had earlier tossed aside the Department's memo about the operation without ever reading it. After stumbling right into the trap, Marteen kept his job only because of a tight relationship with the Department Captain. His employment as a detective was hanging by a thread.

The entire episode humiliated Esmerelda but she forgave Marteen. Partly because she still loved him and partly because she was not at all certain that any other man would ever find her attractive. The incident prompted Esmerelda to try a new approach.

Armed with makeup for the first time, Esmerelda felt rejuvenated. She loosened the bobby pins holding her hair in its customary bun and let her brunette strands fall down to their natural shoulder length. Perhaps she could still salvage what was left of their marriage and make her husband excited about her again. Esmerelda could not escape visions of a romantic evening with Marteen on the Champs-Elysees and convinced herself that Paris Nights was just the magic potion to get her there.

Now done with applying her mismatched cosmetics, Esmerelda cast one last glance into the murky mirror. She thought she looked fabulous. Like a movie star. Vanessa Williams maybe.

"Well, not Vanessa Williams *now* of course," conceded Esmerelda, who had just watched the movie "Eraser." "But this might be what Vanessa Williams will look like when she is fifty-five," she reasoned assuredly.

Just then the phone rang. Esmeralda answered it, then handed it to Marteen. He was now semi-retired from the New Orleans police force, but was working part time as a detective with the Plaquemines Parish Sheriff's office. They were happy to have him.

"Uh-huh," Marteen said as he listened intently to the voice on the other end of the line.

"Ok, the east shore of Lake Hermitage? I'll be down there as fast as I can," he continued and hung up the phone.

"Honey, what is it?" asked Esmeralda, as she turned to face Marteen, proudly displaying her transformation so that Marteen had a birds-eye view of the entire elaborate production.

"Some human bones were found buried just off the shore of Lake Hermitage," Marteen responded, not bothering to look up. "I need to get over there and take a look. I'll be back late. Don't wait up for me."

Then as he moved quickly towards the front door, Marteen stopped, turned and faced his wife.

"And what is that crap all over your face?" he demanded. "You look like a damn Ringling Brothers circus clown. Ain't nobody in their right mind ever gonna put you on a Mardi Gras float, I can guarantee that."

Then Marteen sighed and whispered to himself but loud enough so Esmerelda could hear him. "Hell, I don't know why I even bother coming home anymore."

Esmerelda was crushed.

She resolved not to cry openly in front of Marteen, but a couple of tears flowed down her checks right into the accumulated mass of Paris Nights slathered all over her lips.

Esmerelda waited in excruciating agony, not daring to raise her chin until she heard the front door close. Mercifully, it finally did with an emphatic thud.

"He doesn't really mean it. He's just . . . he's just overworked," Esmerelda sobbed to herself, once again going out of her way to make excuses for Marteen's behavior. "He's just tired, that's all. He'll come back to me when he's had a chance to think things over."

Chapter 81

Marteen Cortez made his way through rural Plaquemines Parish to the outskirts of J&E Rag Ranch owned by Jonathan and Evelyn Delacroix. As the local Parish sheriff secured the area, the coroner began to exhume the remains. Cortez looked on, gazing intently.

When the coroner started to load the remains into a van, Cortez eyed a silver chain weathered by exposure to soil and water, still dangling from what appeared to be the neck area of the mass of cartilage. The pendant featured a gold fleur-de-lis with six diamonds, one on each pedal.

The coroner noticed Cortez's interest in the necklace and asked if anything was wrong.

"Nuthin wrong," said Cortez as he puffed on a cigar, "but I've seen that chain and pendant before. And I know whose neck it was around the last time I saw it."

"I expect that when you are done with your examination," Cortez continued, "you're going to tell me that these bones belong to Alvarez Pope. Asshole formerly led a major New Orleans crime syndicate. Drug dealing, prostitution, business extortion, you name it, Pope had his fingers on it. He disappeared a few years back and hasn't been heard from since. I'm not surprised that somebody turned his lights out. I am surprised though that he ended up clear down here in Plaquemines."

"Some say he was rubbed out by a rival gang. Others believe the mob got tired of playing games with Pope when he moved in on their territory. Seems that ol' Pope got a little greedy when he expanded his operations from simple street corner dope pushing. Rule number one: when you're running a local operation, know your limits. Don't screw around with the mob. Pope might have gotten too big for his britches."

"Then there's another rumor says Pope got knocked off by an enraged woman. Whatever happened to him, nobody's seen hide nor hair of him for going on eight years now. New Orleans' own little Jimmy Hoffa mystery you might say. Hasn't stopped the crime syndicates or drug wars though. Fools out there still killing each other every day like nobody's business."

"Now that we have confirmation that Pope's history, we have to answer the 'who' and 'why' part. That should keep me busy for quite a while."

Secretly, Cortez relished this assignment. He needed a game changer to jump start his career. He was also short on cash, having long since burned through Esmerelda's inheritance. If Cortez could bring Pope's killer to justice, it might restore some of the prestige he had lost among his former New Orleans colleagues, put him in line for a raise and restore his frozen pension.

The coroner looked on in amazement. Law enforcement in Plaquemines Parish typically wanted nothing to do with any organized crime activity coming out of New Orleans. The coroner had never heard of Pope and didn't care to know much more.

"You can tell all of that from a rusted old metal chain?" he asked Cortez.

"That and those gold teeth. We used to call this guy Fort Knox. It's my business to know," Cortez responded. "Mark my words son. You just dug up what's left of Alvarez Pope."

A few days later the phone range at the desk of Norman Broussard, a homicide detective with the New Orleans Police Department. Broussard hurriedly scribbled on his note pad as he listened to the voice on the other end of the line.

After hanging up the phone, Broussard slowly rose from his desk, turned and walked forward, stopping when he reached his secretary's cubicle. He was now within earshot of several other officers.

Broussard paused, then began mumbling to no one in particular. "That skeleton they found in Plaquemines a week ago?" Broussard said. "It's him. It's Alvarez Pope."

Chapter 82

The coroner's final report was not entirely definitive on the cause of Pope's death since all soft tissue of the body had long since decomposed. The coroner's report did, however, note that a .38 caliber slug was found lodged in Pope's sternum.

Broussard was the lead detective on the case. Cortez was assigned to work with him. Armed with more facts and details, but no solid leads, the two detectives returned to the location where Pope's body was found. The pair couldn't have been more different.

Cortez, gruff, abrupt and in his late fifties, resembled an inhabitant of skid row more than anything else. The stubble on his face varied between three and five days growth, and Cortez always looked like he could use a meticulous grooming and a hot bath. He cracked cases through old school methods, often relying on hunches and gut instinct.

Cortez always got straight to the point when interviewing witnesses or persons of interest but sometimes his hastiness got the best of him. Short-tempered and feisty, when his blood ran hot Cortez was not above roughing up a suspect or two if that's what it took to get some answers. He desperately wanted to be the detective who solved this case.

Broussard presented a sharp contrast. Thin, clean-shaven and well-dressed, Broussard was in his early thirties. He was born and raised in Nacogdoches, Texas and obtained a master's degree in criminology from Sam Houston State University. He had been on the New Orleans police force for five years and was considered a rising star.

Broussard solved crimes using the latest high tech investigative tools and represented the future of Louisiana law enforcement. He operated cerebrally and left no stone unturned. Instead of witness intimidation, he built cases through logic and by connecting dots that ultimately led to air tight conclusions. Broussard was meticulous, sometimes annoyingly so, but he always did his homework.

Upon arriving back at the shores of Lake Hermitage, the detectives walked the entire area once again. They noticed nothing unusual. No tattered clothing, old shoes or any other artifacts that might provide leads or clues.

The two next made their way to Earl's Bait Shoppe. Earl's shack, already weathered but further weakened by Katrina, was now leaning to one side with several missing boards and sharp splinters extending from the rotting and broken pieces of wood that remained.

The detectives introduced themselves and made small talk with Earl. They informed Earl they were investigating the circumstances surrounding the body that had been discovered in the area a couple of weeks earlier.

As Cortez conversed with Earl about Katrina and college football, Broussard's eyes scanned Earl's shack; first from right to left, then top to bottom. He noticed a series of old and worn fishing lines protruding down from the shack's ceiling, some with gaping holes in their midst.

"My, my," Broussard thought to himself, "the tales those nets could tell."

Underneath one net was a shelf with different sized fish hooks for sale. Next to the hooks was an aquarium sized glass container filled with mud and labeled "Live Bait."

Broussard continued to survey the inside of the shack. Several fishing poles were perched on one wall. Directly across the shack on the opposite wall dangled a half dozen or so old license plates. Hanging in the middle of the wall at the back of the shack was an autographed picture of a smiling Earl and Parish attorney and judge Emile Martin III.

Next to the picture of Earl and the judge swiveling from a loose nail was a rusted, bullet-punctured Route 66 highway sign. The sign hung nearly upside down, at times more resembling a 99 than a 66.

Broussard's eyes continued to wander around the damp room. He noticed a rectangular wooden board that served as the shack's counter beneath the open window in the front. The panel was circumscribed by a couple of dozen bottle caps nailed to the wood. The names on the rusted caps evoked memories of summers long since passed and included such forgotten soda brands as Kickapoo Joy Juice, Big Star Cola, Dixie Grape, Cactus Cooler, Delaware Punch, and Johnny Ryan Birch Beer. Broussard smiled as he imagined barefoot youngsters, fishing poles in hand, washing down the last bite of their fried oyster po' boy sandwiches with a bottle of cold pop.

Broussard now stared blankly into space. He was puzzled. There was something about the collection of items inside the shack that just didn't add up. Some inconsistency or contradiction about the shack's contents. It stumped and frustrated him and he didn't like it. Try as he might though, Broussard could not put his finger on what was bugging him.

"Something here's just not right," Broussard thought to himself, once again taking stock of the whole scene inside the shack. "Something's out of place, something's missing. Maybe something's here that shouldn't be."

Whatever it was, it bothered Broussard to his core and he couldn't let it go.

Broussard asked Earl if he remembered or noticed anything unusual in the area several years earlier about the time the detectives suspected the crime had been committed. Earl, who was now in his late sixties, at times had trouble remembering what happened yesterday, so he wasn't much help.

Earl expressed surprise, however, to learn that human remains had been found buried less than a couple of hundred yards from his shack. "Not much goes on 'round here without me knowing about it," Earl said proudly.

Not being able to glean much from Earl, the detectives moved on, Broussard reluctantly so, to the Myrtle Grove Marina. They wanted to question boat owners, local fisherman and dock hands about the gruesome discovery. They found no credible leads.

Most of those interviewed were preoccupied with salvaging whatever property they could in Katrina's aftermath including their boats, many of which were beyond repair. There was little interest in discussing the apparent murder and disappearance of an inner city crime lord that most knew nothing about, committed years earlier.

One individual claimed to have witnessed the entire episode of Pope's killing and hasty burial while hiding in a patch of nearby reeds. The same man had earlier boasted to one of the Parish newspapers about riding out Hurricane Katrina in the Gulf of Mexico on his dinghy.

The detectives soon discovered that he was known in the area for telling tall tales at every opportunity. When the detectives confirmed that the man was hunkered down in a shelter when Katrina hit and had been holding on for dear life like everyone else, his claims of having witnessed Pope's shooting were quickly dismissed.

Broussard and Cortez had reached a dead end.

Chapter 83

After coming up empty in Myrtle Grove, Cortez suggested that they head for home and start anew the next morning. Broussard, however, was not quite ready to call it a day.

"Let's go back to Earl's," he said. "I want to take one more look around."

Cortez mildly protested. It was Tuesday and Cortez had planned on dining that evening at LeBeau's Crab Shack and Pool Hall, a popular bar and grill in Empire, a couple of miles down the road from where Cortez maintained an apartment in Nairn, for his Plaquemines Parish assignments.

LeBeau's offered an All You Can Eat Dinner Special each week night for $8.95. Tuesdays, however, was the only evening that fried frog legs were included in the buffet. Cortez loved frog legs. He also liked the waitresses at LeBeau's. Cortez openly flirted with them and managed to convince himself that they flirted back. No, Cortez did not want to be late to LeBeau's. Thus, he was not pleased with Broussard's request to return to Earl's to take another look around, especially since it could wait until morning.

Ultimately, a grumbling Cortez relented. In the short time he worked with Broussard, Cortez knew that once Broussard had something on his mind, he was not going to rest until it had been resolved to his satisfaction. Cortez would just have to show up at LeBeau's whenever he could get there and hope that one of his waitress friends had set aside some frog legs just for him.

With the sun now sinking slowly in the west, the detectives headed back towards Earl's place. Cortez, who usually moved at a snail's pace, was nearly in full gallop. If they were going back to Earl's he figured, they might as well make it quick. The pair reached Earl's shop just as Earl was shutting down for the evening.

"Hey Earl," said Broussard. "Can I take another quick look inside?"

"Be my guest," said Earl, "but I want to close up in five minutes."

"Should only take a second or two," replied Broussard.

After entering the shack, Broussard once again scanned the scene. In a couple of minutes or so, Broussard nodded his head slightly and smiled to himself. He had identified what was bothering him.

"Hey Earl," Broussard yelled gleefully. "You from Arkansas?"

"No, South Florida" Earl replied. "Why?"

Broussard pointed to the Arkansas license plate on the shack's wall. The other plates, from Louisiana, Mississippi and Texas, were rusted, fading and disfigured. The Arkansas plate had splotches of dried mud on it, but was otherwise nearly new and in good condition. In addition, the plate still had its license tags intact, the only license plate in the bunch with that particular piece of additional identification. The tags indicated a 1997 registration.

"Oh that," said Earl. "I forgot to mention it, but I found that plate in the marshes several years ago. I'd say it was about a hundred and fifty yards from my shop. Now that I think about it, I found it shortly after I had to replace my lock."

"You replaced your lock?" said Broussard. "Why?"

"Came into work one morning," recalled Earl. "and the lock and the door were broken. Also, one of my shovels was missing. And a pair of my mud boots."

"I think that was about four or five years ago," Earl continued "but it could have been longer. I'm not sure anymore. And I'll tell you something else. Whoever broke in left a $20 bill on the counter. Sure did. How about that?" Earl laughed. "An honest thief. I've held onto it all these years. Just in the case whoever left it comes back and needs a loan. I'm not paying them interest though," said Earl with a quick wink.

"You mean you have the $20 bill that was left in your place after it was vandalized?" said Broussard, scarcely believing his luck.

"Why sure, it's right over here," said Earl opening one of his bait drawers. "I keep it in this envelope, but I haven't looked at it for a while. Hopefully the storm didn't soak it."

Cortez's ears perked up. Perhaps they were getting closer to solving the case than he had thought. His mind raced forward. Cortez envisioned himself arresting the suspect, seeing him convicted at trial and then being commended by the entire department and his fellow officers. He eagerly reached for the envelope Earl was holding, anxious to get his hands on it.

"Not so fast," Broussard admonished Cortez. "This is evidence. We have to be careful how we handle it. I'll seal it in a plastic bag and then we'll have the lab technicians test it for prints."

Cortez pressed Earl for additional details about the break-in, but Earl's memory bank was exhausted. He had done well to remember as much as he did.

The detectives thanked Earl and told him they would need to take the envelope holding the $20 bill as potential evidence along with the license plate, which Earl grudgingly handed over.

As the detectives left his shack, Earl gave them a parting shot about the shovel the $20 was intended to replace.

"Hey, what about my twenty dollars?" he said.

Broussard was so excited, he gave Earl two twenties. "We'll need to have someone come out and take your fingerprints Earl," he said, "so we can isolate any fingerprints on the bill that aren't yours. You've been a big help."

Chapter 84

Lab tests revealed a right thumbprint on one side of the $20 bill and an index finger print on the other side, neither of which belonged to Earl. There was no match for the prints in the national database. As for the license plate, the Arkansas Department of Motor Vehicles was able to trace it to a car purchased by Zephyr's Rental Cars in Kenner, a couple of miles from the New Orleans airport.

Cortez and Broussard arrived at Zephyr's the next day. They asked one of the clerks about the car, a tan Ford Mercury Sable that had been leased a number of years before.

The clerk had only been employed at Zephyr's for a year, so she referred the men to Todd, her manager who she said had worked there longer than anyone else.

The detectives found Todd in a small office towards the back of the facility, seated at his desk which faced a side wall. Todd squashed a cigarette butt into an ashtray already full of them and began typing on his computer as the detectives silently entered the room.

He had been the on-site manager at this Zephyr's location for nearly a decade, having stuck around when upper management inferred years earlier on several occasions that Todd was in line for a promotion to regional supervisor. It never came. Once his superiors decided to move in a different direction, they attempted to appease Todd by tossing him a bone and upping his annual paid vacation from two weeks to two and a half weeks. Todd had never forgotten or forgiven them.

Bitter at what he viewed as management's betrayal, Todd only exerted himself on the job when he had to. He delegated work as often as he could and took liberties with "borrowing" company pens, pencils, envelopes and staplers. Although he was rarely selected to travel on company business, Todd falsified his expense reports whenever he did. He figured the company owed him and he was determined to extract every cent from his employer that he could get away with.

Todd spent most of his time at work placing bets on local horse races. He despised senior management at every level, especially those younger employees who had been promoted over him. He had not aged well and gradually increased his smoking habit to two packs a day. Now forty-three years old but looking every bit of sixty, Todd was screwed and he knew it.

The detectives moved closer but Todd, in his own world, never noticed. Cortez, ever curious, peered over Todd's shoulder and noticed a display on the computer screen of odds for the day's races at the New Orleans Fair Grounds.

Broussard cleared his throat to draw Todd's attention. A startled Todd jumped up and quickly retracted his computer monitor, placing his elbow squarely in the middle of the folded computer top so no one could see what was on his screen. He wheeled around to face the detectives.

"Something I can do for you fellas?" Todd asked nervously.

"We're with the police," Broussard answered, as he and Cortez flashed their badges for Todd to see. "We'd like to ask you a few questions."

Todd's heart sank when he heard those words. He was eighteen months behind in his child support payments, but figured it would take the court system at least a couple of years to catch up with him.

"Damn it," Todd thought to himself, realizing there was no escape route past the two holstered men occupying the space between him and the doorway.

Broussard asked Todd if Zephyr's retained records of prior year's rentals.

Todd breathed a sigh of relief. He could scarcely believe his good fortune. The detectives apparently were not here to question him about his delinquent minor support obligations. He happily agreed to help.

"We sure do," a suddenly rejuvenated Todd said beaming from ear to ear. "But we rent damn near 300 cars a month, so if you are looking for any particular rental, that will be like trying to find a needle in a haystack."

"Ok," Cortez said slowly. "This one would be a Mercury Sable and it would have been returned with a missing Arkansas license plate. I know it's a long shot, but it would have happened about eight years ago."

Todd paused for a few seconds. "Now you're talking," he said. "I remember it. Was rented by a nice-lookin' black fella. Well-spoken but he wasn't from around here. I noticed the missing plate right away when he pulled up. He seemed to be in quite a hurry though. I told him he would have to pay for the plates. It's a hassle for us to replace plates, especially one from out-of-state."

"The guy said he didn't have time to discuss it. He was a little edgy and got his nose all pushed out of shape about it. Not sure why. I didn't lose the plate, he lost it. Know what I mean?"

"Anyway, when I brought the paper work out for him to sign, he just gave me $1,000 cash on the spot and asked if that would cover it. Can you believe that?"

"Most customers returning cars, why you'd have a rat's ass helluva time getting fifty bucks out of 'em to cover chipped paint or a cracked windshield. This dude, a thousand dollars no questions asked, in hundred dollar bills no less. The most Benjamin Franklin's I've seen in all my years. Never happened before, never happened since. That's how come I remember him."

Todd didn't tell the detectives that the Arkansas Department of Motor Vehicles had charged Zephyr's $615 to replace the lost license plate and that he had pocketed the remaining $385.

"What was this guy's name?" asked Broussard.

"Oh I don't remember that," said Todd. "Like you said, it was a long time ago."

"Well now that we seem to have refreshed your memory, can you please check your records and figure out who he was?" pressed Cortez, becoming more agitated by the minute. "We think the rental may have occurred in October of 1997."

"We should have records from that far back" replied Todd. "We keep 'em for ten years."

Having avoided any questioning about his delinquent child support payments, Todd instantly shifted gears, thinking now that he might actually profit from his encounter with the detectives. He quickly and correctly surmised that they needed something only he could provide. For one evanescent moment, the detectives were desperate seekers of information.

And Todd was the only seller.

"I'm awful busy today though," Todd said. "Reeeeeal busy. I'm afraid it will be a while before I can dig that information up for y'all," he said smiling.

Cortez paced a bit and chomped on his cigar which was now a mere stub of rolled tobacco leaves. Exasperated, he reached into his pocket to retrieve his wallet.

Out of the corner of his eye Todd noticed Cortez start to pull out a $20 bill. Todd cleared his throat and then raised his voice. $20 was not going to do the trick.

"Like I mentioned before, we are real busy today and I just won't be able to get to it," said Todd, almost shouting to make sure the detectives understood just *how busy* he was.

Todd continued to play his hand by expressing something he had not cared about for years. A desire to provide excellent customer service.

"Of course you boys realize I got a business to run and customers are waiting," Todd stated emphatically. "Y'all understand that I'm sure. Time is money."

The customers hadn't mattered a few minutes earlier when Todd was placing his horse bets, Cortez thought, but Todd's assessment of the situation proved accurate. The detectives needed his assistance so they were willing to further indulge Todd, up to a point anyway.

Cortez maneuvered his thumb around inside his billfold and pulled out an additional $20 to go with the $20 already visible. Todd smiled, clearly pleased that he had managed to manipulate the situation to his advantage.

"Course I might be able to make some time to look," said Todd as he quickly snatched the two $20 bills out of Cortez's hands. "I'll certainly see what I can do. You boys call me in a week or so and I'll let you know what I found out."

This was more than Cortez could take.

"Damn it son, next week is not good enough," he seethed. "You've got to do better than that."

Fists clenched, Cortez moved threateningly in Todd's direction. He was about ready to put Todd in a full nelson. Broussard gently slid his arm diagonally across Cortez's chest from behind to restrain him. He motioned towards the door.

"Easy, easy," Broussard said to Cortez, hoping to defuse his partner before Cortez catapulted himself into a human powder keg. "Come on let's go outside to cool off."

As the detectives were about to leave, Broussard paused, then turned around.

"One more thing Todd," he said. "I'd hate to have to come back here and start poking into some other things that I just don't have time for right now."

"You see there's this nasty rumor floating around the precinct about some local scumbag that is using a rental car joint as a front for taking illegal bets on his bookmaking operations."

"And get this. The guy really thinks he's slick. He's also a deadbeat, skipping out on his child support payments. So while his kids go hungry, the lousy piece of filth is raking in dough while running numbers on the ponies."

"The things you hear out on the street," Broussard said as he laughed to himself. "Can you imagine that?"

"Well anyway, the Department has asked me to look into it, but I'm tied up right now. Now the way I figure it, maybe the jerk gets wise and cleans up his act. If his kids get their money, then by the time I get around to it, there won't be much left to investigate. Who knows? The whole thing might just disappear at that point."

"Anyway, good day Todd," said Broussard as he finished up. "We'll be in touch."

"Hold on a second fellas," said a worried but suddenly cooperative Todd. "Let me go check those records right now to see what I can find. You know I always said I'm a law abiding citizen ready to help the police in any way I can. Yessireee, y'all can count on ol' Todd. I'll be right back."

Chapter 85

Todd appeared from the office's record storage room twenty minutes later. "I got a name for ya" he said. "That car was rented by a gentleman named Bryan Stirling from Los Angeles, California. Here's his California driver's license number if you want it."

The detectives grudgingly thanked Todd for his assistance and wrote down the information he provided about Bryan. As they started back to their car, Cortez grumbled about being out $40 while Broussard just laughed.

On the drive back to Belle Chase, Broussard kept repeating, "Bryan Stirling, now where have I heard that name?"

"All new to me," said Cortez. "Never heard of him."

When they reached Cortez's office, Broussard asked to borrow Cortez's computer. Broussard googled "Bryan Stirling," and then snapped his fingers.

"I knew it," he said. "I knew I had heard that name before. Our Mr. Stirling is famous. He's a stud lawyer in California who just got appointed to the state Supreme Court. Youngest guy in history. I saw a feature on him a couple of weeks ago on CNN. Don't you ever read the paper or watch the news?" Broussard asked Cortez.

"Not really," shrugged Cortez.

"I figured as much," Broussard said under his breath. He continued.

"Now why is a big-time California lawyer like that renting a car here in New Orleans right about the time Pope disappeared? And how did his license plate end up on the wall in Earl's Shack a few yards from where Pope's body was found?" pondered Broussard as he tapped his pencil on a note pad. "Well, well. What do ya think about that?"

Chapter 86

Hoping they might now be on to something, the detectives began to work at a fever pitch. They researched the professional history of Bryan Stirling and soon obtained a lengthy dossier. Broussard read from the report aloud while sitting in Cortez's office with his feet up on Cortez's desk.

"Graduated top 5% of his class from Westchester School of Law in 1994. Passed the bar the first time. Worked with the DA right out of law school. Switched to an environmental defense firm in 1996. Married in 2002. Divorced in 2003. Recently appointed to the California Supreme Court by the Governor. Nothing here all that unusual, except that he's about as polished as they come."

"Wait a minute. Get this. Summer internship in Natchez in 1993. Might be interesting to find out a little more about that?"

"Impressive credentials," said Cortez. "But just because he was in Natchez in 1993 don't have nothing to do with happened to Pope in 1997."

"Maybe, maybe not," said Broussard. "That's what we get paid to find out. I'll grant you that he looks impeccable on paper. But we know he was here in 1997 because he rented a car from Zephyr's. That's a fact, assuming you believe Zephyr's records. And Todd seemed pretty certain. Now what was our Mr. Stirling doing in New Orleans then?"

Chapter 87

Try as they might, the detectives were unable to nail down any firm connection between Bryan and New Orleans. As a result, they requested a search warrant from a local magistrate to review Bryan's cell phone records during the time of his rental from Zephyr's.

The magistrate perused their warrant application. The detectives' request was based on Bryan's rental of the car, his return of the car without a license plate and the discovery of the plate near the location where Pope's body was found.

The magistrate called the detectives into his office. He adjusted his glasses forward to the bridge of his nose. His eyes frowned skeptically over the top rim at Cortez and Broussard.

"You fellas been smoking some of that imported herb?" he asked, "because I'm not seeing much here. You know the rest of the country thinks all we do is run a good ol' boy network down here anyway. Hick sheriffs, hick detectives and if you have your way, a damned hick magistrate burrowing down the possum hole right behind the bumbling two of you. I'd hate to give them Yankees more evidence that they're right. If you want this warrant, you've got to be serious about it."

"We're on to something," said Broussard, who didn't appreciate his professionalism being questioned. "You've got to trust us. There is something here that is going to help us solve a murder. I know it. You won't regret helping us out."

"Murder? Sheeeeett, come on. You mean Alvarez Pope?" replied the magistrate. "Good riddance as far as I'm concerned. Hell, whoever knocked off that sumbitch did us all a favor. The world's a better place without him in it. It's made our lives here in the Parish a lot easier these last few years. Yours too. Now you want me to grant a search warrant for a California Supreme Court judge's phone because it might, and I emphasize *might*, have something to do with Pope's killing? Then you present me with this cockamamie connection based on a wild premonition that you can't even explain? As Dusty Springfield once sang gentlemen, 'wishin' and hopin' never solved a damn thing, or something like that."

Broussard squirmed uncomfortably. He was bothered by the magistrate's insinuation that vigilante justice may have been appropriately served on Pope. Broussard considered himself the consummate professional. It was his job to solve crimes, not to determine if the victim got what he, or she, deserved.

Broussard was even more concerned though that the magistrate might deny the request. The magistrate was right and he knew it. There were at least a dozen holes in their theory. Broussard didn't like to take wild shots in the dark and he didn't appreciate being chastised about slipshod detective work. If he could get the magistrate to bend a little this one time, however, Broussard was certain that going out on a limb would pay off.

"Alright detectives," the magistrate continued after some additional scolding. "I'm going with you two on this one. But only for communications that were made while Mr. Stirling was in Louisiana. I've got no jurisdiction over anything else and you can't go snooping into every detail of the man's life just because you have an inkling. One other thing. There's going to be hell to pay if you're wrong. Your necks are on the line. Mine too, which they have been trying to chop off for years by the way. We'll all be tarred and feathered if you screw this one up and yours truly will be the first to go."

"Don't make me look bad," he lectured as Broussard and Cortez eagerly started towards the door. "You better be right. This guy's got some political muscle behind him and he could embarrass all of us if this turns out to be a wild goose chase."

Having secured the search warrant, Broussard and Cortez immediately served it on Bryan's wireless phone carrier. After a week or so, the carrier provided a summary of Bryan's phone calls while he was in Louisiana. The records showed several calls made to a local 504 area code number in October 1997. There were also a few other communications to and from that same number a couple of years later using a new technology called "short message service" or SMS, more commonly known as "text messages."

Within minutes, the detectives determined that the 504 number belonged to Kathryn Duvall, a local registered nurse with no criminal record.

The detectives decided to pay Ms. Duvall a visit.

Chapter 88

Katy answered the knock on her door early one Thursday evening at about 6:30. She had spent most of the day moving her mother to Nana Bernard's farmhouse after the destruction of Francine's Lafitte apartment.

"Can I help you?" Katy asked the two gentlemen standing in front of her.

"Ms. Duvall, I presume?" asked Broussard.

"Yes, I'm Kathryn Duvall," Katy answered. "Who are you and what do you want?"

"Ma'am, I'm Detective Cortez and this is Detective Broussard" said Cortez, as the two showed their badges and Cortez blew a puff of cigar smoke skyward. "Can we come in and speak with you for a moment?"

"I guess that would be alright," said Katy, "but what's this about? And please don't smoke in my apartment."

"My apologies, ma'am," said Cortez as he extinguished his cigar and then started to chomp on the wet stub still in his mouth.

"Ma'am, are you familiar with a Bryan Stirling?" asked Broussard.

Katy was slow to answer. Finally she spoke.

"I think I have heard of him," she said cautiously. "Why yes. He's famous I think. He's been on television a lot lately. Isn't he a California Supreme Court justice or something like that?"

"Correct," answered Broussard. "We are interested in finding out if you know Mr. Stirling personally."

Katy knew they would not be asking if they hadn't already established that she knew Bryan.

"Oh, well . . . yes," Katy said slowly. "Bryan, I mean Mr. Stirling, and I are old friends. We met more than ten years ago when he was passing through New Orleans on his way back to California from Natchez. Why do you ask?"

Broussard nodded in Cortez's direction. There was something to Bryan's visit to Natchez after all.

"Well when was the last time you saw him?" asked Broussard.

"I think it was a few years ago," said Katy. "Mr. Stirling was in Louisiana on a business trip and we met briefly for an hour or so while he was here," Katy continued, lying about the date she last saw Bryan and neglecting to disclose her recent visit to California.

"Would you have seen him in October of 1997?" asked Broussard.

"I don't know," said Katy. "Maybe. I'm not very good with dates though."

"Where did you meet?" asked Broussard as Cortez occupied himself by strolling around Katy's apartment, examining her family pictures and peering in and out of vacant rooms.

"Please stop walking through my home," Katy said sternly to Cortez, who cut short his tour of the premises and sauntered back over to where Katy and Broussard were standing.

"We had dinner somewhere in the French Quarter," Katy responded, casting a stern glare in Cortez's direction. "I don't remember what restaurant."

"Do you meet him in the French Quarter or did he pick you up?" pressed Broussard. He could sense Katy's hesitancy so he wanted to be precise with his questions and tie down as many facts as he could before Katy completely shut down.

Katy started to fidget and began tugging on the sleeve of her sweatshirt.

"I believe he may have picked me up," she said, "but it was so long ago I can't be sure. I might have caught a cab. I just don't know. What's this all about anyway?"

"We have information that Mr. Stirling obtained a rental car here in New Orleans," Broussard said, pulling out a copy of the rental agreement and handing it to Katy. "He rented a Mercury Sable as you can see. Does this jog your memory any? Now, I'll ask you again. Did you catch a cab to dinner or did Mr. Stirling pick you up in a Mercury Sable?"

"How I am supposed to remember what type of car he rented. It was a number of years ago. Anyway, I caught a cab to the restaurant. I'm pretty certain about that," said Katy, shoving the rental agreement back into Broussard's mid-section.

Suddenly, Cortez decided to join in the line of questioning. He cut straight to the point.

"Did y'all have any occasion to take a drive down to Plaquemines Parish?" Cortez blurted out, drawing a wicked stare from an exasperated Broussard who didn't want the foundation he was trying to build undercut by Cortez's impatience.

The mention of Plaquemines Parish terrified Katy. Could the detectives possibly know something about Pope's killing, Katy's role in it, the use of Bryan's rental car and the disposal of the body in the Louisiana swamp? Over the past eight years, Katy thought about that evening constantly. She had also heard the news that human remains had recently been discovered near Lake Hermitage. She now had a very real concern that her long kept secret was about to be exposed.

Katy took a deep breath and tried to restore her equilibrium. She now spoke very deliberately. She didn't want to trip herself up.

"As I recall, Mr. Stirling and I drove around a bit after dinner," she responded. "Whether his car was a Mercury Sable or not, I don't know. But like I said, it was a long time ago and I can't really remember exactly where we went."

This was all a lie of course. Katy remembered every detail.

"Will that be all gentlemen?" she asked, hoping in vain to put an abrupt end to the grilling. Katy realized that the detectives standing in front of her would not be pushovers like Officers Marshall and Teague.

"Just a few more questions Ms. Duvall," replied Broussard, sensing that Katy was becoming cornered. He did not want to let her off the hook. "Do you happen to know if Mr. Stirling owns a revolver?"

Katy paused, ran her fingers through her hair a couple of times and then tugged on her sleeves some more.

"I would have no way of knowing whether or not Mr. Stirling owns a gun. Need I remind you gentlemen that he lives in California?"

Cortez again interjected, cutting straight to the chase. "Did Mr. Stirling have a gun with him on the night the two of you drove around Plaquemines Parish in 1997?" he huffed.

"I never said we drove to Plaquemines Parish did I?" responded Katy.

"Well, do you own a gun?" piped Cortez.

That last question hit closer to home.

"As a matter of fact I do," said Katy, figuring that Broussard and Cortez already knew the answer. "Me and 75% of the people in New Orleans. Single girl living alone in the big city's gotta protect herself you know. A nine millimeter. Is that a crime?"

"We would like to see it if you don't mind. Run a ballistics check. Just routine police business," said Broussard.

"Happy to hand it over to you," said Katy, now extremely thankful that she had tossed the .38 special pistol she used to shoot Pope, into the Mississippi from the Crescent City Bridge years earlier.

Even though Katy knew there would be no ballistics match with whatever bullet the detectives intended to test against her pistol, she realized her treachery was on the verge of being uncovered. Her little game of hide the ball had just about run its course. Further coyness was likely to be pointless. Katy knew where Broussard was going and Broussard knew that Katy knew.

Broussard continued to probe. He wanted to unnerve Katy as much as possible.

"Oh and Ms. Duvall, did you know an Alvarez Pope by any chance?"

The circle was getting tighter.

Again, Katy was slow to answer. She could see the dots being connected right in front of her eyes.

"Why yes, I have certainly heard of him," she responded. "I'm sure you two know that New Orleans has enough street thugs to fill Angola," Katy said referencing Louisiana's most notorious prison and hoping that the penitentiary was not her future destination. "Pope was one of them. Why do you ask?"

"Well," said Broussard, who was immediately cut off by an impatient Cortez.

"Because Pope vanished from the scene right around the time you and your boyfriend were in New Orleans and later cruised around Plaquemines Parish in the rental car," he said, prematurely revealing the detective's theory of the case.

His impetuousness drew a frigid glare from Broussard, who didn't appreciate Cortez's telegraphing where he was going.

"I asked you before what this was all about," said Katy. "I'm going to call my lawyer," knowing full well she didn't have a criminal attorney. "I think you gentlemen should leave."

"Very well," said Broussard. "We'll go, but you will be seeing us again."

Broussard had one last surprise for Katy before he left.

"By the way," he said on his way out, "when was the last time you saw Earl?"

Katy froze. She was caught completely off guard by the question. "They know about Earl?" she thought to herself. Things were worse than she had imagined.

Realizing that Broussard was still waiting for an answer, all that a shell-shocked Katy could manage was a weak and unconvincing "Earl who?"

Katy didn't wait for a response or any more questions. She was anxious to shut the door behind the detectives.

Cortez, sensing that Katy was rapidly becoming constricted by her own answers, stuck his nose in Katy's face on his way out.

"Let me tell you something Miss Duvall," he said, still holding what remained of the wet cigar stub in his hand.

"We're leaving, but we'll be back. And you and your California judge boyfriend better get your stories straight."

As the detectives walked back to their car, Cortez was frustrated. He was ready to make an immediate arrest.

"She didn't admit to anything yet," he said to his partner, "but we'll get her."

"We may already have," replied Broussard flashing the rental agreement in front of Cortez. "I played a hunch and printed out this bogus agreement right before we came over here. The only fingerprints on it are mine . . . and now Kathryn Duvall's. We've got something to compare against the prints on the $20 bill we took from Earl's place."

Chapter 89

By the time the detectives left her apartment, Katy's concern had turned to panic. She was convinced the detectives suspected her in Pope's murder. But did they have any proof to back it up?

Katy wasn't worried about the ballistics match. Any bullets the police recovered from Pope's body or anywhere else would not match her current weapon. That gun had only been fired at the target range. And even though Katy and Bryan had broken into Earl's shack to steal a shovel, Earl had not been there when it happened, so Earl could not place Katy or Bryan at the scene. Still, it bothered Katy that the detectives seemed so smug about their case. That would have been unlikely if they didn't already possess some evidence that raised suspicions about her and Bryan.

A multitude of thoughts raced through Katy's mind. She reassured herself that she had acted in self-defense. She was just trying to protect her brother. And besides, Pope had threatened her. Anybody in her situation would have reacted the same way.

"No reasonable jury in the world will convict you," Katy told herself, not believing a word of it and certainly not wanting to put that belief to the test.

Then there was Bryan. Should Katy call him? The two had not spoken in a week or so but Katy knew that the oven was starting to broil. She couldn't keep Bryan in the dark but she also realized that any hint of a major scandal could ruin Bryan's career. And what if her communications were being monitored by the police? Katy resolved to do everything she could to protect Bryan, but she was still only guessing about precisely what the detectives knew and what they were doing with the information they had.

Meanwhile, the detectives were in fact zeroing in on Bryan. They knew he must have some involvement in the entire episode but were not sure what, or why. The Arkansas license plate hanging innocently in Earl's shack, detached from a car that Bryan rented, plus the numerous calls and texts between Katy and Bryan, spoke volumes. The detectives were slowly binding the two of them together like Bonnie and Clyde.

Chapter 90

"I think we got her," Broussard said to Cortez as both of them sat in Cortez's office. "There's a fingerprint match on that $20 bill we took from Earl's. Kathryn Duvall's prints are all over it. I guess that shows she has a conscious and didn't want Earl to foot the cost of having to replace his shovel. Admirable perhaps, but sometimes altruism can get you in trouble. Anyway, it's not our problem. Now if we could just figure out Bryan Stirling's role in this whole thing, we'll be in business."

"Let's go pick her up," responded Cortez. "Lean on her some more. Hard. And maybe we'll find out."

"First things first," replied Broussard. "Let's see what the DA thinks."

The next day the detectives held a meeting to present their evidence to Gunter Hudson, an associate District Attorney who had never tried a murder case.

"It's not perfect," said Hudson. "She probably did it, but there are some holes. We can go forward, but I can't guarantee a conviction. What's Stirling's involvement? Do you have anything on him?"

"He drove Duvall out to Lake Hermitage to bury Pope," replied Broussard. "At least that's what we think happened since his rental car was used. It would have been awfully difficult for Duvall to have driven all the way out to Plaquemines with Pope's body in the trunk, knock down the locked door at Earl's shack, drag the body up an incline, dig a grave and then bury it, with no help. There are still a couple of moving parts that we haven't figured out yet though."

"We may have to seek extradition from California to get Stirling out here to find out. Not sure the good judge is going to come voluntarily. Plus we need to anticipate all the roadblocks he'll throw up. Once it becomes public that a sitting state Supreme Court justice is involved, the lid of this thing will be blown completely off and all hell's gonna break loose. But we didn't create these bizarre circumstances. We're just following the evidence where it leads us."

Hudson nodded. "Well, we don't need to have a case against Stirling yet to try Kathryn Duvall. Alright, let's do it," he said.

Later that Thursday evening, the detectives descended upon Katy's apartment. They were armed with a warrant for Katy's arrest. The charge was first degree murder.

Chapter 91

Meredith Bascom couldn't quite get the key lined up square with the lock to open her apartment's front door. Balancing two bags of groceries with her purse slung over her shoulder, Meredith lifted her left leg up so that her knee bent and pinned the bags against the door. She then guided the key into the lock with her right hand.

Suddenly one bag slipped slightly. Meredith tried to compensate by pushing her knee up further, which only caused the other bag to teeter as

Meredith was turning the key in the lock. She lost her balance when the door gave way, scattering groceries out of both bags as Meredith fell onto the entry way floor of her apartment.

"I should have just made two trips," she thought to herself as oranges ricocheted around the sidewalk like pinballs and a dozen eggs lay crushed just outside her welcome mat.

The commotion alerted two men who were standing at the door of Meredith's neighbor, Katy Duvall. They both rushed to Meredith's aid.

"Did someone call 9-1-1 for the rescue squad," joked the well-dressed, clean-cut gentleman who was first on the scene, as he extended his hand to lift Meredith up. "This is quite a mess. We're happy to help you clean it up. My name's Norman Broussard and this is my partner Marteen Cortez. We're with the New Orleans police."

"Meredith Bascom. Nice to meet you both," replied Meredith, struggling to stand up and regain her balance. The detectives then proceeded to retrieve the oranges and the other scattered groceries that were spread across the walkway and under some nearby bushes.

After a few minutes of intense clean-up, order was restored.

"By the way," said Broussard somewhat nonchalantly as he finished washing away the egg residue from the area around Meredith's front door. "We were hoping to catch up with your neighbor Kathryn Duvall, but she doesn't appear to be home. Do you know her? Any idea what time she might be coming back?"

Meredith had just moved into her apartment two months earlier. She had gotten to know Katy a little and the two found that they had several common interests. As helpful as the detectives had been though and as thankful as Meredith was to have assistance, she was not ready to volunteer any information about Katy, although she really didn't know much anyway.

"I'm not sure," said Meredith. "Katy is usually home in the evenings, so she must have run an errand or something. I'll let her know you were here when she gets back."

Not satisfied that Broussard's little exchange with Meredith was producing enough information, an impatient Cortez decided to pursue his own line of questioning.

"Uh, Ms. Bascom," he said clearing his voice. "In your conversations with Ms. Duvall, did she every mention any regrets? Maybe, well . . . like something from her past that she would change if she could."

Broussard cast an icy stare in Cortez's direction. Now he fully understood why several of his colleagues had sarcastically wished him "good luck," upon learning that Cortez had been assigned to work with him on the case. Broussard could not believe Cortez's sloppiness.

"No need to worry about any of that, ma'am," interjected Broussard, before a stunned Meredith could address the question. "We'll just catch up with Ms. Duvall at another time. Have a good night," he nodded in Meredith's direction.

After Meredith got settled in her apartment and put away the groceries salvaged from the spill, she thought more about the detectives' interest in Katy. Meredith didn't want to pry, but that last question by Cortez disturbed her. She had developed enough of a bond with Katy to think that she should at least forewarn Katy about the police being there. After all, if the situation were reversed she assumed that Katy would do the same for her.

Not wanting her neighbor to be ambushed or surprised upon returning home, Meredith called Katy that Thursday evening and gave her a rundown of her encounter with Broussard and Cortez outside the apartment. Katy was at the Bernard family farm at the time, visiting her mother and grandmother. She thanked Meredith and told her how appreciative she was.

In Katy's mind, the return of the detectives was a bad sign. Perhaps they wanted to make an arrest, although Katy thought that was unlikely. There couldn't possibly be a ballistics match and Katy could not think of any other incriminating evidence that the detectives might have. She was completely unaware that the detective had her fingerprints and had already matched them with the $20 bill at Earl's shack. Katy had totally forgotten all about leaving that money for Earl to replace his shovel.

Katy was convinced it was time to hire an attorney. She had no interest in another meeting with the detectives and didn't see how anything good could come out of it.

But first she needed to talk to Bryan.

Chapter 92

As Katy contemplated the reappearance of the detectives, she thought about the questions they had previously asked about Bryan. Were they circling the wagons around him also? Katy didn't know. She also did not want to bother Bryan unnecessarily, but things could now be nearing a crises stage. Katy decided to send Bryan a text. The message was cryptic.

"Call me at Nana's tomorrow morning. Cayenne."

"Cayenne" was Bryan and Katy's secret code word. They had agreed that the word was only to be used when there was a dire emergency. Bryan had forgotten his cell phone at work and therefore did not see the message until the next morning when he arrived at the judge's chambers. At first, he didn't know what to make of it and thought that Katy must be playing some kind of practical joke on him.

Then Bryan started to wonder. It was not like Katy to use their secret code word unless it was warranted. In fact, the word had only come up when they were discussing the secrets of Louisiana cooking after he made jambalaya for Katy on her recent visit to California.

Almost as a joke, Katy had said that if she were ever in trouble, she would let Bryan know by using the word "cayenne" to indicate that things were getting hot. Bryan barely remembered that conversation, but the sight of the word in a text message jogged his memory. Maybe something serious was going on.

Puzzled by Katy's message, Bryan booted up his computer and searched for recent articles about any developments in Plaquemines Parish. What he found shocked him. Indeed, a body had been discovered in Plaquemines Parish days after Hurricane Katrina swept through. A week later, the body had been identified as that of the long-missing New Orleans crime lord Alvarez Pope.

Bryan stared at his computer screen in disbelief. He pulled up article after article to get as many details as he could. Then he came across a video of a press conference held by the detectives who were working the case. A tall, thin younger man spoke first.

"We're making progress in the investigation," the man said. "It's tough sledding with a case this old, but we're working round the clock to solve it."

Before the man could finish, another man, this one gruff, stocky and chewing on a cigar, grabbed the microphone.

"We intend to have a suspect or suspects in custody shortly," the second man boldly predicted. "And I think a lot of people are going to be surprised where this all ends up. We may have a high profile out-of-state arrest," he continued with an arrogant grin.

Those last words were particularly chilling. What did this man know, Bryan wondered? Could he himself be the "high profile out-of-state arrest" the detective referred to? That wasn't clear, but the man's cockiness unnerved Bryan.

Suddenly, there was a knock on his door. It was Molly, Bryan's court clerk.

"Opening session in five minutes Judge," Molly said cheerfully. Bryan was usually one of the first justices seated, so Molly was not used to having to come to his chambers to get him. Hastily Bryan exited out of the articles and closed his computer. But the discovery stayed with him the rest of the day.

As soon as court ended that afternoon, Bryan called Katy. She informed him that two detectives had questioned her and asked her whether or not she knew Bryan. Bryan realized that the investigation was further along, and much more dire, than he thought.

"Then, they showed up at my apartment last night again," said Katy, "but I wasn't there. I think they may be trying to track me down for more questioning," she continued, completely unaware that a warrant had been issued for her arrest.

"Ok," said Bryan. "I'll be on a flight out tonight and then we can figure out what to do next."

"I think you should stay in California," said Katy. "Whatever happens here is going to happen anyway. There is no sense in you getting into this any deeper."

Bryan was wary of returning to Louisiana, but his fear of being arrested in California, maybe even in the Supreme Court courtroom itself, prompted him to take action. If that happened, it would be career ending. Perhaps he could get to New Orleans and forestall events, or meet with the local authorities and come to some sort of arrangement that would keep his name out of the public eye. Maybe it was time for he and Katy to come clean and explain that the whole thing was indeed an accident.

Bryan didn't have all of the facts in front of him regarding where the Louisiana authorities were in their investigation or what they knew, but ultimately he decided that action was better than inaction. The damage to his reputation from an arrest would be immense under any circumstances but was something he could not survive if it occurred on his home turf.

Since the weekend was approaching, Bryan knew he could catch a redeye that evening to New Orleans, land on Saturday morning, meet with Katy and figure out what to do next, even if that meant going to the police. Then hopefully he would fly back to California on Sunday and be back in court Monday morning. Even if he had to take Monday off, it might be worth the gamble to go to New Orleans and get out in front of whatever next steps the police might be planning against him.

So late that night Bryan headed to the airport, donning dark shades and wearing a black leather baseball cap pulled low and tight over his eyes. He obscured his neck and the rest of his face with a thick scarf, snuggly tucked into his jacket. Upon arriving at the ticket counter, Bryan purchased a seat at the rear of the plane in the last row for the nonstop midnight flight to New Orleans.

As Bryan boarded the aircraft, he couldn't escape thoughts of his trip to Louisiana eight years earlier. He could not help but wonder if a similar disaster awaited him.

Chapter 93

Bryan's flight landed in New Orleans early Saturday morning. After picking up his rental car, he called Nana's Bernard's landline.

Katy answered the phone.

"Katy, this is Bryan. I'm at Louis Armstrong. Can you talk?" he said.

"Bryan, we or at least I, am in deep trouble," Katy said, after having learned overnight that an arrest warrant had been issued.

"I don't have time to explain. I need you to get on I-10 and come across the Lake Pontchartrain Causeway like we've done before when you've come out to Nana's house. Follow the signs for highway

433/Little Lagoon. Take 433 south. When you get to highway 90, cross over and park on 5th Street. I'll meet you there. Please hurry!"

"But Katy," Bryan said as he heard the line on the other end go dead while he was trying to scribble the directions Katy rattled off at warp speed.

Again Bryan pondered what to do. Was he walking into a trap? There was no way Katy would betray him. But Katy was clearly in distress. Bryan decided to follow the directions Katy gave him as best he could. Within forty minutes he arrived at the location that Katy had described on the shores of Lake Pontchartrain. The Lake's vastness, spread out in front of him like a panorama, was ocean-like.

As he exited his car, Katy appeared from nowhere and wrapped him in a tight embrace.

"Bryan, they know," she screamed. "They know."

"Who knows?" said Bryan, "and what do they know?" although at this juncture he had a pretty good idea of what Katy was talking about.

"They know what we, what I did. They know I shot Pope and they know you were with me. And there is a warrant out for my arrest."

Just then, the faint sound of sirens could be heard in the distance. The blaring grew louder with each passing second.

"Katy, where are we?" asked Bryan.

"We're at The Rigolets," said Katy. "On the north shore of Lake Pontchartrain. They're coming after us. If we can just buy a day, a half a day, so we can talk and I can figure out what to do. Then I'll turn myself in. But this has all happened so suddenly. I thought the police had just a few more questions for me and the next thing I know they are on their way out to Nana's to arrest me. I left just before they got there, but obviously they followed me."

Katy pointed to a small body of water that bordered them on the east.

"We need to swim across this inlet to reach West Double Bayou on the other side. My uncle used to work in a warehouse over there and we can hide out until the police leave."

"But Katy," Bryan protested.

"Bryan, let's go," said Katy. "NOW!"

Bryan continued to balk, but the sirens were getting louder. He was not ready to acquiesce to an arrest if he could avoid it.

Bryan threw off his jacket and jumped into the water after Katy. The two began making their way across the two hundred or so meters separating them from the other side as the sound of the wailing sirens grew louder.

Chapter 94

The rippling waves tossed Bryan around the lake like a rollercoaster. Katy, the stronger swimmer, was several feet ahead of him. Unsure of his whereabouts and losing his bearings, Bryan was swallowing water. Twenty-four hours with no sleep had left him drained, physically and mentally.

Bryan entered full panic mode. Then he saw the shore in the distance. It was only 30 or 40 yards away, but he was tiring quickly. He could barely muster the strength to keep his arms churning but willed himself to keep swimming. A few more labored strokes just might get him to safety. He didn't want to lose it all now.

Suddenly Bryan felt a tug on his left ankle then a sharp pain as if needles were lacerating his flesh. Bryan shook his leg and cried out as the pain intensified. He couldn't free his foot. Someone, or *something* was trying to drag him under . . .

Hearing Bryan's screams, Katy turned and swam back. She was petrified by what she saw. A juvenile alligator, about two and half feet long, had Bryan's foot lodged in its mouth. Katy knew that alligators had been recently spotted in the Lake, but didn't dare think they would encounter one. This one was small enough that it would not be able to drag Bryan down, but the sight was still terrifying.

The reptile had turned over on its back in an attempt to roll over and pull Bryan under. Bryan thrashed madly in the water, now realizing what was happening, but he couldn't shake the gator loose. Were there more, he thought? Could he escape?

Instantly, Katy applied a hard kick to the gator's soft underbelly. It immediately let go of Bryan's foot and disappeared into the murky depths below.

The exhausted pair continued to swim across the narrow channel, blood now oozing from Bryan's punctured foot. They were now just yards from the other side, with Bryan barely able to keep his head above the surface.

The shore was in sight.

And then they heard another siren, one that sounded awfully close. They looked up directly into a police airboat that pulled right beside them.

It was over. There would be no escape.

Chapter 95

Showing no mercy, a gleeful Cortez reached over the side of the boat, yanked Bryan out of the water and body slammed him with a thud onto the boat's wire mesh floor.

Cortez was proud of himself. At long last he was convinced that he would have the last laugh. Visions of vindication danced in his head. Certainly he would be lauded and honored within the Department for solving the murder of one of New Orleans' most notorious crime figures and capturing the perpetrators.

"You should have stayed your ass in California," he yelled derisively at Bryan. Then he taunted, "your honor!"

Katy was also lifted out of the water. They were both read their rights by Broussard. Katy was charged with one count of murder. Bryan was charged as an accessory.

The headlines in the Sunday morning San Francisco Advocate exposed Bryan's humiliation to all the world. Appearing in large, bold print with capitalized letters across the top of the front page were the words "SUPREME COURT JUSTICE ARRESTED IN LOUISIANA

SWAMP." Underneath the headlines was the picture of a shackled Bryan sitting on the edge of the airboat, his blood-soaked, heavily-bandaged foot hanging limply over the edge of the watercraft for all to see.

Chapter 96

Adele Olivier was presented as a New Orleans debutante at the 1993 Knights of Columbus winter Cotillion. A sophomore in college at the time, Adele attended Xavier University in New Orleans. She had been the salutatorian of her high school class and a regular member of the school's honor roll. After college, the charming, statuesque native of Zachary, Louisiana graduated third in her class from Tulane Law School in 1998.

She changed her last name to "Oliver" shortly thereafter, telling others that a three syllable last name was long enough for a prominent lawyer, which Adele had every intention of becoming. Those who know her best, however, suspected that Adele really wanted to sever any remaining ties with her father, Cyril Bonaparte Olivier, who had recently divorced Adele's mother after 31 years of marriage to run off with his much younger mistress. Adele was determined to make a name for herself. She resolved that no credit for her success would be afforded to Cyril Bonaparte or to the name "Olivier."

By the time Katrina hit Louisiana in 2005, Adele was rapidly earning a reputation as one of the finest criminal defense attorneys in southern

Louisiana, stretching all the way from the Atchafalaya Basin to New Orleans. Thus, it was no surprise that Katy and her family moved quickly to retain Adele's services after Katy was arrested and charged with Pope's murder.

The former Ms. Olivier did not come cheap, however. In addition to taking out a loan against her 401(k) savings, Katy also borrowed money from several family members including a small sum from her father, in order to pay Adele's retainer. Adele would have told you she was well worth the price.

At her meeting with Katy in the local jail, Adele reviewed the facts of the case and potential strategies. Katy told Adele everything, but was adamant that Bryan, who had been released on bail, should not be implicated. Katy's gesture came too late for Bryan, however, who had taken a temporary leave of absence from the Court amidst calls for his resignation.

"There are two ways to go," Adele told Katy. "The first is to attack the prosecution's case as insufficient to support a conviction. They have your fingerprints on a $20 dollar bill left in Earl's shack, allegedly on the night Pope was buried. The prosecution is also aware that Pope's organization was recruiting Jerome. That would provide a motive. Then there is the bullet recovered from Pope's sternum that is the same caliber as a gun you used to own. In my opinion, that is not going to be enough to support a conviction. My recommendation is to let the prosecution put on their case. It will end in a big 'so what'?"

"And the second option?" questioned Katy. "What is that?"

"You could testify and tell the jury the story you just told me. You shot Pope, but in self-defense. The potential problem there is that Pope was unarmed and even though there was a confrontation, when you shot him technically there was no physical contact between you and Pope. There is some risk in admitting you pulled the trigger. You still have a good story, but I would say the odds of a conviction go up a bit. A good prosecutor can make a lot of hay out of why you shot Pope once you admit you've done it. The first option requires them to show you actually did something other than leave $20 for Earl."

"And what about Bryan? Which option will limit his involvement?"

"Bryan is not my client," answered Adele, "but under Option 1, the prosecution may put on a case without Bryan or they could try to compel him to testify as to what he saw. If Bryan testifies and places you at the scene, at that point we shift into full on self-defense mode. Anyway, I'm not concerned about Bryan. He'll survive. Or, we could choose the second option. Under Option 2, you would admit shooting Pope so Bryan's involvement would probably be minimal.

"Option 2," said Katy. "That's what I want to do. After all Bryan and I have been through, I owe him that much. There's no need for his further involvement in any of this."

"Katy, as your lawyer, I strongly recommend the first path. Make them prove their case. Bryan's an adult. They may or may not call him as a witness and who knows if he will cooperate. He could also take the fifth. If he agrees to testify, his testimony may not hurt you that much and he'll survive. At some point you need to think about yourself. I'm also going to request a speedy trial, which is your right. That will force the District Attorney to get its case together in a hurry and that will work to our advantage."

"Ok," said Katy. "I'm not sure about any of this. But for now at least, I'm going to trust you and follow your advice."

Chapter 97

Adele's trial philosophy was simple. She was there to win and to win at all costs. She relied on strategic ruthlessness. She was careful not to run afoul of any legal ethics, but bent the rules as much as she needed to and did so in such a subtle fashion that you were never quite sure if it was intentional or not. It was.

In Louisiana, murder convictions need not be unanimous but only require guilty votes from ten of the twelve jurors. Thus, Adele had the daunting task of trying to identify multiple potential jurors who might vote "not guilty" under the right circumstances. Her strategy was to try to stack the jury with as many elderly gentlemen as possible. Adele knew that both she and Katy were attractive women and she needed a demographic who might let that fact sway them in a close case. She ended up placing two widowed men and one man in his seventies on the jury.

Adele did not intend to be flirtatious. That tactic was reserved for those occasions when she was in front of judges known to have a wandering eye. Her strategy in this case was for both Katy and herself to dress as conservatively as possible, to be polite and to at every opportunity cast the prosecution's aggressiveness as bullying. She also intended to make light of any mistakes that DA Hudson might make, well aware that this was his first capital case. She intended to make Hudson feel that he was out of his league.

The trial started twenty days after Katy's arrest. Adele fired the first salvo. "I am requesting that the DA drop its case and release my client immediately," she boldly stated in front of the jury. "There is no evidence of a crime here. The jurors' time is being wasted and Kathryn Duvall has been locked up far too long for something that the prosecution knows she did not do."

The theatrics of course went nowhere and the judge quickly dismissed her motion. But Adele had made her point and sown the first seeds of doubt in the minds of the jurors, especially the three hand-picked men she was counting on.

Chapter 98

When Earl took the stand at Katy's trial, he was visibly uncomfortable. The prosecutors wanted Earl to recite his account of how he came into possession of the $20 bill that bore Katy's fingerprints. Once Earl fully realized that he was being used to place Katy near the scene of where Pope's body was found, he balked, stumbled and claimed he no longer could remember anything about the twenty dollars.

The prosecutors then reminded Earl of what he had told them earlier. Earl continued to stonewall, clearly not wanting to do anything that might hurt Katy. Katy cringed as she watched the nearly seventy-year old Earl struggle on the stand. Hudson eventually threatened to hold Earl in contempt if he didn't regenerate his memory. A dejected Earl then acknowledged that the currency had been left in his shack on the same evening that someone broke in and stole one of his shovels. He also admitted that Katy had been to his shack nearly a dozen times on her previous fishing trips to the lake.

As the trial progressed, the DA continued his negotiations with Bryan. By now, Hudson had a pretty good idea of what actually happened the night of Pope's murder. He would feel a whole lot better about his chances for conviction if he could get Bryan to testify about what he witnessed in Pope's driveway. The prosecution needed to firmly establish Katy presence at Pope's residence. The easiest way to do that was to simply have Bryan recite the facts and describe what he saw happen outside Pope's house.

Hudson's first offer included a promise of no prosecution for Bryan on the accessory charge if Bryan agreed to testify. Bryan refused. His resentment for the price he was paying from his involvement with Katy was growing, but he would not turn on her. Also, Bryan had recently resigned from the California Supreme Court in shame and embarrassment, so he figured he didn't have that much left to lose anyway.

When Bryan declined Hudson's initial offer, Hudson threatened Bryan with a contempt citation. This raised the stakes for Bryan quite a bit. Bryan still retained his license to practice law. It was about the only professional dignity he still maintained. Was he also willing to risk losing that in order to protect Katy?

"I would think that as a California Supreme Court justice . . . former justice that is," continued Hudson further rubbing the humiliation right into Bryan's face, "you would have the utmost respect for the law. You have a duty as an officer of the court to testify," he scolded.

Bryan remained non-cooperative, but he did not want to be held in contempt. He knew that things could get worse for him if the California State Bar Association allowed a contempt citation to serve as grounds for disbarment.

Katy was more interested in seeking updates from her lawyer regarding Bryan's status than she was about how her own case was proceeding. Adele was under an ethical obligation to provide truthful responses to Katy's inquiries.

"Will Bryan be forced to take the stand?" Katy asked.

"In my opinion, yes," Adele answered. "In all honesty, I don't see how he can continue his refusal to comply. He's been offered immunity. Therefore, he has no standing to assert the Fifth Amendment to keep from testifying. If he doesn't, he could be in real trouble, although I'm not sure about whether his license to practice law in California will be jeopardized if he continues to refuse to cooperate. He's in a real pickle. But like I said before, I'm not sure his testimony will be all that damaging, especially if he saw Pope threaten you."

Katy considered the implications of taking the stand. If she did nothing, there was a good chance she would walk out of the courtroom scot-free. But Bryan would likely be forced to take the witness stand and suffer additional ridicule. If Katy testified, Bryan would be spared the spectacle of being grilled as a witness to a murder and having to admit he helped bury Pope in the swamps.

But testifying, in the worst case could mean prison for Katy. Then there would be no chance that she and Bryan would ever be together again. At this point, that possibility was a long shot anyway, but Katy did not want to completely foreclose it. She still held out the faintest hope of a life with Bryan.

Katy agonized over her decision. Finally, after much thought and with no small measure of resignation, Katy made up her mind. She had to take the path that would spare Bryan being on the witness stand, whatever consequences that might have for her and any fading chance of a reunion with Bryan.

"I'm going to testify and tell the truth," she told Adele. "It may mean that Bryan and I will never be together again but if taking that chance will keep him off the witness stand, I have to do it. Please don't try to stop me. But I need you to do everything in your power to keep me out of prison."

Adele cringed, but she could tell Katy meant it. She also relished the challenge that Katy had put before her.

At the start of court proceedings the next morning, Katy noticed a sullen Bryan sitting in the back of the court room. She instructed Adele to request a recess and a meeting of all parties in the judge's chambers. Adele complied.

Once in front of the judge, Katy asked if she could give testimony.

"Yes Ms. Duvall," the judge replied. "You are permitted to testify in your own defense. But I would urge you to consult with counsel before taking that step."

"I've already discussed it with my lawyer," Katy replied. Then she turned to Hunter. "If I get on the stand and acknowledge shooting Pope and tell you exactly what happened, will you drop your demand to have Bryan Stirling give testimony?"

"That depends on what you have to say," replied Hunter.

Katy then told the prosecutor her story.

"If you testify to what you just told me," Hunter said, "then we will not need Bryan Stirling's testimony. But, and you should understand this, we will still pursue charges against you. I may consider a lesser offense, but based on what you just told me, you will still need to serve time if convicted."

Then Katy turned to the judge.

"Will you cancel the contempt citation against Bryan?" she asked.

"Yes Ms. Duvall. If the prosecution no longer intends to call Mr. Stirling as a witness, then there is no need to consider contempt proceedings."

"Fine, that's what I want to do," said Katy. "I'm ready to take the stand."

The court proceedings resumed. Bryan Stirling was never called as a witness. Katy spared him the burden of having to take the witness stand, but not much else. Bryan felt that he had lost everything.

Chapter 99

Adele calmly and deliberately led Katy through her testimony. Katy explained in great detail how distressed she and her mother were about

Jerome's presumed affiliation with the crime syndicate and how she probably overreacted in choosing to confront Pope.

"I wish I had acted differently for a lot of reasons," Katy said, "but I never intended to shoot Pope and would not have aimed the gun at him if he hadn't rushed me and reached for my hand. Plus after the gun failed to fire the first two times I pulled the trigger, I pulled it again thinking it would not discharge the third time either. I just wanted Pope to stop charging me and simply go back inside so I could leave."

After Katy finished her testimony, she was subjected to a withering cross examination by Hunter.

Hunter got Katy to acknowledge that Pope was unarmed. Then he asked Katy why she even pulled the gun out of her purse at all. Katy didn't have a good answer but stated she merely wanted to threaten Pope so he would take her seriously and stop preying on Jerome and other young men in the New Orleans projects.

"So you were not being threatened when you decided to pull the revolver out of your purse."

"Those are your words, not mine," Katy replied. "I certainly felt threatened."

"But you acknowledge Ms. Duvall don't you, that there never could have been a threat if you had not placed yourself on Mr. Pope's property in the first place?" Again, Katy was forced to admit that Hunter's statement was accurate.

Hunter then concluded his questioning of Katy with a statement.

"So based on your testimony Miss Duvall, you introduced a loaded firearm into a situation where you were not being threatened because you wanted to 'scare' somebody. I think we would all agree that Mr. Pope would be alive today if you hadn't gone out to his home, uninvited no less, with a concealed pistol in your purse and then pulled that pistol out for no reason."

Adele Oliver, however, had come prepared. She understood from the beginning that there was a distinct possibility that Katy would reverse her position and ultimately fall on her sword to protect Bryan. Adele had been head over heels in love once, but things hadn't worked out. So Adele knew there was very little that could be done to stop the irrational actions of someone under the influence of an affair of the heart.

And so at the end of Hunter's cross examination of Katy, Adele produced a surprise witness from a local hospital who specialized in gunshot wounds. The witness testified that the bullet hole in Pope's sternum was unlikely to have been fatal.

"I can't tell whatever else may have happened to this man," the witness said, "since all we have is a skeleton, but I can tell you that the bullet lodged in his breastbone probably did not kill him."

A short time later, the dueling attorneys gave their closing arguments. Hunter realized this was his moment. He shook off any prior intimidation he felt from Adele's tactics and delivered a summation of the case as if his future depended on it, which it partially did.

"Only one of the two people involved in that shooting is here to tell their story," Hunter began, seeking to use Katy's testimony against her.

"The other lay buried in a Plaquemines Parish marsh for more than seven years. Through all that time, Miss Duvall uttered not a word to police that might have spared the Pope family additional anguish. If the incident was truly an accident as Ms. Duvall now claims, she should have come forward. She certainly did not act like an innocent person. Do we want to live in a community where vigilante justice reigns supreme or do we want to live under the rule of law? Because if we want to live under the rule of law, then you have no other choice but to find Kathryn Duvall guilty of murdering Alvarez Pope."

Adele was just as adamant in her defense, essentially putting Pope on trial and highlighting all of the pain and misery he and his operation had caused in New Orleans. Then pointing directly at Katy, Adele emphasized that there was really no reason for Katy to lie about what happened.

It was the medical examiner's testimony though, that gave jurors sympathetic to Katy, the "out" they needed to find reasonable doubt. After three days of deliberations, the jury told the judge they were hopelessly deadlocked. The prosecution had fallen one vote short of the ten they needed for conviction. The final tally: nine votes guilty, three votes not guilty. One of the widowers and the seventy year-old man had voted not guilty.

The third vote for acquittal came from an unlikely source, one that Adele had not counted on. Juror number seven, Karyna Breaux didn't think much of Katy or Adele but she was convinced that Katy's entire testimony was fabricated to protect Bryan, the real shooter.

Breaux had been a problem in the jury box from Day One. She was frustrated at not having been excused so she could spend time with her newborn granddaughter. Nevertheless, she vowed to uphold her civic duty. At the beginning of jury deliberations, Breaux announced that she would be voting not guilty. Bryan was the real perpetrator, Breaux explained. Therefore Katy was innocent of the crime she was charged with. Unwilling to even consider changing her mind, Breaux then proceeded to knit a pair of pink booties while the other jurors deliberated the case for three days.

When two of Adele's hand-selected jurors joined Breaux in voting not guilty, the hung jury result was assured. Katy walked out of the courtroom a free woman, at least for the time being. It might have been by the skin of her teeth, but she left with her freedom and not in chains or handcuffs.

The widowed male juror who voted in Katy's favor clearly had no sympathy for Pope. "If I had the chance, I would have shot his ass myself," he remarked, focusing on Pope's reputation for fomenting violence in the impoverished New Orleans neighborhoods. "The prosecution needs to leave those two ladies alone."

Hunter though, vowed to retry the case so Katy wasn't home free. Not by any means.

Broussard and Cortez observed the entire trial from the back row of the courtroom, but through different sets of lenses. Broussard had gradually developed a soft spot for Katy. He wasn't completely certain if Katy was believable or if her actions met the standard of self-defense, but guilty or not, he was convinced of her decency.

Cortez on the other hand just wanted a conviction. He didn't have time to concern himself with whether a guilty verdict was just or not. His career, and his pocketbook needed a boost and playing a prominent role in solving a high profile murder would have put him back on the right track.

After the judge declared a mistrial, Cortez just shook his head.

"Everybody's carrying ice in New Orleans," he said, disappointed that he would not be able to use Katy's conviction to resurrect his standing among his colleagues. "You can't convict the drug lords because of witness intimidation and now you can't convict the killers of the drug lords because everyone's sympathetic. We laid out the case for the state. All they had to do was follow our blueprint."

"You win some, you lose some," said Broussard not all that disappointed at the verdict. "Sometimes things just have a way of working out the way they're supposed to. Who knows? Maybe this was one of those times."

After the paperwork for her release was processed and Katy signed some documents, she was free to be reunited with her family and Adele on the courthouse steps. Amidst all the handshakes and hugs, Katy continuously looked over and around those in front of her, scouring the crowd for a glimpse of Bryan. Her search was futile. Bryan was nowhere to be found.

Frantic, Katy asked everyone in sight if they knew where Bryan was. All answered in the negative. Desperate, Katy then approached one of the bailiffs who was standing a short distance away at a city bus stop. Katy recognized him as Sam, the man who on most days escorted her in shackles, from her jail cell to the courtroom. She asked him if he had seen Bryan.

"I've been here waiting for the bus for close to half an hour," Sam said. "About fifteen minutes ago, Mr. Stirling came and stood beside me and started flagging down taxis. When one stopped I heard him say to the cab driver, 'Louis Armstrong International please.' So I think he was headed for the airport."

Sam paused. He debated whether to tell Katy what else Bryan said knowing it would hurt her. Reluctantly, Sam continued. "And Mr. Stirling said he was never coming back. I'm sorry Miss Katy, real sorry." Sam still did not have the heart to tell Katy everything Bryan said. He mercifully left out Bryan's remarks that he regretted ever coming to Louisiana.

Then Sam spoke again. "But I sure am glad you are not going to prison."

A brief and quiet "thank you" were the only words Katy could summon. Then she stumbled as if punched in the gut. Katy sank slowly towards the earth until seated by herself on the lonely bus stop bench, a prisoner of the moment while jubilant family and friends celebrated her freedom in the distance.

Katy held her head in her hands. It was too much to take. She had found love, lost it, miraculously rediscovered it and now lost it again. Her eyes focused downward and stared blankly at the buckling, weed strewn pavement beneath her where dozens of fire ants traversed in, around and over her slip-on shoes. As Katy became indifferent to their painful stings, the marauding ants were stymied only by the occasional splash of a tear dropped from above.

Chapter 100

Q sat alone in one of the spare bedrooms of Pope's house. He spent a lot of his time there as he found Pope's extra space much more comfortable than his own small apartment at the Magnolia Housing Project. He often wondered about the future of Pope's organization and his place within the group. Pope talked a lot about "taking back the streets" and his "all for one and one for all" philosophy, but where did Q fit into that grand scheme?

Q was rapidly coming to the conclusion that Pope had become satisfied with success. And why not? Pope was at the top of the food chain. He had made it. He didn't have the same motivation and drive that he had when he first started his quest to rule the New Orleans streets. But where did that leave the up and comers in the organization like Q? Would they ever get the nice house and the fancy cars? Or were they just disposable foot soldiers, doing the grunt work like worker bees to make sure money got funneled to the top? Q wondered and the more he wondered, the more he questioned the status quo.

Q was certain there were other areas of the city ripe for expansion and takeover by Pope's operations. If Pope moved aggressively, new sources of funds could be tapped. In theory, this would allow more members of the organization to share in a bigger pot. But now that Pope was basking in success, he seemed overly cautious, passive almost. Had Pope lost his drive now that he had reached the apex?

As Q strolled through Pope's house, he heard the doorbell ring. Pope motioned for him to answer it. Through the peephole, Q could see a very attractive woman that he knew he had seen before.

Q opened the door and recognized the woman as Katy Duvall, the woman he had previously encountered at Jose's restaurant.

"Is Alvarez in? Katy asked.

Q looked Katy up and down, then left the room to confer with Pope. After securing Pope's approval, Q then escorted Katy through the dining room and past the living room into the den where Pope sat watching television from his recliner.

"There's a visitor here to see you from the 'hood," Q announced, leading Katy into the den. "Only she ain't one of us," Q laughed. Pope and Katy exchanged tepid greetings as Q retreated back to the bedroom. On his way back, he overheard Pope refer to him as the "hired help" who had acted in an "overzealous" fashion. Who the hell was Pope to call him the "hired help?" That's the thanks he got, Q thought to himself, for putting it all on the line every day so that the Popes of the world could live like royalty.

As Q got dressed to go out for the evening, he could hear the voices from the den rising to an angry and heated crescendo. The discussion was becoming intense and Q heard an adamant Katy tell Pope, "I'm warning you. Leave Jerome the hell alone."

With the voices in the background becoming louder, Q prepared to leave to roam the streets. He grabbed his "chopper" the street name in New Orleans for assault rifles like AK-47s, along with a home-made silencer he had previously assembled out of PVC pipe and duct tape from instructions he found in a paramilitary magazine. Q was rarely out at night without it.

Q slipped out through the rear door and circled around the exterior of the house back towards the front. To his surprise, there were Pope and Katy screaming at each other in the driveway. Someone Q didn't know was sitting behind the wheel of a car parked in Pope's driveway. Q bent down and moved closer to observe the unfolding drama, hidden by a clump of bushes. His black pants and a black leather jacket provided additional camouflage from the deepening darkness of the sinister night.

Suddenly, Q saw Katy reach into her purse, pull out a pistol and point it directly at Pope. Instinctively, Q raised his rifle and trained it on Katy, her torso now clearly visible through the makeshift scope crafted weeks earlier for him by a cousin just released from prison.

Q had never shot a woman before, but his leader was being threatened and must be protected. That was part of the organization's doctrine. If the circumstances called for him to take out a female, so be it, especially someone like Katy who had previously insulted him and for whom he had no love lost. Q wrapped his index finger around the trigger, checked his aim again to make sure Katy was in his sights and prepared to fire.

Then, suddenly Q's thoughts shifted. He began to question his blind loyalty to Pope. Why was he willing to protect Pope at all costs, he asked himself? What was he going to get out of it?

The self-reflection transformed Q to a deeper, darker place. Where seconds earlier he sought to protect, he now sought to conquer. In the blink of an eye, Q saw an opportunity to rid himself of Pope. He could eliminate what was holding him back, the one impediment to his ability to climb the ladder and assume the mantle of power, influence and wealth.

This was the perfect time and place to carry out the deed Q had been thinking about in the back of his mind for weeks. Instantly, Q shifted the barrel of his rifle from Katy to Pope. With one shot, he could erase Pope from the scene. Q took careful aim at Pope's chest through the scope.

Then Q stopped. He had another idea. Why fire a shot at all? Why not just let things play out the way they seemed to be developing? Q might get lucky and have Pope eliminated by someone else. Q lowered his rifle. He would simply watch the scene unfolding in front of him and let events take their course without intervention.

As Q looked on, Pope repeatedly cursed Katy. Q could see Katy tremble and wince. Just then, Pope took a quick jab step at Katy and yelled, "I will kill you if you ever set foot on my property again."

Q watched Katy, still shaking, place her finger around the trigger of her pistol. Pope advanced further. Katy pointed her gun in the air and twice attempted to fire. Nothing happened.

Pope advanced. "Stop, I'm warning you," Katy screamed.

And then a firecracker seemed to explode from the end of Katy's pistol. Q saw the bright orange flash before he heard the sound. The unthinkable had happened. Katy had actually pulled the trigger and discharged her weapon. Pope collapsed to the ground with a resounding thud.

Chapter 101

As Q continued to survey the scene in Pope's driveway, he saw a shaken Katy quickly climb into the car's front passenger seat aided by the driver. Whoever the driver was, he gunned the engine and peeled out, leaving skid marks on the driveway as the car sped off into the darkness.

Q left his perch and slowly approached Pope's lifeless body. As he got closer, Q noticed a twitch. *Pope was moving.* Q stopped in his tracks and watched.

Pope put his hands on the asphalt and slowly tried to lift himself up.

"Uh . . . uh," Pope uttered as he gasped for air and strained to right himself. Pope fell back down and lay still for several seconds. Then he tried to lift himself up again. Q could see the front of Pope's shirt, soaked in blood.

This time, Pope was able to raise his head and look around. He saw Q and extended his trembling hand.

"Help me," Pope said, barely audible. "Help me, my brother."

Pope started to stagger to his feet, blood now flowing from the corner of his mouth. "Help me," he repeated again as he reached out his arm towards Q.

Q looked around to make sure no one was watching. He then slowly raised his rifle and pointed it directly at Pope.

"Q?" Pope said. "Q?" he repeated with a quizzical look on his face.

Q aimed the barrel of the gun squarely at Pope's chest. One squeeze of the trigger and the throne was his. That was all it would take. A mere twenty feet now separated the two of them. Without an ounce of remorse, Q fired. Pope fell, dead in his tracks.

At that moment, Q recalled the ascension to the throne of his favorite movie character, Scar from the "The Lion King." Scar's words were etched in Q's memory. He repeated them, albeit with his own embellishment.

"The king is dead, damn it," Q said, as he lowered his rifle. "Long live the mother fuckin' king."

Just then, Q noticed car lights approaching the property. He ducked and ran towards the edge of the house tightly clutching his chopper. He scampered around the corner just before the lights could illuminate his fleeing silhouette.

Chapter 102

Once Q had rid himself of Pope, he reorganized Pope's business operations. Q became more aggressive and ventured into areas that put him in direct competition with local gangs and even the larger, big city syndicates. It was a risky way to make a living.

Like most businesses, Q sought to cut unnecessary expenses. This included Pope's 10% periodic profit payments to Axel Lanier. Q felt no obligation to honor a bad deal Pope had made years earlier. As far as Q was concerned, that agreement was now null and void. The deal, Axel and any evidence of their prior collaboration, had to go. Q hatched a plan to rid himself of his one major creditor. He fully intended to carry it out; unless someone else got to Axel first.

Chapter 103

In a banquet suite at one of New Orleans' most trendy hotels, Q and his buddies saluted themselves with shots of Crown Royal.

"To us, the new kings of New Orleans," Q proclaimed.

Q's toast was followed by a chorus of "hell yeahs" from his newly-minted lieutenants, several of whom were engaged in a spirited game of craps. They rolled the dice with extra vigor across a felt-covered surface with peculiar, leather stitching that Q had broken out for the special occasion.

"I've never played craps on the inside of a briefcase before," one of them joked. "Hey Q, where the hell did you get this dice board. And why does it have all these checkers," he continued, not realizing the entire apparatus was an elegant backgammon set.

"Jamaica," replied Q, who had never been to the Caribbean in his life.

"Laissez les bon temps rouler," another bystander exclaimed, while raising his glass.

"Laissez les bon temps rouler indeed," Q said to himself as he looked on in triumphant satisfaction at the new world order.